**CHARLOTTE PERKINS GILMAN,** feminist, author, critic, and theorist, was born on July 3, 1860, in Hartford, Connecticut. Although she was a descendant of the famous theologian Lyman Beecher, Charlotte Perkins's early life was characterized by dire poverty and an unstable home: her family moved nineteen times in eighteen years after her father abandoned them. In 1884 she married Charles Walter Stetson, gave birth to a daughter the following year, and was subsequently overcome by bouts of depression, which nearly caused her complete breakdown. Finally she fled to California and created a scandal by obtaining a divorce and granting custody of her daughter to her husband. In 1892 her story "The Yellow Wallpaper" appeared, and she began her writing and social activism in earnest. She became a contributing editor to *The American Fabian* and fought for reforms based on her socialist and feminist ideals. Her most famous book, *Women and Economics* (1898), was translated into seven languages, winning her international recognition. In 1900 she married George Houghton Gilman. For seven years she wrote and edited her own magazine, *The Forerunner,* and she wrote ten more books, including *The Home* (1902), *Human Works* (1904), and *The Man-Made World: Our Androcentric Culture* (1911). Her famous utopian novel, *Herland,* appeared in 1915. She committed sucide in 1935 while dying from breast cancer.

Bantam Classics
Ask your bookseller for these other American Classics

O PIONEERS!, Willa Cather

THE AWAKENING, Kate Chopin

THE LAST OF THE MOHICANS, James Fenimore Cooper
THE DEERSLAYER, James Fenimore Cooper

THE RED BADGE OF COURAGE, Stephen Crane
MAGGIE: A GIRL OF THE STREETS AND OTHER SHORT FICTION,
   Stephen Crane

SISTER CARRIE, Theodore Dreiser

THE AUTOBIOGRAPHY & OTHER WRITINGS, Benjamin Franklin

THE FEDERALIST PAPERS, Alexander Hamilton, James Madison,
   John Jay

THE SCARLET LETTER, Nathaniel Hawthorne
THE HOUSE OF THE SEVEN GABLES, Nathaniel Hawthorne

THE TURN OF THE SCREW AND OTHER SHORT FICTION, Henry James
THE PORTRAIT OF A LADY, Henry James

THE CALL OF THE WILD and WHITE FANG, Jack London
THE SEA WOLF, Jack London
MARTIN EDEN, Jack London
TO BUILD A FIRE AND OTHER STORIES, Jack London

MOBY-DICK, Herman Melville
BILLY BUDD, SAILOR AND OTHER STORIES, Herman Melville

THE TELL-TALE HEART AND OTHER WRITINGS, Edgar Allan Poe

TEN DAYS THAT SHOOK THE WORLD, John Reed

THE JUNGLE, Upton Sinclair

UNCLE TOM'S CABIN, Harriet Beecher Stowe

WALDEN AND OTHER WRITINGS, Henry David Thoreau

THE ADVENTURES OF HUCKLEBERRY FINN, Mark Twain
THE ADVENTURES OF TOM SAWYER, Mark Twain
THE PRINCE AND THE PAUPER, Mark Twain
LIFE ON THE MISSISSIPPI, Mark Twain
A CONNECTICUT YANKEE IN KING ARTHUR'S COURT, Mark Twain
PUDD'NHEAD WILSON, Mark Twain
THE COMPLETE SHORT STORIES OF MARK TWAIN

THE HOUSE OF MIRTH, Edith Wharton
ETHAN FROME AND OTHER SHORT FICTION, Edith Wharton

FOUR GREAT AMERICAN CLASSICS: THE SCARLET LETTER, THE
   ADVENTURES OF HUCKLEBERRY FINN, THE RED BADGE OF
   COURAGE, BILLY BUDD, SAILOR

# The Yellow Wallpaper and Other Writings by Charlotte Perkins Gilman

With an Introduction by
LYNNE SHARON SCHWARTZ

BANTAM BOOKS

NEW YORK · TORONTO · LONDON · SYDNEY · AUCKLAND

THE YELLOW WALLPAPER AND OTHER WRITINGS
*A Bantam Classic Book / November 1989*

*Cover painting "Contemplation" by Gertrude Fiske (1878-1961), courtesy of Vose Galleries of Boston. Photo by Clive Russ.*

**ISBN 0-553-21375-X**

*Published simultaneously in the United States and Canada*

---

*Bantam Books are published by Bantam Books, a division of Bantam Doubleday Dell Publishing Group, Inc. Its trademark, consisting of the words "Bantam Books" and the portrayal of a rooster, is Registered in U.S. Patent and Trademark Office and in other countries. Marca Registrada. Bantam Books, 666 Fifth Avenue, New York, New York 10103.*

---

PRINTED IN THE UNITED STATES OF AMERICA

O    0 9 8 7 6 5 4 3 2

# CONTENTS

# INTRODUCTION

"Life is a verb," Charlotte Perkins Gilman wrote at the dawn of the twentieth century.[1] From girlhood to old age, she invented new forms of the verb her own living might take. "Here I am," she declares as a teenager, "in the world, conscious, able to do this or that. What is it all about? How does it work? What is my part in it, my job—what ought I to do?"[2] She calls her autobiography, published after her death in 1935, *The Living of Charlotte Perkins Gilman,* and the unexpected rhythm of its title is a deliberate choice, active gerund rather than static noun.

At the close of that book, looking back on almost half a century of writing, lecturing, and traveling, she notes tersely the waning demand for her services. The "market" for lecturers "has declined before the advance of the radio." She had "not unreasonably expected" to be invited to the Connecticut College for Women, near her home in

Norwich. Not unreasonably: her books had gone through numerous editions and been translated into half a dozen languages; she was recognized as a leading thinker in the women's movement, a socialist and supporter of the labor movement. "With so much that was new and strong to say to the coming generation, it seemed to me a natural opportunity. It did not seem so to the college."[3] Perhaps it did not because with the attainment of suffrage the urgency of the women's movement had abated, at least in the public eye. But Gilman's ambitions for women—and men—went far beyond the right to vote. Voting by itself, she might have said, cannot reinvent a society.

Decades later a new generation of feminists discovered Gilman and treasured her, not only for her work, though that remained as strong and pertinent as ever, but also for her life. Impelled by principle, it was a more vivid example than any book. What especially touched readers coming of age in the 1960s and 1970s was her delight in spontaneous quest, her passion for intellectual adventure. In childhood her mind and imagination had been hampered; as an adult, she was impatient with stodgy, habitual grooves of thought.

> Education has diligently endeavored to enforce upon each brain precisely that mass and order of impressions considered as beneficial in the past. . . . The tendency of the race towards its own vanguard—the young—has been that of a heavy old gentleman throwing himself solidly down on an active child, and seeking to smother him and pin him to the earth.[4]

Her reputation today rests largely on "The Yellow Wallpaper" (1892), the classic and often anthologized story of a trapped woman's mental disintegration. Yet Gilman saw herself primarily as a sociologist, anthropologist, and social philosopher; her books outline radical ideas on the meaning and ramifications of human work, on the institutions of marriage and the family (distinct and not always mutually supporting, she warns), on motherhood, and on childrearing in particular, which she vehemently believed should be entrusted to trained professionals, not left to the volatilities of "maternal instinct."

Though her ideas were advanced for her time, she was far from an isolated voice. Born in Hartford, Connecticut in 1860, Charlotte Perkins was raised in an atmosphere where independent thinking and social activism were familiar—indeed, familial. Her great-grandfather on her father's side was the religious leader, Lyman Beecher, and his children, Henry Ward Beecher, Harriet Beecher Stowe, Catherine Beecher, and Isabella Beecher Hooker, along with their circle of friends, were, variously, rebels, writers, feminists, and freethinkers. Among these New England intellectuals the transcendental strain was still powerful—Emerson's and Margaret Fuller's idealism, Thoreau's smug purity and political orneriness.

The final decades of the nineteenth century, when Gilman matured and flourished, saw enormous social change and intellectual ferment: industrialization and immigration destabilized social patterns and gave impetus to the labor movement; the conglomeration of the railroads in the West concentrated new wealth in the hands of a few; the suffrage movement stirred up controversy, while the work of Jane Addams at Chicago's Hull House and that of others in what we now term the "private sector" forced attention to the horrors of poverty. Edward Bellamy's fantasy, *Looking Backward,* which projected a world redeemed by science and socialism, had a tremendous vogue; Gilman was among the many influenced by his utopian dream.

In a more deeply unsettling way, the intellectual climate had been altered forever—heated up, swirled into modernity—by the irreverent trio of Marx, Freud, and Darwin. Like every serious thinker, Gilman had to take them into account, develop a stance toward the news they brought. For the most part her stance was aloof, resistant.

While she drew on Darwinian natural selection in discussing marriage and "improving" the species, she regarded "the struggle for existence" and "the survival of the fittest" as unfortunate branches from the male roots of combat and competition. And though her own motif of collective ownership seems a variant of Marxism's "to each according to his needs, from each according to his abilities," she took pains to abjure communism, a "flat and uniform world, of no ambition, no distinction, no privacy, no private property, and therefore no life worth having."[5] As for Freud, no mythology could be more antithetical; her weapons against lifelong bouts with depression were old-fashioned reason and self-discipline—Emersonian self-reliance.

Gilman makes an easy mark for Freudian-style analysis: no educated modern temperament can fail to perceive her guilt, rage, repression, denial—our comforting, if reductive, insignia. A more fertile approach to her life, though, might be along the lines suggested by feminist critic Phyllis Rose:

> Often the most radical perspective you can adopt on a
> person's experience is his or her own. . . . Each of us,
> influenced perhaps by one ideology or another, generates
> our own plot, our own symbolic landscape, a highly
> individual configuration of significance through which
> we view our own experience and which I call a personal
> mythology.[6]

Gilman's personal myth turns on the themes of rational decision and calculated acts, the power of the will in service of a social ideal. That is, she stuck to the challenge she had set herself as a girl—to find her work and do it.

\*     \*     \*

Frederick Beecher Perkins, a literary man and later librarian of the San Francisco Public Library, left his family when Charlotte and her brother were small children. In her autobiography, she primly attributes the break to her mother's physical weakness—bearing more children would kill her—but surely there were more subtle tensions and dissatisfactions. Although Charlotte kept in touch (she wrote to her father often, asking advice about her studies), she always resented his defection, a resentment mixed awkwardly with admiration. She treats the men in her fiction in likewise ambivalent fashion: sometimes as irresponsible, downright dense creatures, occasionally as victims of spiritual asphyxiation.

With scant aid from her husband, Mary Westcott Perkins raised her children in one Rhode Island lodging after another, often living with relatives, a peripatetic, moneyless way of life Charlotte would continue. The childhood sketched in her autobiography is cold—strictly supervised, emotionally meager. Some poignant, if not perspicacious, lines tell volumes about her mother:

> Her method was to deny the child all expression of affection as far as possible, so that she should not be used to it or long for it. "I used to put away your little hand from my cheek when you were a nursing baby," she told me in later years; "I did not want you to suffer as I had suffered." She would not let me caress her, and would not caress me, unless I was asleep. This I discovered at last, and then did my best to keep awake till she came to bed, even using pins to prevent dropping off, and sometimes succeeding. Then how carefully I pretended to be sound asleep, and how rapturously I enjoyed being gathered into her arms, held close and kissed.[7]

Charlotte lived an intense fantasy life, until she decided her bedtime visions were somehow "wrong" and set about rationing them: strange and lovely things one night a week, "wonders" once a month. "This program was soon forgotten, but it shows conscience wrestling with fantasy at an early age.''[8] They were to wrestle all her life, with conscience, predictably, the usual victor. If granted the proverbial three wishes, this prudent child's first would be, '' 'I wish that everything I wish may be Right!' To be right was the main thing in life.''[9] So it remained. The compulsion to be right inevitably congeals into righteousness, a tone acutely late Victorian and never entirely absent from Gilman's work.

Through lack of money and Mary Perkins's close surveillance, Charlotte was largely self-educated. Then at eighteen, overcoming her mother's objections, she went to the Rhode Island School of Design to study art and painting, which gave her a livelihood, doing commercial illustrations. She was enthusiastic about gymnastics and running; she taught Sunday school, she tutored children; most of all she read to prepare for her life's work, whatever that might be. Finally: "Twenty-one. My own mistress at last. No one on earth had a right to ask obedience of me. I was self-supporting of course, a necessary base for freedom which the young revolters of today often overlook.''[10] Relief bounces audibly through the phrases.

Just one year later, in 1882, she met Walter Stetson, a young painter who pursued her with tenacity. After two years of agonizing, analyzing, and vacillating, she married him. Puzzling, yes, that a young woman so avid for freedom should take the conventional path. In light of the social pressures brought to bear, however, along with Stetson's flattering eagerness, not quite so puzzling. (Years later she would stringently dissect such pressures.)

Her doubts were well founded. Before marrying she was reading literature, philosophy, and feminist journals, learning French and German, writing stories and poetry. Immediately afterward, lassitude, fretfulness, and fits of weeping overtook her, and upon the birth of her daughter, Katharine, in 1885, she sank into a severe depression, hardly able to read or do domestic work, not to mention care for a child.

Her journal entries for that period are a pathetic record of collapse and guilt: "teary," "tremulous," "downcast," a string of dreary days spent lying on the sofa with forbearing Walter bringing cups of tea. She tried travel, visiting her brother in Utah and her friend Grace Channing in California, and her spirits lifted. But as soon as she returned to husband, home, and child the depression tugged her back down.

In the end she saved herself. She left Walter, taking their daughter out West to a California uncannily like the state we know today, "peculiarly addicted to swift enthusiasms, . . . a seed-bed of all manner of cults and theories, taken up, and dropped, with equal speed."[11] There she supported herself (barely) by lecturing, writing for small magazines, and running a boardinghouse (something a number of her fictional heroines do too, as it was one of the few acceptable paths then open to single women). A few years later the Stetsons divorced, and Gilman, already a public figure, sent her daughter to live with Walter and his new wife, Grace Channing (still Gilman's close friend). For this decision she was, to her lasting chagrin, excoriated by the press as an "unnatural mother."

The conflicts triggering her breakdown were never resolved, and spells of morbid depression continued to plague her. In her autobiography Gilman dwells on her illness, understandably, since at the time it was neither acknowledged as such nor accorded much sympathy. She was seldom able to read for more than an hour or so at a stretch; her nerves were "wilted," her mind "like a piece of boiled spinach."[12]

> To see, to hear, to think, to remember, to do anything, is incredible effort, as if trying to rise and walk under a prostrate circus tent, or wade in glue. It brings a heavy darkness, every idea presenting itself as a

misfortune; an irritable unease which finds no rest, and an incapacity of decision which is fairly laughable.

For all the years in which I have had to pack a suitcase and start on a trip, that packing is dreaded; and often finds me at midnight, after several hours' attempt, holding up some article and looking at it in despair, utterly unable to make up my mind whether to take it or not. In one of the worst times, in 1896, I stood on a street corner for fifteen minutes, trying in vain to decide whether or not to take the car home.[13]

Besides navigating this wretched tightrope, she lived in perpetual debt, "as propertyless and as desireless as a Buddhist priest, almost, though needing something more than a yellow robe and begging bowl."[14] With such handicaps, the sheer quantity of her writings and activities is prodigious: *Women and Economics: A Study of the Economic Relation Between Men and Women* (1898), which *The Nation* called "the most significant utterance on the subject since Mill's *Subjection of Women*";[15] *Concerning Children* (1900); *The Home: Its Work and Influence* (1902); *Human Work* (1904); *The Man-Made World: Our Androcentric Culture* (1911); numerous lectures and essays; and several volumes of poetry. In 1909 she started *The Forerunner,* a monthly magazine she wrote and published singlehandedly for seven years—poems, topical pieces, humor, stories, and serialized novels, among them the utopian *Herland*.

Today Gilman's breakdown does not seem baffling but rather archetypal, with the pattern and inevitability of fiction. It did in fact become fiction—"The Yellow Wallpaper," her only story that gives literary shape to private torment and ranks among American classics. She drew on her treatment at the hands of the Philadelphia neurologist, S. Weir Mitchell, whose "rest cure" had been widely used on women with nervous disorders; one shudders to imagine the undocumented cases. The cure consisted of the patient's doing nothing, certainly no more than an hour's daily reading or writing or stimulating talk. It drove Gilman nearly mad; the fictional patient does not have the resources to save herself.

In naively ironic fashion, the narrator of "The Yellow Wallpaper" simultaneously chronicles and reflects her voyage to insanity. A virtual prisoner of her husband, a supposedly well-meaning physician, she queries innocently, *"perhaps* that is one reason I do not get well faster." With her environment restricted to her room, she grows mesmerized by its patterned wallpaper, at first merely sinister, then gradually an emblem of confinement. In the end, reality and symbol hurtle into each other. As an account of the dynamics of delusion, the story is more than superbly shocking; it is physically painful to read, and was so when first published, in 1892, in *The New England Magazine.* "Such a story ought not to be written," one reader wrote. "It was enough to drive anyone mad to read it." In 1920 William Dean Howells included it in his *Great Modern American Stories* as a horror story. Reissuing it in *The Forerunner* in 1913, Gilman added a personal statement answering her many appalled readers, doctors among them:

> Using the remnants of intelligence that remained, . . .
> I cast the noted specialist's advice to the winds and
> went to work again—work, the normal life of every
> human being; work, in which is joy and growth and
> service, without which one is a pauper and a parasite—
> ultimately recovering some measure of power. . . . It
> was not intended to drive people crazy, but to save
> people from being driven crazy, and it worked.[16]

Whatever her intentions, Gilman offered something more than a remedy: a masterpiece. Just as the crucial themes of her life—autonomy, marriage, work, the struggle of enlightenment against restriction—converged in her breakdown, they converge, transformed, in a perfectly balanced, emotionally charged narrative structure. None of her other fiction approaches "The Yellow Wallpaper"; nowhere else did she venture to that inner space where the boundaries dividing imagination, feeling, and conviction fall away.

Once Gilman's life is firmly centered in work and she is something of a celebrity (around the 1890s), the tone of her autobiography loses its timbre. Introspection and passion are replaced, disappointingly, by an itinerary of trips, lectures, and oddly stiff encounters with friends and colleagues, many of them famous names of the period. Even her marriage, in 1900, to her cousin, G. Houghton Gilman, is mentioned perfunctorily, although by all accounts they spent thirty years in a companionable union of equals, her own utopian model for marriage. The self-portrait shows a well-functioning finished product, no longer porous but lacquered, immune to the trafficking between world and self, the reshaping and recombinations that make the succulent heart of adult life.

The obverse of that image appears in Gilman's voluminous diaries and in the letters written to her second husband before their marriage; these are pulsing with intimate revelations. From them, some scholars have imagined a different woman entirely, emotionally fluid, even turbulent, engaged in many passionate friendships—possibly love affairs—with those lifeless figures in her autobiography. Critics disagree, as well, over her attitude about sex— whether she enjoyed it freely, if secretly, or was puritanically repressed or simply uninterested; whether her close women friends were also lovers. Gilman would certainly have scorned such intriguing speculation. Publicly she maintained that the sexual instinct was overdeveloped, with romantic love occupying far too prominent a place in private fantasies and social arrangements.

Her personal myth, in any event, was not about romance but salvation—through work—from imprisoning dogma. Freed by her own initiative, the myth's heroine,

naturally always right, undertakes to lead society to freedom. Reason and discipline triumph over the murky, unreliable impulses of emotion and tradition. Between the lines
we may—we are obliged to—see conflict and perplexity.
For one thing, the woman who extolled motherhood chose
not to raise her own child: not an unnatural mother, but
perhaps an ordinary ambivalent one. And why did she say
so little of her second marriage if it illustrated her ideals?
Contradictions are rampant, as in any valorous life. Yet in
the larger sense, her myth was accurate. She did battle
successfully with fate, and given her aspirations, her work
*was* eminently right.

\*   \*   \*

Any coherent feminist theory must study and span the
social pillars of economics and sexuality—Freud's subjec-
tive "love and work" gone public. Unlike many feminists
today, Gilman stresses the economics and downplays the
sex: economic independence is her first and indispensable
requirement for personal freedom. But more fundamental
than either is a vision of history and society to account for
the present and to project the future. *The Man-Made World,*
her most original and farsighted book (though critics give
top billing to *Women and Economics*), traces that vision.

Its premise is that historically, the notion of human
characteristics has been mistakenly and disastrously restricted to what are actually male qualities. Small wonder,
since in our "androcentric" culture, history has been "made
and written" by men; also no wonder that its themes have
been desire and combat, the propelling male instincts.
Once men succeeded in "monopolizing" human activities,
naming them man's work, women effectively dropped out
of history, out of production, out of everything except a
service role. So *The Man-Made World* seeks, slightly dis-
ingenuously, to isolate specifically male qualities from the
more fundamental traits common to all. To defend this

undertaking, Gilman acidly cites the many treatises seeking to define women, some even debating whether they are persons at all or merely females.

From this half tongue-in-cheek opening develops a witty and pointed analysis of social institutions: the family, originally evolved for the nurture of children, has become "the vehicle of his comfort, power and pride"; history and literature, notably popular fiction, rooted in love and adventure (desire and combat again), are oblivious of the real adventures of more than half the race. Even women's love for men, as shown in fiction, "is largely a reflex; it is the way he wants her to feel, expects her to feel. Not a fair representation of how she does feel." Law and government are cumbersome, authoritarian, and competitive; the lust for combat exalts warfare, making "each man-managed nation an actual or potential fighting organization."

These sweeping judgments focus less on particular manifestations than on the spirit that informs society and conceives and achieves its destiny. That this spirit can be more fully human, more humane, has always been a revolutionary idea. Gilman does not suggest it is found exclusively in women—quite the contrary—simply that it has been undervalued if not ignored. "The female is the race-type—the man the variant" may sound high-handed but, under the circumstances, is an effort to right the balance. She was influenced, too, by the work of Lester Ward, the pioneering American sociologist who claimed that woman "is the unchanging trunk of the great genealogical tree upon which the male is simply grafted."[17]

*Women and Economics* was Gilman's most widely read book, going through seven American editions, translated into seven languages, and bringing her renown in Western European feminist circles. Its version of marriage no doubt appalled many readers: after demonstrating that wives are neither paid servants nor equal partners nor professional mothers, she coolly likens their services to those of prostitutes. In brief, "the female of the genus homo is economically dependent on the male. He is her food supply.''

According to Gilman, since primitive times, when men first set this pattern by force, women have been ''modified'' and shaped accordingly, their sexual attractions overprized and other talents left dormant. Her analysis is uncharitable toward the middle- or upper-class wife, consumer par excellence by necessity, whose idleness and social amusements are unproductive of anything but her continued comfort. Change the social conditions, Gilman briskly advises—Darwinian for the moment—and the women will change soon enough.

On the subject of the home she is even more outrageous: no ''haven in a heartless world,'' but rather a narrow, confining space generating wearisome friction. Home life is minimal life; ideally it should prepare young people to step into the world—*into, not out to,* she carefully distinguishes—and make wider social connections. To facilitate this more worldly life, she would eliminate the home's sacred center, the kitchen, in favor of communal eating establishments. (Curiously, some urban apartments designed for single people or young working couples nowadays have cursory kitchens or none at all; Gilman would approve of them, if not of the gourmet restaurants supplanting the vanquished kitchens.)

Her thoughts on domestic life and food preparation (simple, nutritious, en masse) were elaborated in *The Home,* published in 1902, the year in which, according to the social historian Carl Degler, President Theodore Roosevelt

> castigated the educated classes in general and college-trained women in particular for what he called ''race suicide,'' for . . . even if the ''new women'' married, they bore few or no children. The reasons for this undeniable shunning of marriage and childbearing by the new women are too complex to analyze here.[18]

Surely they did not appear so very complex to Gilman, who leaves little doubt as to why women who could be independent might so choose. Still, she consistently held that given the chance to live full, productive lives under conditions of equality, most women would gladly marry and bear children too.

*Human Work* (1904), which she regarded as her most important book, is Gilman's socialist blueprint. She opens by cajoling her readers to accept the need for change, in precisely the tone of one assuring a child that the feared medicine will help, not hurt—a telling gauge of inferred resistance. Her pervasive theme is optimistic: our unity as a species and interdependence as parts of a living organism; her faith in human reason and malleability is remarkable. The new order requires no uprising, violent or otherwise, merely "certain simple, swift, and easy changes of mind by which we may alter our processes as to avoid . . . suffering and promote our growth and happiness."[19] Poverty, crime, disease, and ignorance are "rudiments" sure to vanish when "economic errors and superstitions" are corrected.

The errors turn out to be the foundations of capitalism: the ethic of "getting" as opposed to "doing," of self-aggrandizement through making money; the principle of supply and demand; the rich man's notion that adversity— for the poor—builds character. Gilman would substitute a radically idealistic concept of human work. Work has gotten a bad name, she asserts, starting from Adam's curse in Genesis and right up to the present, when hiring or enslaving others to do one's work is a source of pride: here she echoes Thorstein Veblen, whose *Theory of the Leisure Class,* published in 1899, complemented her ideas. In truth, work is the highest human function and delight, the process binding society together, an "expression of social energy for social use."[20]

With collective—but not government—ownership of the means of production, a new society would "ensure to the individual those things which are essential to his social service."[21] The product would belong to the consumer, as much of it as needed. This is transcendentalized Marxism, as it were, class struggle replaced by community and mutual concern, economic reform as a means to the happier evolution of humanity. "Working is humanity's growing. In the act of working the individual is modified, and by the work accomplished humanity is modified."[22]

Gilman's utopianism finds full expression in the novel, *Herland*, which she serialized in *The Forerunner* in 1915. Situated in an inaccessible valley near a "great river," in "savage" territory, Herland is an all-female nation—the men died out thousands of years before through natural disaster, war, and female rebellion. Three American adventurers representing male types—the "macho," the romantic, and the objective sociologist serving as narrator —stumble upon it half accidentally, to be taken captive in the most civilized manner. Their encounters with Herland's women, customs, and culture provide the framework for a sketch of the ideal society.

Herland's guiding principle is motherhood, which may seem curious from an author whom motherhood plunged into depression. Then again, motherhood minus the trappings of husband, home (kitchen), and family is quite another matter. The women are mothers "not in our sense of helpless involuntary fecundity . . . but in the sense of Conscious Makers of People. Mother-love with them was not a brute passion, a mere 'instinct,' a wholly personal feeling; it was—a religion." Babies are conceived in a most ingenious way: a Herland instructor explains,

> "before a child comes to one of us there is a period of utter exaltation—the whole being is uplifted and filled with a concentrated desire for that child." When a woman chose to be a mother, she allowed the childlonging to grow within her till it worked its natural miracle.

> When she did not so choose she put the whole thing
> out of her mind, and fed her heart with the other
> babies.

The smooth running of otherwise naturalistic Herland rests on this expedient but preposterous modus operandi. Yet most utopias rely on elements of the absurd, so *Herland* need not be an exception. In any case, parthenogenesis allows Gilman to dispense with men entirely—the issue of sex and marriage was vexing enough in her own life—and thereby dispense with the dilemmas of men and women finding a viable way to be together.

Herland's children need no surnames: they are the children of all the mothers, raised communally, taught by specialists with a natural gift for the work. (Gilman would not have joined feminists today in supporting the biological mother in the Baby M case, though who can say, seeing her inventiveness, what she would have made of surrogate motherhood?) Children are limited to one per woman—birth control posing no problem but that of will— to avoid the evils of overpopulation.

Herland is an almost perfect place, presented lightheartedly, and touching in its way. With the best will in the world—human nature having been refined to a faultless state—its residents have admirably arranged every facet of public and private life: gardens, farms, and forests thrive, redolent of fruit-bearing trees; cities and towns are sensibly and skillfully designed and well kept, with charming, convenient houses; education is humane and enjoyable, food wholesomely simple, clothing practical and comfortable. Everyone works at suitable, useful, and healthy tasks. The government, though hierarchical, is democratic, with no apparatus for punishment—the rare wrongdoers are regarded as ill and treated accordingly. Nor do judgment and damnation have any place in religion: the Loving Power is maternal; religious feeling filial. Rather like the young Charlotte Perkins, the Herlanders, being nothing if not practical, . . . set their keen and active minds to discover the kind of conduct expected of them. This worked out in a most admirable system of ethics. The principle of Love was universally recognized—and used.

. . . They had no ritual, no little set of performances called "divine service." . . . But they had a clear established connection between everything they did—and God. Their cleanliness, their health, their exquisite order, the rich peaceful beauty of the whole land, the happiness of the children, and above all the constant progress they made—all this was their religion.

One of the many refractory human traits that have quite disappeared is sexual desire. Aside from the urge to motherhood, the women have only vestigial sexual instincts and no coquetry whatsoever, which make. .or droll scenes when the three intruders fall in love: courtship is stymied if women will not entice in order to succumb. (Some scenes are not so droll. When Terry, a lady-killer type, tries to force sex on his Herland wife, he gets kicked in the groin and universally denounced as a monster.) Gilman chided her contemporaries for being "oversexed," meaning that the whole spectrum of sociosexual rites was emphasized disproportionately, yet its absence in Herland is disproportionate too. Or at least begs the question. On the other hand, her aim was to illustrate how women, left to their own devices, can create a superior society.

*Herland* is a clever book. It avoids a good deal of didacticism by setting its argument in an adventure story with a narrative line, dramatic structure, and suspense. Gilman deftly exploits the transforming possibilities of context: commonplace American mores are shown up as absurd and unjust when seen through Herlanders' eyes. Cultural contrasts make for wit, if occasionally of too easy a sort. Above all, the novel is brimming with the cheerful, resolute faith in progress shared by most reformers of the era.

Gilman was the first to grant that her fiction was not the stuff of great literature. "I have never made any pretense of being literary. As far as I had any method in mind, it was to express the idea with clearness and vivacity, so that it might be apprehended with ease and pleasure."[23] Of her seven novels serialized in *The Forerunner* she remarks, "I definitely proved that I am not a novelist."[24]

Apart from "The Yellow Wallpaper," her short stories are exercises in problem-solving, parables reminiscent—in form only—of perennially popular women's magazine fiction. The difference is that, far from urging the beleaguered housewife to stretch her patience further and adapt, Gilman's solutions are innovative, aimed at getting people out of self-destructive ruts, not deeper in.

When Mary Main, in "An Honest Woman" (1911), is abandoned by the disreputable father of her child, she seems doomed to the role of fallen woman. Instead she moves to another town, runs a boardinghouse, educates her daughter, and earns a reputation for probity. Years later the prodigal lover returns to find himself unneeded, unwanted. Similarly, in "Turned" (1911), on realizing that her husband has gotten the naive servant girl pregnant, well-bred Mrs. Marroner's first response is to weep despairingly—a "struggling mass of emotion." But she quickly pulls herself together to resolve on a course of action. Eventually the two women and the baby form an independent unit; in a devastating closing scene, the treacherous man is dismissed as superfluous. Perhaps in writing these parallel and very righteous scenes, Gilman was rectifying or avenging a cruelty to her own mother: when dying of cancer Mary Perkins had begged to see her former husband once more, but he never came.

"Making a Change" (1911) is a story somewhat closer to the bone. Julia Gordins, former musician and now distraught housebound mother of a wailing infant, is driven to a suicide attempt. Her wise mother-in-law, who has a talent for babies, saves her by starting a day-care center (as recommended in *Women and Economics*) and sending Julia back to work—all unbeknownst to the simpleminded husband. When he discovers their solution, his manly pride is hurt, but only for a moment; then he marvels at their ingenuity.

Again, in "The Widow's Might" (1911), the older woman proves more daring and imaginative than the young. While three meanspirited children bicker over which will bear the burden of their newly widowed mother—"all of fifty . . . and much broken," one laments—the vigorous widow turns out to have resources and plans of her own. And in a reversed situation, "Mr. Peebles' Heart" (1914) looks at the plight of a man stifled by a pampered, idle wife and rescued by his sister-in-law, a doctor, who shows the way to a freer life and a better marriage in the bargain.

These fictional resolutions, invariably affirmative and invigorating, are possible only when reason governs character, with no ambiguity permitted to balk common sense. In other words, Gilman's exemplary stories are self-justifying: if she reclaimed her future by logic and will, why shouldn't everyone else? Why not society as a whole? Not only her brilliant nonfiction, then, but even her less brilliant fiction reflects its creator: rigorous and farseeing; long on reason and short on psychological penetration; immensely optimistic and intelligent; shaped by the contradictions at the heart of her life. Few writers have so truly mirrored themselves.

In many ways, some noble, some constricting, Gilman was a typical progressive of her time. Her splendid originality lay in keeping faith with her convictions to their natural results, in living as well as in writing. In dying too, for when, in 1932, she learned that she had breast cancer, she determined to end her life when her usefulness had ended, which she did in 1935.

The time is approaching when we shall consider it abhorrent to our civilization to allow a human being to die in prolonged agony. . . . Believing this open choice to be of social service in promoting wiser views on this question, I have preferred chloroform to cancer.[25]

In her vision and struggles, she set a pattern for a more sane and rich human life and fulfilled her own myth. The succeeding generations she longed to reach have yet to summon the wits and resilience to follow where she led.

—LYNNE SHARON SCHWARTZ

## Notes

1. *Human Work.* (New York: McClure, Philips and Co.,1904, p. 201.)
2. *The Living of Charlotte Perkins Gilman.* (New York: Arno Press, 1935, p. 39.)
3. *Ibid.,* pp. 332–333.
4. *Human Work*, pp. 29, 32.
5. *Ibid.,* p. 331.
6. *Writing of Women.* (Middletown, CT: Wesleyan University Press, 1985, pp. 78–79.)
7. *The Living of Charlotte Perkins Gilman,* p.10.
8. *Ibid.,* p. 20.
9. *Ibid.,* p. 21.
10. *Ibid.,* p. 70.
11. *Ibid.,* p. 122.
12. *Ibid.,* pp. 102, 99.
13. *Ibid.,* p. 102.
14. *Ibid.,* p. 186.
15. *The Nation,* (June 8th, 1899), p. 443.
16. "Why I Wrote 'The Yellow Wallpaper'?" *The Forerunner* (October 1913).
17. Lester F. Ward, "Out Better Halves." *The Forerunner* (1888), p. 275.
18. Carl Degler, in Introduction to *Women and Economics.* (New York: Harper and Row, pp. xxv–xxvi.)
19. *Human Work*, p. 16.
20. *Ibid.,* p. 206.

21. *Ibid.*, p. 319.
22. *Ibid.*, p. 258.
23. *The Living of Charlotte Perkins Gilman*, pp. 284–285.
24. *Ibid.*, p. 306.
25. *Ibid.*, p. 333.

# THE YELLOW WALLPAPER

It is very seldom that mere ordinary people like John and myself secure ancestral halls for the summer.

A colonial mansion, a hereditary estate, I would say a haunted house, and reach the height of romantic felicity—but that would be asking too much of fate!

Still I will proudly declare that there is something queer about it.

Else, why should it be let so cheaply? And why have stood so long untenanted?

John laughs at me, of course, but one expects that in marriage.

John is practical in the extreme. He has no patience with faith, an intense horror of superstition, and he scoffs openly at any talk of things not to be felt and seen and put down in figures.

John is a physician, and *perhaps*—(I would not say it

to a living soul, of course, but this is dead paper and a great relief to my mind)—*perhaps* that is one reason I do not get well faster.

You see he does not believe I am sick!

And what can one do?

If a physician of high standing, and one's own husband, assures friends and relatives that there is really nothing the matter with one but temporary nervous depression—a slight hysterical tendency—what is one to do?

My brother is also a physician, and also of high standing, and he says the same thing.

So I take phosphates or phosphites—whichever it is, and tonics, and journeys, and air, and exercise, and am absolutely forbidden to "work" until I am well again.

Personally, I disagree with their ideas.

Personally, I believe that congenial work, with excitement and change, would do me good.

But what is one to do?

I did write for a while in spite of them; but it *does* exhaust me a good deal—having to be so sly about it, or else meet with heavy opposition.

I sometimes fancy that in my condition if I had less opposition and more society and stimulus—but John says the very worst thing I can do is to think about my condition, and I confess it always makes me feel bad.

So I will let it alone and talk about the house.

The most beautiful place! It is quite alone, standing well back from the road, quite three miles from the village. It makes me think of English places that you read about, for there are hedges and walls and gates that lock, and lots of separate little houses for the gardeners and people.

There is a *delicious* garden! I never saw such a garden—large and shady, full of box-bordered paths, and lined with long grape-covered arbors with seats under them.

There were greenhouses, too, but they are all broken now.

There was some legal trouble, I believe, something about the heirs and coheirs; anyhow, the place has been empty for years.

That spoils my ghostliness, I am afraid, but I don't care—there is something strange about the house—I can feel it.

I even said so to John one moonlight evening, but he said what I felt was a *draught,* and shut the window.

I get unreasonably angry with John sometimes. I'm sure I never used to be so sensitive. I think it is due to this nervous condition.

But John says if I feel so, I shall neglect proper self-control; so I take pains to control myself—before him, at least, and that makes me very tired.

I don't like our room a bit. I wanted one downstairs that opened on the piazza and had roses all over the window, and such pretty old-fashioned chintz hangings! but John would not hear of it.

He said there was only one window and not room for two beds, and no near room for him if he took another.

He is very careful and loving, and hardly lets me stir without special direction.

I have a schedule prescription for each hour in the day; he takes all care from me, and so I feel basely ungrateful not to value it more.

He said we came here solely on my account, that I was to have perfect rest and all the air I could get. "Your exercise depends on your strength, my dear," said he, "and your food somewhat on your appetite; but air you can absorb all the time." So we took the nursery at the top of the house.

It is a big, airy room, the whole floor nearly, with windows that look all ways, and air and sunshine galore. It was nursery first and then playroom and gymnasium, I should judge; for the windows are barred for little children, and there are rings and things in the walls.

The paint and paper look as if a boys' school had used it. It is stripped off—the paper—in great patches all around the head of my bed, about as far as I can reach, and in a great place on the other side of the room low down. I never saw a worse paper in my life.

One of those sprawling flamboyant patterns committing every artistic sin.

It is dull enough to confuse the eye in following, pronounced enough to constantly irritate and provoke study, and when you follow the lame uncertain curves for a little distance they suddenly commit suicide—plunge off at outrageous angles, destroy themselves in unheard of contradictions.

The color is repellent, almost revolting; a smouldering unclean yellow, strangely faded by the slow-turning sunlight.

It is a dull yet lurid orange in some places, a sickly sulphur tint in others.

No wonder the children hated it! I should hate it myself if I had to live in this room long.

There comes John, and I must put this away,—he hates to have me write a word.

We have been here two weeks, and I haven't felt like writing before, since that first day.

I am sitting by the window now, up in this atrocious nursery, and there is nothing to hinder my writing as much as I please, save lack of strength.

John is away all day, and even some nights when his cases are serious.

I am glad my case is not serious!

But these nervous troubles are dreadfully depressing.

John does not know how much I really suffer. He knows there is no *reason* to suffer, and that satisfies him.

Of course it is only nervousness. It does weigh on me so not to do my duty in any way!

I meant to be such a help to John, such a real rest and comfort, and here I am a comparative burden already!

Nobody would believe what an effort it is to do what little I am able,—to dress and entertain, and order things.

It is fortunate Mary is so good with the baby. Such a dear baby!

And yet I *cannot* be with him, it makes me so nervous.

I suppose John never was nervous in his life. He laughs at me so about this wallpaper!

At first he meant to repaper the room, but afterwards he said that I was letting it get the better of me, and that nothing was worse for a nervous patient than to give way to such fancies.

He said that after the wallpaper was changed it would be the heavy bedstead, and then the barred windows, and then that gate at the head of the stairs, and so on.

"You know the place is doing you good," he said, "and really, dear, I don't care to renovate the house just for a three months' rental."

"Then do let us go downstairs," I said, "there are such pretty rooms there."

Then he took me in his arms and called me a blessed little goose, and said he would go down to the cellar, if I wished, and have it whitewashed into the bargain.

But he is right enough about the beds and windows and things.

It is an airy and comfortable room as any one need wish, and, of course, I would not be so silly as to make him uncomfortable just for a whim.

I'm really getting quite fond of the big room, all but that horrid paper.

Out of one window I can see the garden, those mysterious deepshaded arbors, the riotous old-fashioned flowers, and bushes and gnarly trees.

Out of another I get a lovely view of the bay and a

little private wharf belonging to the estate. There is a beautiful shaded lane that runs down there from the house. I always fancy I see people walking in these numerous paths and arbors, but John has cautioned me not to give way to fancy in the least. He says that with my imaginative power and habit of story-making, a nervous weakness like mine is sure to lead to all manner of excited fancies, and that I ought to use my will and good sense to check the tendency. So I try.

I think sometimes that if I were only well enough to write a little it would relieve the press of ideas and rest me.

But I find I get pretty tired when I try.

It is so discouraging not to have any advice and companionship about my work. When I get really well, John says we will ask Cousin Henry and Julia down for a long visit; but he says he would as soon put fireworks in my pillow-case as to let me have those stimulating people about now.

I wish I could get well faster.

But I must not think about that. This paper looks to me as if it *knew* what a vicious influence it had!

There is a recurrent spot where the pattern lolls like a broken neck and two bulbous eyes stare at you upside down.

I get positively angry with the impertinence of it and the everlastingness. Up and down and sideways they crawl, and those absurd, unblinking eyes are everywhere. There is one place where two breaths didn't match, and the eyes go all up and down the line, one a little higher than the other.

I never saw so much expression in an inanimate thing before, and we all know how much expression they have! I used to lie awake as a child and get more entertainment and terror out of blank walls and plain furniture than most children could find in a toy-store.

I remember what a kindly wink the knobs of our big,

old bureau used to have, and there was one chair that always seemed like a strong friend.

I used to feel that if any of the other things looked too fierce I could always hop into that chair and be safe.

The furniture in this room is no worse than inharmonious, however, for we had to bring it all from downstairs. I suppose when this was used as a playroom they had to take the nursery things out, and no wonder! I never saw such ravages as the children have made here.

The wallpaper, as I said before, is torn off in spots, and it sticketh closer than a brother—they must have had perseverance as well as hatred.

Then the floor is scratched and gouged and splintered, the plaster itself is dug out here and there, and this great heavy bed which is all we found in the room, looks as if it had been through the wars.

But I don't mind it a bit—only the paper.

There comes John's sister. Such a dear girl as she is, and so careful of me! I must not let her find me writing.

She is a perfect and enthusiastic housekeeper, and hopes for no better profession. I verily believe she thinks it is the writing which made me sick!

But I can write when she is out, and see her a long way off from these windows.

There is one that commands the road, a lovely shaded winding road, and one that just looks off over the country. A lovely country, too, full of great elms and velvet meadows.

This wallpaper has a kind of sub-pattern in a different shade, a particularly irritating one, for you can only see it in certain lights, and not clearly then.

But in the places where it isn't faded and where the sun is just so—I can see a strange, provoking, formless sort of figure, that seems to skulk about behind that silly and conspicuous front design.

There's sister on the stairs!

*    *    *

7

Well, the Fourth of July is over! The people are all gone and I am tired out. John thought it might do me good to see a little company, so we just had Mother and Nellie and the children down for a week.

Of course I didn't do a thing. Jennie sees to everything now.

But it tired me all the same.

John says if I don't pick up faster he shall send me to Weir Mitchell in the fall.

But I don't want to go there at all. I had a friend who was in his hands once, and she says he is just like John and my brother, only more so!

Besides, it is such an undertaking to go so far.

I don't feel as if it was worth while to turn my hand over for anything, and I'm getting dreadfully fretful and querulous.

I cry at nothing, and cry most of the time.

Of course I don't when John is here, or anybody else, but when I am alone.

And I am alone a good deal just now. John is kept in town very often by serious cases, and Jennie is good and lets me alone when I want her to.

So I walk a little in the garden or down that lovely lane, sit on the porch under the roses, and lie down up here a good deal.

I'm getting really fond of the room in spite of the wallpaper. Perhaps *because* of the wallpaper.

It dwells in my mind so!

I lie here on this great immovable bed—it is nailed down, I believe—and follow that pattern about by the hour. It is as good as gymnastics, I assure you. I start, we'll say, at the bottom, down in the corner over there where it has not been touched, and I determine for the thousandth time that I *will* follow that pointless pattern to some sort of a conclusion.

I know a little of the principle of design, and I know this thing was not arranged on any laws of radiation, or alternation, or repetition, or symmetry, or anything else that I ever heard of.

It is repeated, of course, by the breadths, but not otherwise.

Looked at in one way each breadth stands alone, the bloated curves and flourishes—a kind of "debased Romanesque" with *delirium tremens*—go waddling up and down in isolated columns of fatuity.

But, on the other hand, they connect diagonally, and the sprawling outlines run off in great slanting waves of optic horror, like a lot of wallowing seaweeds in full chase.

The whole thing goes horizontally, too, at least it seems so, and I exhaust myself in trying to distinguish the order of its going in that direction.

They have used a horizontal breadth for a frieze, and that adds wonderfully to the confusion.

There is one end of the room where it is almost intact, and there, when the crosslights fade and the low sun shines directly upon it, I can almost fancy radiation after all,—the interminable grotesques seem to form around a common centre and rush off in headlong plunges of equal distraction.

It makes me tired to follow it. I will take a nap I guess.

I don't know why I should write this.

I don't want to.

I don't feel able.

And I know John would think it absurd. But I *must* say what I feel and think in some way—it is such a relief!

But the effort is getting to be greater than the relief.

Half the time now I am awfully lazy, and lie down ever so much.

John says I mustn't lose my strength, and has me take cod liver oil and lots of tonics and things, to say nothing of ale and wine and rare meat.

Dear John! He loves me very dearly, and hates to have me sick. I tried to have a real earnest reasonable talk with him the other day, and tell him how I wish he would let me go and make a visit to Cousin Henry and Julia.

But he said I wasn't able to go, nor able to stand it after I got there; and I did not make out a very good case for myself, for I was crying before I had finished.

It is getting to be a great effort for me to think straight. Just this nervous weakness I suppose.

And dear John gathered me up in his arms, and just carried me upstairs and laid me on the bed, and sat by me and read to me till it tired my head.

He said I was his darling and his comfort and all he had, and that I must take care of myself for his sake, and keep well.

He says no one but myself can help me out of it, that I must use my will and self-control and not let any silly fancies run away with me.

There's one comfort, the baby is well and happy, and does not have to occupy this nursery with the horrid wallpaper.

If we had not used it, that blessed child would have! What a fortunate escape! Why, I wouldn't have a child of mine, an impressionable little thing, live in such a room for worlds.

I never thought of it before, but it is lucky that John kept me here after all, I can stand it so much easier than a baby, you see.

Of course I never mention it to them any more—I am too wise,—but I keep watch of it all the same.

There are things in that paper that nobody knows but me, or ever will.

Behind that outside pattern the dim shapes get clearer every day.

It is always the same shape, only very numerous.

And it is like a woman stooping down and creeping about behind that pattern. I don't like it a bit. I wonder—I begin to think—I wish John would take me away from here!

It is so hard to talk with John about my case, because he is so wise, and because he loves me so.

But I tried it last night.

It was moonlight. The moon shines in all around just as the sun does.

I hate to see it sometimes, it creeps so slowly, and always comes in by one window or another.

John was asleep and I hated to waken him, so I kept still and watched the moonlight on that undulating wall-paper till I felt creepy.

The faint figure behind seemed to shake the pattern, just as if she wanted to get out.

I got up softly and went to feel and see if the paper *did* move, and when I came back John was awake.

"What is it, little girl?" he said. "Don't go walking about like that—you'll get cold."

I thought it was a good time to talk, so I told him that I really was not gaining here, and that I wished he would take me away.

"Why darling!" said he, "our lease will be up in three weeks, and I can't see how to leave before.

"The repairs are not done at home, and I cannot possibly leave town just now. Of course if you were in any danger, I could and would, but you really are better, dear, whether you can see it or not. I am a doctor, dear, and I know. You are gaining flesh and color, your appetite is better, I feel really much easier about you."

"I don't weigh a bit more," said I, "nor as much; and my appetite may be better in the evening when you are here, but it is worse in the morning when you are away!"

"Bless her little heart!" said he with a big hug, "she shall be as sick as she pleases! But now let's improve the shining hours by going to sleep, and talk about it in the morning!"

"And you won't go away?" I asked gloomily.

"Why, how can I, dear? It is only three weeks more and then we will take a nice little trip of a few days while

Jennie is getting the house ready. Really dear you are better!''

"Better in body perhaps—" I began, and stopped short, for he sat up straight and looked at me with such a stern, reproachful look that I could not say another word.

"My darling," said he, "I beg of you, for my sake and for our child's sake, as well as for your own, that you will never for one instant let that idea enter your mind! There is nothing so dangerous, so fascinating, to a temperament like yours. It is a false and foolish fancy. Can you not trust me as a physician when I tell you so?''

So of course I said no more on that score, and we went to sleep before long. He thought I was asleep first, but I wasn't, and lay there for hours trying to decide whether that front pattern and the back pattern really did move together or separately.

On a pattern like this, by daylight, there is a lack of sequence, a defiance of law, that is a constant irritant to a normal mind.

The color is hideous enough, and unreliable enough, and infuriating enough, but the pattern is torturing.

You think you have mastered it, but just as you get well underway in following, it turns a back-somersault and there you are. It slaps you in the face, knocks you down, and tramples upon you. It is like a bad dream.

The outside pattern is a florid arabesque, reminding one of a fungus. If you can imagine a toadstool in joints, an interminable string of toadstools, budding and sprouting in endless convolutions—why, that is something like it.

That is, sometimes!

There is one marked peculiarity about this paper, a thing nobody seems to notice but myself, and that is that it changes as the light changes.

When the sun shoots in through the east window—I always watch for that first long, straight ray—it changes so quickly that I never can quite believe it.

That is why I watch it always.

By moonlight—the moon shines in all night when there is a moon—I wouldn't know it was the same paper.

At night in any kind of light, in twilight, candle light, lamplight, and worst of all by moonlight, it becomes bars! The outside pattern I mean, and the woman behind it is as plain as can be.

I didn't realize for a long time what the thing was that showed behind, that dim sub-pattern, but now I am quite sure it is a woman.

By daylight she is subdued, quiet. I fancy it is the pattern that keeps her so still. It is so puzzling. It keeps me quiet by the hour.

I lie down ever so much now. John says it is good for me, and to sleep all I can.

Indeed he started the habit by making me lie down for an hour after each meal.

It is a very bad habit I am convinced, for you see I don't sleep.

And that cultivates deceit, for I don't tell them I'm awake—O no!

The fact is I am getting a little afraid of John.

He seems very queer sometimes, and even Jennie has an inexplicable look.

It strikes me occasionally, just as a scientific hypothesis,—that perhaps it is the paper!

I have watched John when he did not know I was looking, and come into the room suddenly on the most innocent excuses, and I've caught him several times *looking at the paper!* And Jennie too. I caught Jennie with her hand on it once.

She didn't know I was in the room, and when I asked her in a quiet, a very quiet voice, with the most restrained manner possible, what she was doing with the paper—she turned around as if she had been caught stealing, and looked quite angry—asked me why I should frighten her so!

Then she said that the paper stained everything it touched, that she had found yellow smooches on all my clothes and John's, and she wished we would be more careful!

Did not that sound innocent? But I know she was studying that pattern, and I am determined that nobody shall find it out but myself!

Life is very much more exciting now than it used to be. You see I have something more to expect, to look forward to, to watch. I really do eat better, and am more quiet than I was.

John is so pleased to see me improve! He laughed a little the other day, and said I seemed to be flourishing in spite of my wallpaper.

I turned it off with a laugh. I had no intention of telling him it was *because* of the wallpaper—he would make fun of me. He might even want to take me away.

I don't want to leave now until I have found it out. There is a week more, and I think that will be enough.

I'm feeling ever so much better! I don't sleep much at night, for it is so interesting to watch developments; but I sleep a good deal in the daytime.

In the daytime it is tiresome and perplexing.

There are always new shoots on the fungus, and new shades of yellow all over it. I cannot keep count of them, though I have tried conscientiously.

It is the strangest yellow, that wallpaper! It makes me think of all the yellow things I ever saw—not beautiful ones like buttercups, but old foul, bad yellow things.

But there is something else about that paper—the smell! I noticed it the moment we came into the room, but with so much air and sun it was not bad. Now we have had a week of fog and rain, and whether the windows are open or not, the smell is here.

It creeps all over the house.

I find it hovering in the dining-room, skulking in the parlor, hiding in the hall, lying in wait for me on the stairs.

It gets into my hair.

Even when I go to ride, if I turn my head suddenly and surprise it—there is that smell!

Such a peculiar odor, too! I have spent hours in trying to analyze it, to find what it smelled like.

It is not bad—at first, and very gentle, but quite the subtlest, most enduring odor I ever met.

In this damp weather it is awful, I wake up in the night and find it hanging over me.

It used to disturb me at first. I thought seriously of burning the house—to reach the smell.

But now I am used to it. The only thing I can think of that it is like is the *color* of the paper! A yellow smell.

There is a very funny mark on this wall, low down, near the mopboard. A streak that runs round the room. It goes behind every piece of furniture, except the bed, a long, straight, even *smooch*, as if it had been rubbed over and over.

I wonder how it was done and who did it, and what they did it for. Round and round and round—round and round and round—it makes me dizzy!

I really have discovered something at last.

Through watching so much at night, when it changes so, I have finally found out.

The front pattern *does* move—and no wonder! The woman behind shakes it!

Sometimes I think there are a great many women behind, and sometimes only one, and she crawls around fast, and her crawling shakes it all over.

Then in the very bright spots she keeps still, and in the very shady spots she just takes hold of the bars and shakes them hard.

And she is all the time trying to climb through. But

nobody could climb through that pattern—it strangles so; I think that is why it has so many heads.

They get through, and then the pattern strangles them off and turns them upside down, and makes their eyes white!

If those heads were covered or taken off it would not be half so bad.

I think that woman gets out in the daytime!

And I'll tell you why—privately—I've seen her!

I can see her out of every one of my windows!

It is the same woman, I know, for she is always creeping, and most women do not creep by daylight.

I see her on that long road under the trees, creeping along, and when a carriage comes she hides under the blackberry vines.

I don't blame her a bit. It must be very humiliating to be caught creeping by daylight!

I always lock the door when I creep by daylight. I can't do it at night, for I know John would suspect something at once.

And John is so queer now, that I don't want to irritate him. I wish he would take another room! Besides, I don't want anybody to get that woman out at night but myself.

I often wonder if I could see her out of all the windows at once.

But, turn as fast as I can, I can only see out of one at one time.

And though I always see her, she *may* be able to creep faster than I can turn!

I have watched her sometimes away off in the open country, creeping as fast as a cloud shadow in a high wind.

If only that top pattern could be gotten off from the under one! I mean to try it, little by little.

I have found out another funny thing, but I shan't

tell it this time! It does not do to trust people too much.

There are only two more days to get this paper off, and I believe John is beginning to notice. I don't like the look in his eyes.

And I heard him ask Jennie a lot of professional questions about me. She had a very good report to give.

She said I slept a good deal in the daytime.

John knows I don't sleep very well at night, for all I'm so quiet!

He asked me all sorts of questions, too, and pretended to be very loving and kind.

As if I couldn't see through him!

Still, I don't wonder he acts so, sleeping under this paper for three months.

It only interests me, but I feel sure John and Jennie are secretly affected by it.

Hurrah! This is the last day, but it is enough. John to stay in town over night, and won't be out until this evening.

Jennie wanted to sleep with me—the sly thing! but I told her I should undoubtedly rest better for a night all alone.

That was clever, for really I wasn't alone a bit! As soon as it was moonlight and that poor thing began to crawl and shake the pattern, I got up and ran to help her.

I pulled and she shook, I shook and she pulled, and before morning we had peeled off yards of that paper.

A strip about as high as my head and half around the room.

And then when the sun came and that awful pattern began to laugh at me, I declared I would finish it to-day!

We go away to-morrow, and they are moving all my furniture down again to leave things as they were before.

Jennie looked at the wall in amazement, but I told her merrily that I did it out of pure spite at the vicious thing.

She laughed and said she wouldn't mind doing it herself, but I must not get tired.

How she betrayed herself that time!

But I am here, and no person touches this paper but me,—not *alive*!

She tried to get me out of the room—it was too patent! But I said it was so quiet and empty and clean now that I believed I would lie down again and sleep all I could; and not to wake me even for dinner—I would call when I woke.

So now she is gone, and the servants are gone, and the things are gone, and there is nothing left but that great bedstead nailed down, with the canvas mattress we found on it.

We shall sleep downstairs to-night, and take the boat home to-morrow.

I quite enjoy the room, now it is bare again.

How those children did tear about here!

This bedstead is fairly gnawed!

But I must get to work.

I have locked the door and thrown the key down into the front path.

I don't want to go out, and I don't want to have anybody come in, till John comes.

I want to astonish him.

I've got a rope up here that even Jennie did not find. If that woman does get out, and tries to get away, I can tie her!

But I forgot I could not reach far without anything to stand on!

This bed will *not* move!

I tried to lift and push it until I was lame, and then I got so angry I bit off a little piece at one corner—but it hurt my teeth.

Then I peeled off all the paper I could reach standing on the floor. It sticks horribly and the pattern just enjoys

it! All those strangled heads and bulbous eyes and waddling fungus growths just shriek with derision!

I am getting angry enough to do something desperate.
To jump out of the window would be admirable exercise,
but the bars are too strong even to try.

Besides I wouldn't do it. Of course not. I know well
enough that a step like that is improper and might be
misconstrued.

I don't like to *look* out of the windows even—there
are so many of those creeping women, and they creep so
fast.

I wonder if they all come out of that wallpaper as I
did?

But I am securely fastened now by my well-hidden
rope—you don't get *me* out in the road there!

I suppose I shall have to get back behind the pattern
when it comes night, and that is hard!

It is so pleasant to be out in this great room and creep
around as I please!

I don't want to go outside. I won't, even if Jennie
asks me to.

For outside you have to creep on the ground, and
everything is green instead of yellow.

But here I can creep smoothly on the floor, and my
shoulder just fits in that long smooch around the wall, so I
cannot lose my way.

Why there's John at the door!

It is no use, young man, you can't open it!

How he does call and pound!

Now he's crying for an axe.

It would be a shame to break down that beautiful
door!

"John dear!" said I in the gentlest voice, "the key is
down by the front steps, under a plantain leaf!"

That silenced him for a few moments.

Then he said—very quietly indeed, "Open the door,
my darling!"

"I can't," said I. "The key is down by the front door under a plantain leaf!"

And then I said it again, several times, very gently and slowly, and said it so often that he had to go and see, and he got it of course, and came in. He stopped short by the door.

"What is the matter?" he cried. "For God's sake, what are you doing!"

I kept on creeping just the same, but I looked at him over my shoulder.

"I've got out at last," said I, "in spite of you and Jane. And I've pulled off most of the paper, so you can't put me back!"

Now why should that man have fainted? But he did, and right across my path by the wall, so that I had to creep over him every time!

# IF I WERE
# A MAN

"**I**f I were a man, . . ." that was what pretty little Mollie Mathewson always said when Gerald would not do what she wanted him to—which was seldom.

That was what she said this bright morning, with a stamp of her little high-heeled slipper, just because he had made a fuss about that bill, the long one with the "account rendered," which she had forgotten to give him the first time and been afraid to the second—and now he had taken it from the postman himself.

Mollie was "true to type." She was a beautiful instance of what is reverentially called "a true woman." Little, of course—no true woman may be big. Pretty, of course—no true woman could possibly be plain. Whimsical, capricious, charming, changeable, devoted to pretty clothes and always "wearing them well," as the esoteric phrase has it. (This does not refer to the clothes—they do not wear well in the least—but to some special grace of putting them on and carrying them about, granted to but few, it appears.)

She was also a loving wife and a devoted mother possessed of "the social gift" and the love of "society" that goes with it, and, with all these was fond and proud of her home and managed it as capably as—well, as most women do.

If ever there was a true woman it was Mollie Mathewson, yet she was wishing heart and soul she was a man.

And all of a sudden she was!

She was Gerald, walking down the path so erect and square-shouldered, in a hurry for his morning train, as usual, and, it must be confessed, in something of a temper.

Her own words were ringing in her ears—not only the "last word," but several that had gone before, and she was holding her lips tight shut, not to say something she would be sorry for. But instead of acquiescence in the position taken by that angry little figure on the veranda, what she felt was a sort of superior pride, a sympathy as with weakness, a feeling that "I must be gentle with her," in spite of the temper.

A man! Really a man—with only enough subconscious memory of herself remaining to make her recognize the differences.

At first there was a funny sense of size and weight and extra thickness, the feet and hands seemed strangely large, and her long, straight, free legs swung forward at a gait that made her feel as if on stilts.

This presently passed, and in its place, growing all day, wherever she went, came a new and delightful feeling of being *the right size*.

Everything fitted now. Her back snugly against the seat-back, her feet comfortably on the floor. Her feet? . . . His feet! She studied them carefully. Never before, since her early school days, had she felt such freedom and comfort as to feet—they were firm and solid on the ground when she walked; quick, springy, safe—as when, moved by an unrecognizable impulse, she had run after, caught, and swung aboard the car.

Another impulse fished in a convenient pocket for change—instantly, automatically, bringing forth a nickel for the conductor and a penny for the newsboy.

These pockets came as a revelation. Of course she had known they were there, had counted them, made fun of them, mended them, even envied them; but she never had dreamed of how it *felt* to have pockets.

Behind her newspaper she let her consciousness, that odd mingled consciousness, rove from pocket to pocket, realizing the armored assurance of having all those things at hand, instantly get-at-able, ready to meet emergencies. The cigar case gave her a warm feeling of comfort—it was full; the firmly held fountain pen, safe unless she stood on her head; the keys, pencils, letters, documents, notebook, checkbook, bill folder—all at once, with a deep rushing sense of power and pride, she felt what she had never felt before in all her life—the possession of money, of her own earned money—hers to give or to withhold, not to beg for, tease for, wheedle for—hers.

That bill—why, if it had come to her—to him, that is—he would have paid it as a matter of course, and never mentioned it—to her.

Then, being he, sitting there so easily and firmly with his money in his pockets, she wakened to his life-long consciousness about money. Boyhood—its desires and dreams, ambitions. Young manhood—working tremendously for the wherewithal to make a home—for her. The present years with all their net of cares and hopes and dangers; the present moment, when he needed every cent for special plans of great importance, and this bill, long overdue and demanding payment, meant an amount of inconvenience wholly unnecessary if it had been given him when it first came; also, the man's keen dislike of that "account rendered."

"Women have no business sense!" she found herself saying. "And all that money just for hats—idiotic, useless, ugly things!"

With that she began to see the hats of the women in the car as she had never seen hats before. The men's seemed normal, dignified, becoming, with enough variety for personal taste, and with distinction in style and in age, such as she had never noticed before. But the women's—

With the eyes of a man and the brain of a man; with the memory of a whole lifetime of free action wherein the hat, close-fitting on cropped hair, had been no handicap; she now perceived the hats of women.

The massed fluffed hair was at once attractive and foolish, and on that hair, at every angle, in all colors, tipped, twisted, tortured into every crooked shape, made of any substance chance might offer, perched these formless objects. Then, on their formlessness the trimmings—these squirts of stiff feathers, these violent outstanding bows of glistening ribbon, these swaying, projecting masses of plumage which tormented the faces of bystanders.

Never in all her life had she imagined that this idolized millinery could look, to those who paid for it, like the decorations of an insane monkey.

And yet, when there came into the car a little woman, as foolish as any, but pretty and sweet-looking, up rose Gerald Mathewson and gave her his seat. And, later, when there came in a handsome red-cheeked girl, whose hat was wilder, more violent in color and eccentric in shape than any other—when she stood nearby and her soft curling plumes swept his cheek once and again—he felt a sense of sudden pleasure at the intimate tickling touch—and she, deep down within, felt such a wave of shame as might well drown a thousand hats forever.

When he took his train, his seat in the smoking car, she had a new surprise. All about him were the other men, commuters too, and many of them friends of his.

24

To her, they would have been distinguished as "Mary Wade's husband," "the man Belle Grant is engaged to," "that rich Mr. Shopworth," or "that pleasant Mr. Beale." And they would all have lifted their hats to her, bowed, made polite conversation if near enough—especially Mr. Beale.

Now came the feeling of open-eyed acquaintance, of knowing men—as they were. The mere amount of this knowledge was a surprise to her—the whole background of talk from boyhood up, the gossip of barber-shop and club, the conversation of morning and evening hours on trains, the knowledge of political affiliation, of business standing and prospects, of character—in a light she had never known before.

They came and talked to Gerald, one and another. He seemed quite popular. And as they talked, with this new memory and new understanding, an understanding which seemed to include all these men's minds, there poured in on the submerged consciousness beneath a new, a startling knowledge—what men really think of women.

Good, average, American men were there; married men for the most part, and happy—as happiness goes in general. In the minds of each and all there seemed to be a two-story department, quite apart from the rest of their ideas, a separate place where they kept their thoughts and feelings about women.

In the upper half were the tenderest emotions, the most exquisite ideals, the sweetest memories, all lovely sentiments as to "home" and "mother," all delicate admiring adjectives, a sort of sanctuary, where a veiled statue, blindly adored, shared place with beloved yet commonplace experiences.

In the lower half—here that buried consciousness woke to keen distress—they kept quite another assortment of ideas. Here, even in this clean-minded husband of hers, was the memory of stories told at men's dinners, of worse ones overheard in street or car, of base traditions, coarse epithets, gross experiences—known, though not shared.

And all these in the department "woman," while in the rest of the mind—here was new knowledge indeed.

The world opened before her. Not the world she had been reared in—where Home had covered all the map, almost, and the rest had been "foreign," or "unexplored country," but the world as it was—man's world, as made, lived in, and seen, by men.

It was dizzying. To see the houses that fled so fast across the car window, in terms of builders' bills, or of some technical insight into materials and methods; to see a passing village with lamentable knowledge of who "owned it" and of how its Boss was rapidly aspiring in state power, or of how that kind of paving was a failure; to see shops, not as mere exhibitions of desirable objects, but as business ventures, many mere sinking ships, some promising a profitable voyage—this new world bewildered her.

She—as Gerald—had already forgotten about that bill, over which she—as Mollie—was still crying at home. Gerald was "talking business" with this man, "talking politics" with that, and now sympathizing with the carefully withheld troubles of a neighbor.

Mollie had always sympathized with the neighbor's wife before.

She began to struggle violently with this large dominant masculine consciousness. She remembered with sudden clearness things she had read, lectures she had heard, and resented with increasing intensity this serene masculine preoccupation with the male point of view.

Mr. Miles, the little fussy man who lived on the other side of the street, was talking now. He had a large complacent wife; Mollie had never liked her much, but had always thought him rather nice—he was so punctilious in small courtesies.

And here he was talking to Gerald—such talk!

"Had to come in here," he said. "Gave my seat to a

dame who was bound to have it. There's nothing they won't get when they make up their minds to it—eh?''

"No fear!" said the big man in the next seat. "They haven't much mind to make up, you know—and if they do, they'll change it."

"The real danger," began the Rev. Alfred Smythe, the new Episcopal clergyman, a thin, nervous, tall man with a face several centuries behind the times, "is that they will overstep the limits of their God-appointed sphere."

"Their natural limits ought to hold 'em, I think," said cheerful Dr. Jones. "You can't get around physiology, I tell you."

"I've never seen any limits, myself, not to what they want, anyhow," said Mr. Miles. "Merely a rich husband and a fine house and no end of bonnets and dresses, and the latest thing in motors, and a few diamonds—and so on. Keeps us pretty busy."

There was a tired gray man across the aisle. He had a very nice wife, always beautifully dressed, and three unmarried daughters, also beautifully dressed—Mollie knew them. She knew he worked hard, too, and she looked at him now a little anxiously.

But he smiled cheerfully.

"Do you good, Miles," he said. "What else would a man work for? A good woman is about the best thing on earth."

"And a bad one's the worst, that's sure," responded Miles.

"She's a pretty weak sister, viewed professionally," Dr. Jones averred with solemnity, and the Rev. Alfred Smythe added, "She brought evil into the world."

Gerald Mathewson sat up straight. Something was stirring in him which he did not recognize—yet could not resist.

"Seems to me we all talk like Noah," he suggested drily. "Or the ancient Hindu scriptures. Women have their

27

limitations, but so do we, God knows. Haven't we known girls in school and college just as smart as we were?''

"They cannot play our games," coldly replied the clergyman.

Gerald measured his meager proportions with a practiced eye.

"I never was particularly good at football myself," he modestly admitted, "but I've known women who could outlast a man in all-round endurance. Besides—life isn't spent in athletics!"

This was sadly true. They all looked down the aisle where a heavy ill-dressed man with a bad complexion sat alone. He had held the top of the columns once, with headlines and photographs. Now he earned less than any of them.

"It's time we woke up," pursued Gerald, still inwardly urged to unfamiliar speech. "Women are pretty much *people,* seems to me. I know they dress like fools— but who's to blame for that? We invent all those idiotic hats of theirs, and design their crazy fashions, and, what's more, if a woman is courageous enough to wear commonsense clothes—and shoes—which of us wants to dance with her?

"Yes, we blame them for grafting on us, but are we willing to let our wives work? We are not. It hurts our pride, that's all. We are always criticizing them for making mercenary marriages, but what do we call a girl who marries a chump with no money? Just a poor fool, that's all. And they know it.

"As for Mother Eve—I wasn't there and can't deny the story, but I will say this. If she brought evil into the world, we men have had the lion's share of keeping it going ever since—how about that?"

They drew into the city, and all day long in his business, Gerald was vaguely conscious of new views, strange feelings, and the submerged Mollie learned and learned.

# TURNED

In her soft-carpeted, thick-curtained, richly furnished chamber, Mrs. Marroner lay sobbing on the wide, soft bed.

She sobbed bitterly, chokingly, despairingly; her shoulders heaved and shook convulsively; her hands were tight-clenched. She had forgotten her elaborate dress, the more elaborate bedcover; forgotten her dignity, her self-control, her pride. In her mind was an overwhelming, unbelievable horror, an immeasurable loss, a turbulent, struggling mass of emotion.

In her reserved, superior, Boston-bred life, she had never dreamed that it would be possible for her to feel so many things at once, and with such trampling intensity.

She tried to cool her feelings into thoughts; to stiffen them into words; to control herself—and could not. It brought vaguely to her mind an awful moment in the breakers at York Beach, one summer in girlhood when she had been swimming under water and could not find the top.

In her uncarpeted, thin-curtained, poorly furnished chamber on the top floor, Gerta Petersen lay sobbing on the narrow, hard bed.

She was of larger frame than her mistress, grandly built and strong; but all her proud young womanhood was prostrate now, convulsed with agony, dissolved in tears. She did not try to control herself. She wept for two.

If Mrs. Marroner suffered more from the wreck and ruin of a longer love—perhaps a deeper one; if her tastes were finer, her ideals loftier; if she bore the pangs of bitter jealousy and outraged pride, Gerta had personal shame to meet, a hopeless future, and a looming present which filled her with unreasoning terror.

She had come like a meek young goddess into that perfectly ordered house, strong, beautiful, full of goodwill and eager obedience, but ignorant and childish—a girl of eighteen.

Mr. Marroner had frankly admired her, and so had his wife. They discussed her visible perfections and as visible limitations with that perfect confidence which they had so long enjoyed. Mrs. Marroner was not a jealous woman. She had never been jealous in her life—till now.

Gerta had stayed and learned their ways. They had both been fond of her. Even the cook was fond of her. She was what is called "willing," was unusually teachable and plastic; and Mrs. Marroner, with her early habits of giving instruction, tried to educate her somewhat.

"I never saw anyone so docile," Mrs. Marroner had often commented. "It is perfection in a servant, but almost a defect in character. She is so helpless and confiding."

She was precisely that: a tall, rosy-cheeked baby; rich womanhood without, helpless infancy within. Her braided wealth of dead-gold hair, her grave blue eyes, her mighty shoulders and long, firmly moulded limbs seemed those of a primal earth spirit; but she was only an ignorant child, with a child's weakness.

When Mr. Marroner had to go abroad for his firm, unwillingly, hating to leave his wife, he had told her he felt quite safe to leave her in Gerta's hands—she would take care of her.

"Be good to your mistress, Gerta," he told the girl that last morning at breakfast. "I leave her to you to take care of. I shall be back in a month at latest."

Then he turned, smiling, to his wife. "And you must take care of Gerta, too," he said. "I expect you'll have her ready for college when I get back."

This was seven months ago. Business had delayed him from week to week, from month to month. He wrote to his wife, long, loving, frequent letters, deeply regretting the delay, explaining how necessary, how profitable it was, congratulating her on the wide resources she had, her well-filled, well-balanced mind, her many interests.

"If I should be eliminated from your scheme of things, by any of those 'acts of God' mentioned on the tickets, I do not feel that you would be an utter wreck," he said. "That is very comforting to me. Your life is so rich and wide that no one loss, even a great one, would wholly cripple you. But nothing of the sort is likely to happen, and I shall be home again in three weeks—if this thing gets settled. And you will be looking so lovely, with that eager light in your eyes and the changing flush I know so well—and love so well! My dear wife! We shall have to have a new honeymoon—other moons come every month, why shouldn't the mellifluous kind?"

He often asked after "little Gerta," sometimes enclosed a picture postcard to her, joked his wife about her laborious efforts to educate "the child," was so loving and merry and wise—

All this was racing through Mrs. Marroner's mind as

she lay there with the broad, hemstitched border of fine linen sheeting crushed and twisted in one hand, and the other holding a sodden handkerchief.

She had tried to teach Gerta, and had grown to love the patient, sweet-natured child, in spite of her dullness. At work with her hands, she was clever, if not quick, and could keep small accounts from week to week. But to the woman who held a Ph.D., who had been on the faculty of a college, it was like baby-tending.

Perhaps having no babies of her own made her love the big child the more, though the years between them were but fifteen.

To the girl she seemed quite old, of course; and her young heart was full of grateful affection for the patient care which made her feel so much at home in this new land.

And then she had noticed a shadow on the girl's bright face. She looked nervous, anxious, worried. When the bell rang, she seemed startled, and would rush hurriedly to the door. Her peals of frank laughter no longer rose from the area gate as she stood talking with the always admiring tradesmen.

Mrs. Marroner had labored long to teach her more reserve with men, and flattered herself that her words were at last effective. She suspected the girl of homesickness, which was denied. She suspected her of illness, which was denied also. At last she suspected her of something which could not be denied.

For a long time she refused to believe it, waiting. Then she had to believe it, but schooled herself to patience and understanding. "The poor child," she said. "She is here without a mother—she is so foolish and yielding—I must not be too stern with her." And she tried to win the girl's confidence with wise, kind words.

But Gerta had literally thrown herself at her feet and begged her with streaming tears not to turn her away. She would admit nothing, explain nothing, but frantically promised to work for Mrs. Marroner as long as she lived—if only she would keep her.

Revolving the problem carefully in her mind, Mrs. Marroner thought she would keep her, at least for the present. She tried to repress her sense of ingratitude in one she had so sincerely tried to help, and the cold, contemptuous anger she had always felt for such weakness.

"The thing to do now," she said to herself, "is to see her through this safely. The child's life should not be hurt any more than is unavoidable. I will ask Dr. Bleet about it—what a comfort a woman doctor is! I'll stand by the poor, foolish thing till it's over, and then get her back to Sweden somehow with her baby. How they do come where they are not wanted—and don't come where they are wanted!" And Mrs. Marroner, sitting alone in the quiet, spacious beauty of the house, almost envied Gerta.

Then came the deluge.

She had sent the girl out for needed air toward dark. The late mail came; she took it in herself. One letter for her—her husband's letter. She knew the postmark, the stamp, the kind of typewriting. She impulsively kissed it in the dim hall. No one would suspect Mrs. Marroner of kissing her husband's letters—but she did, often.

She looked over the others. One was for Gerta, and not from Sweden. It looked precisely like her own. This struck her as a little odd, but Mr. Marroner had several times sent messages and cards to the girl. She laid the letter on the hall table and took hers to her room.

"My poor child," it began. What letter of hers had been sad enough to warrant that?

"I am deeply concerned at the news you send." What news to so concern him had she written? "You must bear it bravely, little girl. I shall be home soon, and will take care of you, of course. I hope there is not immediate anxiety—you do not say. Here is money, in case you need it. I expect to get home in a month at latest. If you have to go, be sure to leave your address at my office. Cheer up—be brave—I will take care of you.''

The letter was typewritten, which was not unusual. It was unsigned, which was unusual. It enclosed an American bill—fifty dollars. It did not seem in the least like any letter she had ever had from her husband, or any letter she could imagine him writing. But a strange, cold feeling was creeping over her, like a flood rising around a house.

She utterly refused to admit the ideas which began to bob and push about outside her mind, and to force themselves in. Yet under the pressure of these repudiated thoughts she went downstairs and brought up the other letter—the letter to Gerta. She laid them side by side on a smooth dark space on the table; marched to the piano and played, with stern precision, refusing to think, till the girl came back. When she came in, Mrs. Marroner rose quietly and came to the table. ''Here is a letter for you,'' she said.

The girl stepped forward eagerly, saw the two lying together there, hesitated, and looked at her mistress.

''Take yours, Gerta. Open it, please.''

The girl turned frightened eyes upon her.

''I want you to read it, here,'' said Mrs. Marroner.

''Oh, ma'am—No! Please don't make me!''

''Why not?''

There seemed to be no reason at hand, and Gerta flushed more deeply and opened her letter. It was long; it was evidently puzzling to her; it began ''My dear wife.'' She read it slowly.

''Are you sure it is your letter?'' asked Mrs. Marroner. ''Is not this one yours? Is not that one—mine?''

She held out the other letter to her.

''It is a mistake,'' Mrs. Marroner went on, with a hard quietness. She had lost her social bearings somehow, lost her usual keen sense of the proper thing to do. This was not life; this was a nightmare.

''Do you not see? Your letter was put in my envelope

and my letter was put in your envelope. Now we understand it."

But poor Gerta had no antechamber to her mind, no trained forces to preserve order while agony entered. The thing swept over her, resistless, overwhelming. She cowered before the outraged wrath she expected; and from some hidden cavern that wrath arose and swept over her in pale flame.

"Go and pack your trunk," said Mrs. Marroner. "You will leave my house tonight. Here is your money."

She laid down the fifty-dollar bill. She put with it a month's wages. She had no shadow of pity for those anguished eyes, those tears which she heard drop on the floor.

"Go to your room and pack," said Mrs. Marroner. And Gerta, always obedient, went.

Then Mrs. Marroner went to hers, and spent a time she never counted, lying on her face on the bed.

But the training of the twenty-eight years which had elapsed before her marriage; the life at college, both as student and teacher; the independent growth which she had made, formed a very different background for grief from that in Gerta's mind.

After a while Mrs. Marroner arose. She administered to herself a hot bath, a cold shower, a vigorous rubbing. "Now I can think," she said.

First she regretted the sentence of instant banishment. She went upstairs to see if it had been carried out. Poor Gerta! The tempest of her agony had worked itself out at last as in a child, and left her sleeping, the pillow wet, the lips still grieving, a big sob shuddering itself off now and then.

Mrs. Marroner stood and watched her, and as she watched she considered the helpless sweetness of the face; the defenseless, unformed character; the docility and habit of obedience which made her so attractive—and so easily a victim. Also she thought of the mighty force which had swept over her; of the great process now working itself out through her; of how pitiful and futile seemed any resistance she might have made.

She softly returned to her own room, made up a little fire, and sat by it, ignoring her feelings now, as she had before ignored her thoughts.

Here were two women and a man. One woman was a wife: loving, trusting, affectionate. One was a servant: loving, trusting, affectionate—a young girl, an exile, a dependent; grateful for any kindness; untrained, uneducated, childish. She ought, of course, to have resisted temptation; but Mrs. Marroner was wise enough to know how difficult temptation is to recognize when it comes in the guise of friendship and from a source one does not suspect.

Gerta might have done better in resisting the grocer's clerk; had, indeed, with Mrs. Marroner's advice, resisted several. But where respect was due, how could she criticize? Where obedience was due, how could she refuse—with ignorance to hold her blinded—until too late?

As the older, wiser woman forced herself to understand and extenuate the girl's misdeed and foresee her ruined future, a new feeling rose in her heart, strong, clear, and overmastering: a sense of measureless condemnation for the man who had done this thing. He knew. He understood. He could fully foresee and measure the consequences of his act. He appreciated to the full the innocence, the ignorance, the grateful affection, the habitual docility, of which he deliberately took advantage.

Mrs. Marroner rose to icy peaks of intellectual apprehension, from which her hours of frantic pain seemed far indeed removed. He had done this thing under the same roof with her—his wife. He had not frankly loved the younger woman, broken with his wife, made a new marriage. That would have been heart-break pure and simple. This was something else.

That letter, that wretched, cold, carefully guarded,

unsigned letter, that bill—far safer than a check—these did not speak of affection. Some men can love two women at one time. This was not love.

Mrs. Marroner's sense of pity and outrage for herself, the wife, now spread suddenly into a perception of pity and outrage for the girl. All that splendid, clean young beauty, the hope of a happy life, with marriage and motherhood, honorable independence, even—these were nothing to that man. For his own pleasure he had chosen to rob her of her life's best joys.

He would "take care of her," said the letter. How? In what capacity?

And then, sweeping over both her feelings for herself, the wife, and Gerta, his victim, came a new flood, which literally lifted her to her feet. She rose and walked, her head held high. "This is the sin of man against woman," she said. "The offense is against womanhood. Against motherhood. Against—the child."

She stopped.

The child. His child. That, too, he sacrificed and injured—doomed to degradation.

Mrs. Marroner came of stern New England stock. She was not a Calvinist, hardly even a Unitarian, but the iron of Calvinism was in her soul: of that grim faith which held that most people had to be damned "for the glory of God."

Generations of ancestors who both preached and practiced stood behind her; people whose lives had been sternly moulded to their highest moments of religious conviction. In sweeping bursts of feeling, they achieved "conviction," and afterward they lived and died according to that conviction.

When Mr. Marroner reached home a few weeks later, following his letters too soon to expect an answer to either, he saw no wife upon the pier, though he had cabled, and found the house closed darkly. He let himself in with his latch-key, and stole softly upstairs, to surprise his wife.

No wife was there.

He rang the bell. No servant answered it.

He turned up light after light, searched the house from top to bottom; it was utterly empty. The kitchen wore a clean, bald, unsympathetic aspect. He left it and slowly mounted the stairs, completely dazed. The whole house was clean, in perfect order, wholly vacant.

One thing he felt perfectly sure of—she knew.

Yet was he sure? He must not assume too much. She might have been ill. She might have died. He started to his feet. No, they would have cabled him. He sat down again.

For any such change, if she had wanted him to know, she would have written. Perhaps she had, and he, returning so suddenly, had missed the letter. The thought was some comfort. It must be so. He turned to the telephone and again hesitated. If she had found out—if she had gone—utterly gone, without a word—should he announce it himself to friends and family?

He walked the floor; he searched everywhere for some letter, some word of explanation. Again and again he went to the telephone—and always stopped. He could not bear to ask: "Do you know where my wife is?"

The harmonious, beautiful rooms reminded him in a dumb, helpless way of her—like the remote smile on the face of the dead. He put out the lights, could not bear the darkness, turned them all on again.

It was a long night—

In the morning he went early to the office. In the accumulated mail was no letter from her. No one seemed to know of anything unusual. A friend asked after his wife—"Pretty glad to see you, I guess?" He answered evasively.

About eleven a man came to see him: John Hill, her lawyer. Her cousin, too. Mr. Marroner had never liked him. He liked him less now, for Mr. Hill merely handed him a letter, remarked, "I was requested to deliver this to you personally," and departed, looking like a person who is called on to kill something offensive.

"I have gone. I will care for Gerta. Good-bye. Marion."

That was all. There was no date, no address, no postmark, nothing but that.

In his anxiety and distress, he had fairly forgotten Gerta and all that. Her name aroused in him a sense of rage. She had come between him and his wife. She had taken his wife from him. That was the way he felt.

At first he said nothing, did nothing, lived on alone in his house, taking meals where he chose. When people asked him about his wife, he said she was traveling—for her health. He would not have it in the newspapers. Then, as time passed, as no enlightenment came to him, he resolved not to bear it any longer, and employed detectives. They blamed him for not having put them on the track earlier, but set to work, urged to the utmost secrecy.

What to him had been so blank a wall of mystery seemed not to embarrass them in the least. They made careful inquiries as to her "past," found where she had studied, where taught, and on what lines; that she had some little money of her own, that her doctor was Josephine L. Bleet, M.D., and many other bits of information.

As a result of careful and prolonged work, they finally told him that she had resumed teaching under one of her old professors, lived quietly, and apparently kept boarders; giving him town, street, and number, as if it were a matter of no difficulty whatever.

He had returned in early spring. It was autumn before he found her.

A quiet college town in the hills, a broad, shady street, a pleasant house standing in its own lawn, with trees and flowers about it. He had the address in his hand, and the number showed clear on the white gate. He walked up the straight gravel path and rang the bell. An elderly servant opened the door.

"Does Mrs. Marroner live here?"

"No, sir."

"This is number twenty-eight?"

"Yes, sir."

"Who does live here?"

"Miss Wheeling, sir."

Ah! Her maiden name. They had told him, but he had forgotten.

He stepped inside. "I would like to see her," he said.

He was ushered into a still parlor, cool and sweet with the scent of flowers, the flowers she had always loved best. It almost brought tears to his eyes. All their years of happiness rose in his mind again—the exquisite beginnings; the days of eager longing before she was really his; the deep, still beauty of her love.

Surely she would forgive him—she must forgive him. He would humble himself; he would tell her of his honest remorse—his absolute determination to be a different man.

Through the wide doorway there came in to him two women. One like a tall Madonna, bearing a baby in her arms.

Marion, calm, steady, definitely impersonal, nothing but a clear pallor to hint of inner stress.

Gerta, holding the child as a bulwark, with a new intelligence in her face, and her blue, adoring eyes fixed on her friend—not upon him.

He looked from one to the other dumbly.

And the woman who had been his wife asked quietly:

"What have you to say to us?"

# THE
# COTTAGETTE

"Why not?" said Mr. Mathews. "It is far too small for a house, too pretty for a hut, too—unusual—for a cottage."

"Cottagette, by all means," said Lois, seating herself on a porch chair. "But it is larger than it looks, Mr. Mathews. How do you like it, Malda?"

I was delighted with it. More than delighted. Here this tiny shell of fresh unpainted wood peeped out from under the trees, the only house in sight except the distant white specks on far-off farms, and the little wandering village in the river-threaded valley. It sat right on the turf—no road, no path even, and the dark woods shadowed the back windows.

"How about meals?" asked Lois.

"Not two minutes' walk," he assured her, and showed us a little furtive path between the trees to the place where meals were furnished.

We discussed and examined and exclaimed, Lois holding her pongee skirts close about her—she needn't have been so careful, there wasn't a speck of dust—and presently decided to take it.

Never did I know the real joy and peace of living, before that blessed summer at High Court. It was a mountain place, easy enough to get to, but strangely big and still and far away when you were there.

The working basis of the establishment was an eccentric woman named Caswell, a sort of musical enthusiast, who had a summer school of music and the "higher thought." Malicious persons, not able to obtain accommodations there, called the place High C.

I liked the music very well, and kept my thoughts to myself, both high and low, but the Cottagette I loved unreservedly. It was so little and new and clean, smelling only of its fresh-planed boards—they hadn't even stained it.

There was one big room and two little ones in the tiny thing, though from the outside you wouldn't have believed it, it looked so small; but small as it was, it harbored a miracle—a real bathroom with water piped from mountain springs. Our windows opened into the green shadiness, the soft brownness, the bird-inhabited, quiet, flower-starred woods. But in front we looked across whole counties—over a far-off river—into another state. Off and down and away—it was like sitting on the roof of something—something very big.

The grass swept up to the doorstep, to the walls—only it wasn't just grass, of course, but such a procession of flowers as I had never imagined could grow in one place.

You had to go quite a way through the meadow, wearing your own narrow faintly marked streak in the grass, to reach the town-connecting road below. But in the woods was a little path, clear and wide, by which we went to meals.

For we ate with the highly thoughtful musicians, and highly musical thinkers, in their central boardinghouse nearby. They didn't call it a boardinghouse, which is neither high nor musical; they called it the Calceolaria. There was plenty of that growing about, and I didn't mind what they called it so long as the food was good—which it was, and the prices reasonable—which they were.

The people were extremely interesting—some of them at least; and all of them were better than the average of summer boarders.

But if there hadn't been any interesting ones, it didn't matter while Ford Mathews was there. He was a newspaper man, or rather an ex-newspaper man, then becoming a writer for magazines, with books ahead.

He had friends at High Court—he liked music, he liked the place, and he liked us. Lois liked him too, as was quite natural. I'm sure I did.

He used to come up evenings and sit on the porch and talk.

He came daytimes and went on long walks with us. He established his workshop in a most attractive little cave not far beyond us—the country there is full of rocky ledges and hollows—and sometimes asked us over to an afternoon tea, made on a gipsy fire.

Lois was a good deal older than I, but not really old at all, and she didn't look her thirty-five by ten years. I never blamed her for not mentioning it, and I wouldn't have done so myself on any account. But I felt that together we made a safe and reasonable household. She played beautifully, and there was a piano in our big room. There were pianos in several other little cottages about—but too far off for any jar of sound. When the wind was right, we caught little wafts of music now and then; but mostly it was still, blessedly still, about us. And yet that Calceolaria was only two minutes off—and with raincoats and rubbers we never minded going to it.

We saw a good deal of Ford, and I got interested in

him; I couldn't help it. He was big. Not extra big in pounds and inches, but a man with a big view and grip—with purpose and real power. He was going to do things. I thought he was doing them now, but he didn't—this was all like cutting steps in the icewall, he said. It had to be done, but the road was long ahead. And he took an interest in my work too, which is unusual for a literary man.

Mine wasn't much. I did embroidery and made designs.

It is such pretty work! I like to draw from flowers and leaves and things about me—conventionalize them sometimes, and sometimes paint them just as they are, in soft silk stitches.

All about up here were the lovely small things I needed; and not only these, but the lovely big things that make one feel so strong and able to do beautiful work.

Here was the friend I lived so happily with, and all this fairyland of sun and shadow, the free immensity of our view, and the dainty comfort of the Cottagette. We never had to think of ordinary things till the soft musical thrill of the Japanese gong stole through the trees, and we trotted off to the Calceolaria.

I think Lois knew before I did.

We were old friends and trusted each other, and she had had experience too.

"Malda," she said, "let us face this thing and be rational." It was a strange thing that Lois should be so rational and yet so musical—but she was, and that was one reason I liked her so much.

"You are beginning to love Ford Mathews—do you know it?"

I said yes, I thought I was.

"Does he love you?"

That I couldn't say. "It is early yet," I told her. "He is a man, he is about thirty I believe, he has seen more of life and probably loved before—it may be nothing more than friendliness with him."

"Do you think it would be a good marriage?" she

asked. We had often talked of love and marriage, and Lois
had helped me to form my views—hers were very clear
and strong.

"Why yes—if he loves me," I said. "He has told me
quite a bit about his family, good Western farming people,
real Americans. He is strong and well—you can read clean
living in his eyes and mouth." Ford's eyes were as clear
as a girl's, the whites of them were clear. Most men's
eyes, when you look at them critically, are not like that.
They may look at you very expressively, but when you
look at them, just as features, they are not very nice.

I liked his looks, but I liked him better.

So I told her that as far as I knew, it would be a good
marriage—if it was one.

"How much do you love him?" she asked.

That I couldn't quite tell—it was a good deal—but I
didn't think it would kill me to lose him.

"Do you love him enough to do something to win
him—to really put yourself out somewhat for that purpose?"

"Why—yes—I think I do. If it was something I
approved of. What do you mean?"

Then Lois unfolded her plan. She had been married—
unhappily married, in her youth; that was all over and
done with years ago. She had told me about it long since,
and she said she did not regret the pain and loss because it
had given her experience. She had her maiden name again—
and freedom. She was so fond of me she wanted to give
me the benefit of her experience—without the pain.

"Men like music," said Lois. "They like sensible
talk; they like beauty, of course, and all that—"

"Then they ought to like you!" I interrupted, and, as
a matter of fact, they did. I knew several who wanted to
marry her, but she said "once was enough." I don't think
they were "good marriages," though.

"Don't be foolish, child," said Lois. "This is serious. What they care for most, after all, is domesticity. Of
course they'll fall in love with anything; but what they

want to marry is a homemaker. Now we are living here in an idyllic sort of way, quite conducive to falling in love, but no temptation to marriage. If I were you—if I really loved this man and wished to marry him—I would make a home of this place.''

"Make a home? Why, it *is* a home. I never was so happy anywhere in my life. What on earth do you mean, Lois?"

"A person might be happy in a balloon, I suppose,'' she replied, "but it wouldn't be a home. He comes here and sits talking with us, and it's quiet and feminine and attractive—and then we hear that big gong at the Calceolaria, and off we go slopping through the wet woods—and the spell is broken. Now you can cook.'' I could cook. I could cook excellently. My esteemed Mama had rigorously taught me every branch of what is now called domestic science; and I had no objection to the work, except that it prevented my doing anything else. And one's hands are not so nice when one cooks and washes dishes—I need nice hands for my needlework. But if it was a question of pleasing Ford Mathews—

Lois went on calmly. "Miss Caswell would put on a kitchen for us in a minute; she said she would, you know, when we took the cottage. Plenty of people keep house up here—we can if we want to.''

"But we don't want to,'' I said. "We never have wanted to. The very beauty of the place is that it never had any housekeeping about it. Still, as you say, it would be cosy on a wet night, we could have delicious little suppers, and have him stay—''

"He told me he had never known a home since he was eighteen,'' said Lois.

That was how we came to install a kitchen in the Cottagette. The men put it up in a few days, just a lean-to with a window, sink, and two doors. I did the cooking. We had nice things, there is no denying that: good fresh milk and vegetables particularly. Fruit is hard to get in the country, and meat too—still we managed nicely; the less you have, the more you have to manage—it takes time and brains, that's all.

Lois likes to do housework, but it spoils her hands for practicing, so she can't and I was perfectly willing to do it—it was all in the interest of my own heart. Ford certainly enjoyed it. He dropped in often, and ate things with undeniable relish. So I was pleased, though it did interfere with my work a good deal. I always work best in the morning; but of course housework has to be done in the morning too; and it is astonishing how much work there is in the littlest kitchen. You go in for a minute, and you see this thing and that thing and the other thing to be done, and your minute is an hour before you know it.

When I was ready to sit down, the freshness of the morning was gone somehow. Before, when I woke up, there was only the clean wood smell of the house, and then the blessed out-of-doors; now I always felt the call of the kitchen as soon as I woke. An oil stove will smell a little, either in or out of the house; and soap, and—well, you know if you cook in a bedroom how it makes the room feel differently? Our house had been only bedroom and parlor before.

We baked too—the baker's bread was really pretty poor, and Ford did enjoy my whole wheat, and brown, and especially hot rolls and gems. It was a pleasure to feed him, but it did heat up the house, and me. I never could work much—at my work—baking days. Then, when I did get to work, the people would come with things—milk or meat or vegetables, or children with berries; and what distressed me most was the wheelmarks on our meadow. They soon made quite a road—they had to, of course, but I hated it. I lost that lovely sense of being on the last edge and looking over—we were just a bead on a string like other houses. But it was quite true that I loved this man, and would do more than this to please him. We couldn't go off so freely on excursions as we used, either; when meals are to be prepared, someone has to be there, and to take in things when they come. Sometimes Lois stayed in, she always asked to, but mostly I did. I couldn't let her spoil her summer on my account. And Ford certainly liked it.

He came so often that Lois said she thought it would look better if we had an older person with us, and that her mother could come if I wanted her, and she could help with the work of course. That seemed reasonable, and she came. I wasn't very fond of Lois's mother, Mrs. Fowler, but it did seem a little conspicuous, Mr. Mathews eating with us more than he did at the Calceolaria. There were others of course, plenty of them dropping in, but I didn't encourage it much, it made so much more work. They would come in to supper, and then we would have musical evenings. They offered to help me wash dishes, some of them, but a new hand in the kitchen is not much help. I preferred to do it myself; then I knew where the dishes were.

Ford never seemed to want to wipe dishes, though I often wished he would.

So Mrs. Fowler came. She and Lois had one room, they had to—and she really did a lot of the work; she was a very practical old lady.

Then the house began to be noisy. You hear another person in a kitchen more than you hear yourself, I think—and the walls were only boards. She swept more than we did too. I don't think much sweeping is needed in a clean place like that; and she dusted all the time, which I know is unnecessary. I still did most of the cooking, but I could get off more to draw, out-of-doors, and to walk. Ford was in and out continually, and, it seemed to me, was really coming nearer. What was one summer of interrupted work, of noise and dirt and smell and constant meditation on what to eat next, compared to a lifetime of love? Besides—if he married me—I should have to do it always, and might as well get used to it.

Lois kept me contented, too, telling me nice things that Ford said about my cooking. "He does appreciate it so," she said.

One day he came around early and asked me to go up Hugh's Peak with him. It was a lovely climb and took all day. I demurred a little; it was Monday. Mrs. Fowler thought it was cheaper to have a woman come and wash, and we did, but it certainly made more work.

"Never mind," he said. "What's washing day or ironing day or any of that old foolishness to us? This is walking day—that's what it is." It was really, cool and sweet and fresh—it had rained in the night—and brilliantly clear.

"Come along!" he said. "We can see as far as Patch Mountain I'm sure. There'll never be a better day."

"Is anyone else going?" I asked.

"Not a soul. It's just us. Come."

I came gladly, only suggesting—"Wait, let me put up a lunch."

"I'll wait just long enough for you to put on knickers and a short skirt," said he. "The lunch is all in the basket on my back. I know how long it takes for you women to 'put up' sandwiches and things."

We were off in ten minutes, light-footed and happy; and the day was all that could be asked. He brought a perfect lunch, too, and had made it all himself. I confess it tasted better to me than my own cooking; but perhaps that was the climb.

When we were nearly down, we stopped by a spring on a broad ledge, and supped, making tea as he liked to do out-of-doors. We saw the round sun setting at one end of a world view, and the round moon rising at the other, calmly shining each on each.

And then he asked me to be his wife.

We were very happy.

"But there's a condition!" said he, all at once, sitting up straight and looking very fierce. "You mustn't cook!"

"What!" said I. "Mustn't cook?"

"No," said he, "you must give it up—for my sake."

I stared at him dumbly.

"Yes, I know all about it," he went on. "Lois told me. I've seen a good deal of Lois—since you've taken to cooking. And since I would talk about you, naturally I learned a lot. She told me how you were brought up, and how strong your domestic instincts were—but bless your artist soul, dear girl, you have some others!" Then he smiled rather queerly and murmured, "Surely in vain the net is spread in the sight of any bird.

"I've watched you, dear, all summer," he went on. "It doesn't agree with you.

"Of course the things taste good—but so do my things! I'm a good cook myself. My father was a cook, for years—at good wages. I'm used to it, you see.

"One summer when I was hard up I cooked for a living—and saved money instead of starving."

"Oh ho!" said I. "That accounts for the tea—and the lunch!"

"And lots of other things," said he.

"But you haven't done half as much of your lovely work since you started this kitchen business, and—you'll forgive me, dear—it hasn't been as good. Your work is quite too good to lose; it is a beautiful and distinctive art, and I don't want you to let it go. What would you think of me if I gave up my hard long years of writing for the easy competence of a well-paid cook!"

I was still too happy to think very clearly. I just sat and looked at him. "But you want to marry me?" I said.

"I want to marry you, Malda—because I love you— because you are young and strong and beautiful—because you are wild and sweet and—fragrant, and—elusive, like the wildflowers you love. Because you are so truly an artist in your special way, seeing beauty and giving it to others. I love you because of all this, because you are rational and high-minded and capable of friendship—and in spite of your cooking!''

"But—how do you want to live?"

"As we did here—at first," he said. "There was peace, exquisite silence. There was beauty—nothing but beauty. There were the clean wood odors and flowers and fragrances and sweet wild wind. And there was you—your fair self, always delicately dressed, with white firm fingers sure of touch in delicate true work. I loved you then. When you took to cooking, it jarred on me. I have been a cook, I tell you, and I know what it is. I hated it—to see my woodflower in a kitchen. But Lois told me about how you were brought up to it and loved it, and I said to myself, 'I love this woman; I will wait and see if I love her even as a cook.' And I do, darling: I withdraw the condition. I will love you always, even if you insist on being my cook for life!''

"Oh, I don't insist!" I cried. "I don't want to cook—I want to draw! But I thought— Lois said— How she has misunderstood you!''

"It is not true, always, my dear," said he, "that the way to a man's heart is through his stomach; at least it's not the only way. Lois doesn't know everything; she is young yet! And perhaps for my sake you can give it up. Can you, sweet?''

Could I? Could I? Was there ever a man like this?

# AN HONEST
# WOMAN

"There's an honest woman if ever there was one!" said the young salesman to the old one, watching their landlady whisk inside the screen door and close it softly without letting in a single fly—those evergreen California flies not mentioned by real estate men.

"What makes you think so?" asked Mr. Burdock, commonly known as Old Burdock, wriggling forward, with alternate jerks, the two hind legs which supported his chair, until its backward tilt was positively dangerous.

"Think!" said young Abramson with extreme decision. "I happen to know. I've put up here for three years past, twice a year; and I know a lot of people in this town—sell to 'em right along."

"Stands well in the town, does she?" inquired the other with no keen interest. He had put up at the Main House for eight years, and furthermore he knew Mrs. Main when she was a child; but he did not mention it. Mr.

Burdock made no pretense of virtue, yet if he had one in especial it lay in the art of not saying things.

"I should say she does!" the plump young man replied, straightening his well-curved waistcoat. "None better. She hasn't a bill standing—settles the day they come in. Pays cash for everything she can. She must make a handsome thing of this house; but it don't go in finery—she's as plain as a hen."

"Why, I should call Mrs. Main rather a good-looking woman," Burdock gently protested.

"Oh yes, good-looking enough; but I mean her style—no show—no expense—no dress. But she keeps up the house all right—everything first class, and reasonable prices. She's got good money in the bank, they tell me. And there's a daughter—away at school somewhere—won't have her brought up in a hotel. She's dead right, too."

"I dunno why a girl couldn't grow up in a hotel—with a nice mother like that," urged Mr. Burdock.

"Oh come! You know better 'n that. Get talked about in any case—probably worse. No sir! You can't be too careful about a girl, and her mother knows it."

"Glad you've got a high opinion of women. I like to see it," and Mr. Burdock tilted softly backward and forward in his chair, a balancing foot thrust forth. He wore large, square-toed, rather thin shoes with the visible outlines of feet in them.

The shoes of Mr. Abramson, on the other hand, had pronounced outlines of their own, and might have been stuffed with anything—that would go in.

"I've got a high opinion of good women," he announced with finality. "As to bad ones, the less said the better!" and he puffed his strong cigar, looking darkly experienced.

"They're doin' a good deal towards reformin' 'em, nowadays, ain't they?" ventured Mr. Burdock.

The young man laughed disagreeably. "You can't

reform spilled milk,'' said he. ''But I do like to see an honest, hardworking woman succeed.''

''So do I, boy,'' said his companion, ''so do I,'' and they smoked in silence.

The hotel bus drew up before the house, backed up creakingly, and one passenger descended, bearing a large, lean suitcase showing much wear. He was an elderly man, tall, well-built, but not well-carried, and wore a long, thin beard. Mr. Abramson looked him over, decided that he was neither a buyer nor a seller, and dismissed him from his mind.

Mr. Burdock looked him over and brought the front legs of his chair down with a thump.

''By heck!'' said he softly.

The newcomer went in to register.

Mr. Burdock went in to buy another cigar.

Mrs. Main was at the desk alone, working at her books. Her smooth, dark hair curved away from a fine forehead, both broad and high; wide-set, steady gray eyes looked out from under level brows with a clear directness. Her mouth, at thirty-eight, was a little hard.

The tall man scarcely looked at her, as he reached for the register book; but she looked at him, and her color slowly heightened. He signed his name as one of considerable importance, ''Mr. Alexander E. Main, Guthrie, Oklahoma.''

''I want a sunny room,'' he said. ''A south room, with a fire when I want it. I feel the cold in this climate very much.''

''You always did,'' remarked Mrs. Main quietly.

Then he looked, the pen dropping from his fingers and rolling across the untouched page, making a dotted path of lessening blotches.

Mr. Burdock made himself as small as he could against the cigar stand, but she ruthlessly approached, sold him the cigar he selected, and waited calmly till he started out, the tall man still staring.

Then she turned to him.

"Here is your key," she said. "Joe, take the gentleman's grip."

The boy moved off with the worn suitcase, but the tall man leaned over the counter towards her.

Mr. Burdock was carefully closing the screen door—so carefully that he could still hear.

"Why Mary! Mary! I must see you," the man whispered.

"You may see me at any time," she answered quietly. "Here is my office."

"This evening!" he said excitedly. "I'll come down this evening when it's quiet. I have so much to tell you, Mary."

"Very well," she said. "Room twenty-seven, Joe," and turned away.

Mr. Burdock took a walk, his cigar still unlighted.

"By heck!" said he. "By—heck! And she as cool as a cucumber— That confounded old skeezicks! Hanged if I don't happen to be passin'."

A sturdy, long-legged little girl was Mary Cameron when he first did business with her father in a Kansas country store. Ranch born and bred, a vigorous, independent child, gravely selling knives and sewing silk, writing paper, and potatoes "to help Father."

Father was a freethinker—a man of keen, strong mind, scant education, and opinions which ran away with him. He trained her to think for herself, and she did; to act up to her beliefs, and she did; to worship liberty and the sacred rights of the individual, and she did.

But the store failed, as the ranch had failed before it. Perhaps Old Man Cameron's arguments were too hot for the store loafers; perhaps his freethinking scandalized them. When Burdock saw Mary again, she was working in a San Francisco restaurant. She did not remember him in the least; but he knew one of her friends there and learned of the move to California—the orange failure, the grape failure, the unexpected death of Mr. Cameron, and Mary's self-respecting efficiency since.

"She's doin' well already—got some money ahead—and she's just as straight!" said Miss Josie. "Want to meet her?"

"Oh no," said Mr. Burdock, who was of a retiring disposition. "No, she wouldn't remember me at all."

When he happened into that restaurant again a year later, Mary had gone, and her friend hinted dark things.

"She got to goin' with a married man!" she confided. "Man from Oklahoma—name o' Main. One o' these Healers—great man for talkin'. She's left here, and I don't know where she is."

Mr. Burdock was sorry, very sorry—not only because he knew Mary, but because he knew Mr. Main. First—where had he met that man first? When he was a glib young phrenologist in Cincinnati. Then he'd run against him in St. Louis—a palmist this time; and then in Topeka—"Dr. Alexander," some sort of an "opaththist." Dr. Main's system of therapy varied, it appeared, with circumstances; he treated brains or bones as it happened, and here in San Francisco had made quite a hit, had lectured, had written a book on sex.

That Mary Cameron, with her hard sense and high courage, should take up with a man like that!

But Mr. Burdock continued to travel, and some four years later, coming to a new hotel in San Diego, he had found Mary again, now Mrs. Mary Main, presiding over the affairs of the house, with a small daughter going to school sedately.

Nothing did he say, to or about her. She was closely attending to her business, and he attended to his; but the next time he was in Cincinnati he had no difficulty in hearing of Mrs. Alexander Main—and her three children—in very poor circumstances indeed.

Of Main he had heard nothing for many years—till now.

He returned to the hotel, and walked near the side window of the office. No one there yet. Selecting chewing gum for solace, as tobacco might betray him, he deliberately tucked a camp stool under the shadow of the overhanging rose bush and sat there, somewhat thornily, but well hidden.

"It's none o' my business, but I mean to get the rights o' this," said Mr. Burdock.

She came in about a quarter of ten, as neat, as plain, as quiet as ever, and sat down under the light with her sewing. Many pretty things Mrs. Main made lovingly, but never wore.

She stopped after a little, folded her strong hands in her lap, and sat looking straight before her.

"If I could only see what she's looking at, I'd get the hang of it," thought Mr. Burdock, occasionally peering.

What she was looking at was a woman's life—and she studied it calmly and with impartial justice.

A fearless, independent girl, fond of her father but recognizing his weaknesses, she had taken her life in her own hands at about the age of twenty, finding in her orphanhood mainly freedom. Her mother she hardly remembered. She was not attractive to such youths as she met in the course of business, coldly repellent to all casual advances, and determined inwardly not to marry, at least not till she had made something of herself. She had worked hard, kept her health, saved money, and read much of the "progressive literature" her father loved.

Then came this man who also read—studied—thought, who felt as she felt, who shared her aspirations, who "understood her." (Quite possibly he did—he was a person of considerable experience.)

Slowly she grew to enjoy his society, to depend upon it. When he revealed himself as lonely, not over-strong, struggling with the world, she longed to help him; and when, at last, in a burst of bitter confidence, he had said he must leave her, that she had made life over for him but that he must tear himself away, that she was life and hope to him, but he was not free—she demanded the facts.

He told her a sad tale, seeming not to cast blame on any but himself; but the girl burned deep and hot with indignation at the sordid woman, older than he, who had married him in his inexperienced youth, drained him of all he could earn, blasted his ideals, made his life an unbearable desert waste. She had—but no, he would not blacken her who had been his wife.

"She gives me no provable cause for divorce," he told her. "She will not loosen her grip. I have left her, but she will not let me go."

"Were there any—children?" she asked after a while.

"There was one little girl—" he said with a pathetic pause. "She died—"

He did not feel it necessary to mention that there were three little boys—who had lived, after a fashion.

Then Mary Cameron made a decision which was more credit to her heart than to her head, though she would have warmly denied such a criticism.

"I see no reason why your life—your happiness—your service to the community—should all be ruined and lost because you were foolish as a boy."

"I was," he groaned. "I fell under temptation. Like any other sinner, I must bear my punishment. There is no escape."

"Nonsense," said Mary. "She will not let you go. You will not live with her. You cannot marry me. But I can be your wife—if you want me to."

It was nobly meant. She cheerfully risked all, gave up all, to make up to him for his "ruined life," to give some happiness to one so long unhappy; and when he vowed that he would not take advantage of such sublime unselfishness, she said that it was not in the least unselfish—for she loved him. This was true—she was quite honest about it.

And he? It is perfectly possible that he entered into their "sacred compact" with every intention of respecting it. She made him happier than anyone else ever had, so far.

There were two happy years when Mr. and Mrs. Main—they took themselves quite seriously—lived in their little flat together and worked and studied and thought great thoughts for the advancement of humanity. Also there was a girl child born, and their contentment was complete.

But in time the income earned by Mr. Main fell away more and more; till Mrs. Main went forth again and worked in a hotel, as efficient as ever, and even more attractive.

Then he had become restless and had gone to Seattle to look for employment—a long search, with only letters to fill the void.

And then—the quiet woman's hands were clenched together till the nails were purple and white—then The Letter came.

She was sitting alone that evening, the child playing on the floor. The woman who looked after her in the daytime had gone home. The two "roomers" who nearly paid the rent were out. It was a still, soft evening.

She had not had a letter for a week—and was hungry for it. She kissed the envelope—where his hand had rested. She squeezed it tight in her hands—laid her cheek on it—pressed it to her heart.

The baby reached up and wanted to share in the game. She gave her the envelope.

He was not coming back—ever. . . . It was better that she should know at once. . . . She was a strong woman—she would not be overcome. . . . She was a capable woman—independent—he need not worry about her in that way. . . . They had been mistaken. . . . He had found one that was more truly his. . . . She had been a Great

Boon to him. . . . Here was some money for the child. . . . Good-bye.

She sat there, still, very still, staring straight before her, till the child reached up with a little cry.

Then she caught that baby in her arms, and fairly crushed her with passionate caresses till the child cried in good earnest and had to be comforted. Stony-eyed, the mother soothed and rocked her till she slept, and laid her carefully in her little crib. Then she stood up and faced it.

"I suppose I am a ruined woman," she said.

She went to the glass and lit the gas on either side, facing herself with fixed gaze and adding calmly, "I don't look it!"

She did not look it. Tall, strong, nobly built, softer and richer for her years of love, her happy motherhood, the woman she saw in the glass seemed as one at the beginning of a splendid life, not at the end of a bad one.

No one could ever know all that she thought and felt that night, bracing her broad shoulders to meet this unbelievable blow.

If he had died she could have borne it better; if he had disappeared she would at least have had her memories left. But now she had not only grief but *shame*. She had been a fool—a plain, ordinary, old-fashioned, girl fool, just like so many others she had despised. And now?

Under the shock and torture of her shattered life, the brave, practical soul of her struggled to keep its feet, to stand erect. She was not a demonstrative woman. Possibly he had never known how much she loved him, how utterly her life had grown to lean on his.

This thought struck her suddenly and she held her head higher. "Why should he ever know?" she said to herself, and then, "At least I have the child!" Before that night was over, her plans were made.

The money he had sent, which her first feeling was to tear and burn, she now put carefully aside. "He sent it for the child," she said. "She will need it." She sublet the little flat and sold the furniture to a young couple, friends of hers, who were looking for just such a quiet home. She bought a suit of mourning, not too cumbrous, and set forth with little Mollie for the South.

In that fair land to which so many invalids come too late, it is not hard to find incompetent women, widowed and penniless, struggling to make a business of the only art they know—emerging from the sheltered harbor of "keeping house" upon the troubled sea of "keeping boarders."

Accepting moderate terms because of the child, doing good work because of long experience, offering a friendly sympathy out of her own deep sorrow, Mrs. Main made herself indispensable to such a one.

When her new employer asked her about her husband, she would press her handkerchief to her eyes and say, "He has left me. I cannot bear to speak of him."

This was quite true.

In a year she had saved a little money, and had spent it for a ticket home for the bankrupt lady of the house, who gladly gave her "the goodwill of the business" for it.

Said goodwill was lodged in an angry landlord, a few discontented and largely delinquent boarders, and many unpaid tradesmen. Mrs. Main called a meeting of her creditors in the stiff boardinghouse parlor.

She said, "I have bought this business, such as it is, with practically my last cent. I have worked seven years in restaurants and hotels and know how to run this place better than it has been done so far. If you people will give me credit for six months, and then, if I make good, for six months more, I will assume these back debts—and pay them. Otherwise I shall have to leave here, and you will get nothing but what will come from a forced sale of this third-hand furniture. I shall work hard, for I have this fatherless child to work for." She had the fatherless child at her side—a pretty thing about three years old.

They looked the house over, looked her over, talked a

little with the boarder of longest standing, and took up her offer.

She made good in six months, at the end of the year had begun to pay debts, and now—

Mrs. Main drew a long breath and came back to the present.

Mollie, dear Mollie, was a big girl now, doing excellently well at a good school. The Main House was an established success—had been for years. She had some money laid up—for Mollie's college expenses. Her health was good, she liked her work, she was respected and esteemed in the town, a useful member of a liberal church, of the Progressive Woman's Club, of the City Improvement Association. She had won Comfort, Security, and Peace.

His step on the stairs—restrained—uncertain—eager.

Her door was open. He came in, and closed it softly behind him. She rose and opened it.

"That door stands open," she said. "You need not worry. There's no one about."

"Not many, at any rate," thought the unprincipled Burdock.

She sat down again quietly. He wanted to kiss her, to take her in his arms; but she moved back to her seat with a decided step, and motioned him to his.

"You wanted to speak to me, Mr. Main. What about?"

Then he poured forth his heart as he used to, in a flow of strong, convincing words.

He told of his wanderings, his struggles, his repeated failures; of the misery that had overwhelmed him in his last fatal mistake.

"I deserve it all," he said with the quick smile and lift of the head that once was so compelling. "I deserve everything that has come to me. . . . Once to have had you . . . and to be so blind a fool as to let go your hand! I needed it, Mary, I needed it."

He said little of his intermediate years as to facts, much as to the waste of woe they represented.

"Now I am doing better in my business," he said. "I have an established practice in Guthrie, but my health is not good and I have been advised to come to a warmer climate at least for a while."

She said nothing but regarded him with a clear and steady eye. He seemed an utter stranger, and an unattractive one. That fierce leap of the heart, which, in his presence, at his touch, she recalled so well—where was it now?

"Will you not speak to me, Mary?"

"I have nothing to say."

"Can you not—forgive me?"

She leaned forward, dropping her forehead in her hands. He waited breathless; he thought she was struggling with her heart.

In reality she was recalling their life together, measuring its further prospects in the light of what he had told her, and comparing it with her own life since. She raised her head and looked him squarely in the eye.

"I have nothing to forgive," she said.

"Ah, you are too generous, too noble!" he cried. "And I? The burden of my youth is lifted now. My first wife is dead—some years since—and I am free. You are my real wife, Mary, my true and loving wife. Now I can offer you the legal ceremony as well."

"I do not wish it," she answered.

"It shall be as you say," he went on. "But for the child's sake—I wish to be a father to her."

"You are her father," said she. "That cannot be helped."

"But I wish to give her my name."

"She has it. I gave it to her."

"Brave, dear woman! But now I can give it to you."

"I have it also. It has been my name ever since I—according to my conscience—married you."

"But—but—you have no *legal* right to it, Mary."

She smiled, even laughed.

"Better read a little law, Mr. Main. I have used that name for twelve years, am publicly and honorably known by it; it is mine, legally."

"But Mary, I want to help you."

"Thank you. I do not need it."

"But I want to do for the child—my child—our little one!"

"You may," said she. "I want to send her to college. You may help if you like. I should be very glad if Mollie could have some pleasant and honorable memories of her father." She rose suddenly. "You wish to marry me now, Mr. Main?"

"With all my heart I wish it, Mary. You will?—"

He stood up—he held out his arms to her.

"No," said she, "I will not. When I was twenty-four I loved you. I sympathized with you. I was willing to be your wife—truly and faithfully your wife, even though you could not legally marry me—because I loved you. Now I will not marry you because I do not love you. That is all."

He glanced about the quiet, comfortable room; he had already estimated the quiet, comfortable business; and now, from some forgotten chamber of his honeycombed heart, welled up a fierce longing for this calm, strong, tender woman whose power of love he knew so well.

"Mary! You will not turn me away! I love you—I love you as I never loved you before!"

"I'm sorry to hear it," she said. "It does not make me love you again."

His face darkened.

"Do not drive me to desperation," he cried. "Your whole life here rests on a lie, remember. I could shatter it with a word."

She smiled patiently.

"You can't shatter facts, Mr. Main. People here know

that you left me years ago. They know how I have lived since. If you try to blacken my reputation here, I think you will find the climate of Mexico more congenial.''

On second thought, this seemed to be the opinion of Mr. Main, who presently left for that country.

It was also agreed with by Mr. Burdock, who emerged later, a little chilly and somewhat scratched, and sought his chamber.

''If that galoot says anything against her in this town, he'll find a hotter climate than Mexico—by heck!'' said Mr. Burdock to his boots as he set them down softly. And that was all he ever said about it.

# MAKING A CHANGE

## "Waa-a-a-a-a! Waa-a-a-aaa!"

Frank Gordins set down his coffee cup so hard that it spilled over into the saucer.

"Is there no way to stop that child crying?" he demanded.

"I do not know of any," said his wife, so definitely and politely that the words seemed cut off by machinery.

"*I do,*" said his mother with even more definiteness, but less politeness.

Young Mrs. Gordins looked at her mother-in-law from under her delicate level brows, and said nothing. But the weary lines about her eyes deepened; she had been kept awake nearly all night, and for many nights.

So had he. So, as a matter of fact, had his mother. She had not the care of the baby—but lay awake wishing she had.

"There's no use talking about it," said Julia. "If

Frank is not satisfied with the child's mother, he must say so—perhaps we can make a change."

This was ominously gentle. Julia's nerves were at the breaking point. Upon her tired ears, her sensitive mother's heart, the grating wail from the next room fell like a lash—burnt in like fire. Her ears were hypersensitive, always. She had been an ardent musician before her marriage, and had taught quite successfully on both piano and violin. To any mother a child's cry is painful; to a musical mother it is torment.

But if her ears were sensitive, so was her conscience. If her nerves were weak, her pride was strong. The child was her child, it was her duty to take care of it, and take care of it she would. She spent her days in unremitting devotion to its needs and to the care of her neat flat; and her nights had long since ceased to refresh her.

Again the weary cry rose to a wail.

"It does seem to be time for a change of treatment," suggested the older woman acidly.

"Or a change of residence," offered the younger, in a deadly quiet voice.

"Well, by Jupiter! There'll be a change of some kind, and p. d. q.!" said the son and husband, rising to his feet.

His mother rose also, and left the room, holding her head high and refusing to show any effects of that last thrust.

Frank Gordins glared at his wife. His nerves were raw, too. It does not benefit anyone in health or character to be continuously deprived of sleep. Some enlightened persons use that deprivation as a form of torture.

She stirred her coffee with mechanical calm, her eyes sullenly bent on her plate.

"I will not stand having Mother spoken to like that," he stated with decision.

"I will not stand having her interfere with my methods of bringing up children."

"Your methods! Why, Julia, my mother knows more

about taking care of babies than you'll ever learn! She has the real love of it—and the practical experience. Why can't you *let* her take care of the kid—and we'll all have some peace!"

She lifted her eyes and looked at him; deep inscrutable wells of angry light. He had not the faintest appreciation of her state of mind. When people say they are "nearly crazy" from weariness, they state a practical fact. The old phrase which describes reason as "tottering on her throne" is also a clear one.

Julia was more near the verge of complete disaster than the family dreamed. The conditions were so simple, so usual, so inevitable.

Here was Frank Gordins, well brought up, the only son of a very capable and idolatrously affectionate mother. He had fallen deeply and desperately in love with the exalted beauty and fine mind of the young music teacher, and his mother had approved. She too loved music and admired beauty.

Her tiny store in the savings bank did not allow of a separate home, and Julia had cordially welcomed her to share in their household.

Here was affection, propriety, and peace. Here was a noble devotion on the part of the young wife, who so worshipped her husband that she used to wish she had been the greatest musician on earth—that she might give it up for him! She had given up her music, perforce, for many months, and missed it more than she knew.

She bent her mind to the decoration and artistic management of their little apartment, finding her standards difficult to maintain by the ever-changing inefficiency of her help. The musical temperament does not always include patience, nor, necessarily, the power of management.

When the baby came, her heart overflowed with utter devotion and thankfulness; she was his wife—the mother of his child. Her happiness lifted and pushed within till she longed more than ever for her music, for the free-pouring current of expression, to give forth her love and pride and happiness. She had not the gift of words.

So now she looked at her husband, dumbly, while wild visions of separation, of secret flight—even of self-destruction—swung dizzily across her mental vision. All she said was, "All right, Frank. We'll make a change. And you shall have—some peace."

"Thank goodness for that, Jule! You do look tired, girlie—let Mother see to His Nibs, and try to get a nap, can't you?"

"Yes," she said. "Yes . . . I think I will." Her voice had a peculiar note in it. If Frank had been an alienist, or even a general physician, he would have noticed it. But his work lay in electric coils, in dynamos and copper wiring—not in women's nerves—and he did not notice it.

He kissed her and went out, throwing back his shoulders and drawing a long breath of relief as he left the house behind him and entered his own world.

"This being married—and bringing up children—is not what it's cracked up to be." That was the feeling in the back of his mind. But it did not find full admission, much less expression.

When a friend asked him, "All well at home?" he said, "Yes, thank you—pretty fair. Kid cries a good deal—but that's natural, I suppose."

He dismissed the whole matter from his mind and bent his faculties to a man's task—how he can earn enough to support a wife, a mother, and a son.

At home his mother sat in her small room, looking out of the window at the ground-glass one just across the "well," and thinking hard.

By the disorderly little breakfast table his wife remained motionless, her chin in her hands, her big eyes staring at nothing, trying to formulate in her weary mind some reliable reason why she should not do what she was thinking of doing. But her mind was too exhausted to serve her properly.

Sleep—sleep—sleep—that was the one thing she wanted. Then his mother could take care of the baby all she wanted to, and Frank could have some peace. . . . Oh, dear! It was time for the child's bath.

She gave it to him mechanically. On the stroke of the hour, she prepared the sterilized milk and arranged the little one comfortably with his bottle. He snuggled down, enjoying it, while she stood watching him.

She emptied the tub, put the bath apron to dry, picked up all the towels and sponges and varied appurtenances of the elaborate performance of bathing the first-born, and then sat staring straight before her, more weary than ever, but growing inwardly determined.

Greta had cleared the table, with heavy heels and hands, and was now rattling dishes in the kitchen. At every slam, the young mother winced, and when the girl's high voice began a sort of doleful chant over her work, young Mrs. Gordins rose to her feet with a shiver and made her decision.

She carefully picked up the child and his bottle, and carried him to his grandmother's room.

"Would you mind looking after Albert?" she asked in a flat, quiet voice. "I think I'll try to get some sleep."

"Oh, I shall be delighted," replied her mother-in-law. She said it in a tone of cold politeness, but Julia did not notice. She laid the child on the bed and stood looking at him in the same dull way for a little while, then went out without another word.

Mrs. Gordins, senior, sat watching the baby for some long moments. "He's a perfectly lovely child!" she said softly, gloating over his rosy beauty. "There's not a *thing* the matter with him! It's just her absurd ideas. She's so irregular with him! To think of letting that child cry for an hour! He is nervous because she is. And of course she couldn't feed him till after his bath—of course not!"

She continued in these sarcastic meditations for some time, taking the empty bottle away from the small wet mouth, that sucked on for a few moments aimlessly and then was quiet in sleep.

"I could take care of him so that he'd *never* cry!" she continued to herself, rocking slowly back and forth. "And I could take care of twenty like him—and enjoy it! I believe I'll go off somewhere and do it. Give Julia a rest. Change of residence, indeed!"

She rocked and planned, pleased to have her grandson with her, even while asleep.

Greta had gone out on some errand of her own. The rooms were very quiet. Suddenly the old lady held up her head and sniffed. She rose swiftly to her feet and sprang to the gas jet—no, it was shut off tightly. She went back to the dining-room—all right there.

"That foolish girl has left the range going and it's blown out!" she thought, and went to the kitchen. No, the little room was fresh and clean, every burner turned off.

"Funny! It must come in from the hall." She opened the door. No, the hall gave only its usual odor of diffused basement. Then the parlor—nothing there. The little alcove called by the renting agent "the music room," where Julia's closed piano and violin case stood dumb and dusty—nothing there.

"It's in her room—and she's asleep!" said Mrs. Gordins, senior; and she tried to open the door. It was locked. She knocked—there was no answer; knocked louder—shook it—rattled the knob. No answer.

Then Mrs. Gordins thought quickly. "It may be an accident, and nobody must know. Frank mustn't know. I'm glad Greta's out. I *must* get in somehow!" She looked at the transom, and the stout rod Frank had himself put up for the portieres Julia loved.

"I believe I can do it, at a pinch."

She was a remarkably active woman of her years, but no memory of earlier gymnastic feats could quite cover the exercise. She hastily brought the step-ladder. From its top she could see in, and what she saw made her determine recklessly.

Grabbing the pole with small strong hands, she thrust her light frame bravely through the opening, turning clumsily but successfully, and dropping breathlessly and somewhat bruised to the floor, she flew to open the windows and doors.

When Julia opened her eyes she found loving arms around her, and wise, tender words to soothe and reassure.

"Don't say a thing, dearie—I understand. I *understand,* I tell you! Oh, my dear girl—my precious daughter! We haven't been half good enough to you, Frank and I! But cheer up now—I've got the *loveliest* plan to tell you about! We *are* going to make a change! Listen now!"

And while the pale young mother lay quiet, petted and waited on to her heart's content, great plans were discussed and decided on.

Frank Gordins was pleased when the baby "outgrew his crying spells." He spoke of it to his wife.

"Yes," she said sweetly. "He has better care."

"I knew you'd learn," said he, proudly.

"I have!" she agreed. "I've learned—ever so much!"

He was pleased, too, vastly pleased, to have her health improve rapidly and steadily, the delicate pink come back to her cheeks, the soft light to her eyes; and when she made music for him in the evening, soft music, with shut doors—not to waken Albert—he felt as if his days of courtship had come again.

Greta the hammer-footed had gone, and an amazing French matron who came in by the day had taken her place. He asked no questions as to this person's peculiarities, and did not know that she did the purchasing and planned the meals, meals of such new delicacy and careful variance as gave him much delight. Neither did he know that her wages were greater than her predecessor's. He turned over the same sum weekly, and did not pursue details.

He was pleased also that his mother seemed to have taken a new lease of life. She was so cheerful and brisk, so full of little jokes and stories—as he had known her in his boyhood; and above all she was so free and affectionate with Julia, that he was more than pleased.

"I tell you what it is!" he said to a bachelor friend. "You fellows don't know what you're missing!" And he brought one of them home to dinner—just to show him.

"Do you do all that on thirty-five a week?" his friend demanded.

"That's about it," he answered proudly.

"Well, your wife's a wonderful manager—that's all I can say. And you've got the best cook I ever saw, or heard of, or ate of—I suppose I might say—for five dollars."

Mrs. Gordins was pleased and proud. But he was neither pleased nor proud when someone said to him, with displeasing frankness, "I shouldn't think you'd want your wife to be giving music lessons, Frank!"

He did not show surprise nor anger to his friend, but saved it for his wife. So surprised and so angry was he that he did a most unusual thing—he left his business and went home early in the afternoon. He opened the door of his flat. There was no one in it. He went through every room. No wife; no child; no mother; no servant.

The elevator boy heard him banging about, opening and shutting doors, and grinned happily. When Mr. Gordins came out, Charles volunteered some information.

"Young Mrs. Gordins is out, sir; but old Mrs. Gordins and the baby—they're upstairs. On the roof, I think."

Mr. Gordins went to the roof. There he found his mother, a smiling, cheerful nursemaid, and fifteen happy babies.

Mrs. Gordins, senior, rose to the occasion promptly.

"Welcome to my baby-garden, Frank," she said cheerfully. "I'm so glad you could get off in time to see it."

73

She took his arm and led him about, proudly exhibiting her sunny roof-garden, her sand-pile and big, shallow, zinc-lined pool, her flowers and vines, her seesaws, swings, and floor mattresses.

"You see how happy they are," she said. "Celia can manage very well for a few moments." And then she exhibited to him the whole upper flat, turned into a convenient place for many little ones to take their naps or to play in if the weather was bad.

"Where's Julia?" he demanded first.

"Julia will be in presently," she told him, "by five o'clock anyway. And the mothers come for the babies by then, too. I have them from nine or ten to five."

He was silent, both angry and hurt.

"We didn't tell you at first, my dear boy, because we knew you wouldn't like it, and we wanted to make sure it would go well. I rent the upper flat, you see—it is forty dollars a month, same as ours—and pay Celia five dollars a week, and pay Dr. Holbrook downstairs the same for looking over my little ones every day. She helped me to get them, too. The mothers pay me three dollars a week each, and don't have to keep a nursemaid. And I pay ten dollars a week board to Julia, and still have about ten of my own."

"And she gives music lessons?"

"Yes, she gives music lessons, just as she used to. She loves it, you know. You must have noticed how happy and well she is now—haven't you? And so am I. And so is Albert. You can't feel very badly about a thing that makes us all happy, can you?"

Just then Julia came in, radiant from a brisk walk, fresh and cheery, a big bunch of violets at her breast.

"Oh, Mother," she cried, "I've got tickets and we'll all go to hear Melba—if we can get Celia to come in for the evening."

She saw her husband, and a guilty flush rose to her brow as she met his reproachful eyes.

"Oh, Frank!" she begged, her arms around his neck. "Please don't mind! Please get used to it! Please be proud of us! Just think, we're all so happy, and we earn about a hundred dollars a week—all of us together. You see, I have Mother's ten to add to the house money, and twenty or more of my own!"

They had a long talk together that evening, just the two of them. She told him, at last, what a danger had hung over them—how near it came.

"And Mother showed me the way out, Frank. The way to have my mind again—and not lose you! She is a different woman herself now that she has her heart and hands full of babies. Albert does enjoy it so! And *you've* enjoyed it—till you found it out!

"And dear—my own love—I don't mind it now at all! I love my home, I love my work, I love my mother, I love you. And as to children—I wish I had six!"

He looked at her flushed, eager, lovely face, and drew her close to him.

"If it makes all of you as happy as that," he said, "I guess I can stand it."

And in after years he was heard to remark, "This being married and bringing up children is as easy as can be—when you learn how!"

# MR. PEEBLES'
# HEART

He was lying on the sofa in the homely, bare little sitting room—an uncomfortable stiff sofa, too short, too sharply upcurved at the end, but still a sofa, whereon one could, at a pinch, sleep.

Thereon Mr. Peebles slept, this hot still afternoon; slept uneasily, snoring a little, and twitching now and then, as one in some obscure distress.

Mrs. Peebles had creaked down the front stairs and gone off on some superior errands of her own—with a good palm-leaf fan for a weapon, a silk umbrella for a defense.

"Why don't you come too, Joan?" she had urged her sister, as she dressed herself for departure.

"Why should I, Emma? It's much more comfortable at home. I'll keep Arthur company when he wakes up."

"Oh, Arthur! He'll go back to the store as soon as he's had his nap. And I'm sure Mrs. Older's paper'll be real interesting. If you're going to live here, you ought to take an interest in the club, seems to me.''

"I'm going to live here as a doctor—not as a lady of leisure, Em. You go on—I'm contented.''

So Mrs. Emma Peebles sat in the circle of the Ellsworth Ladies' Home Club, and improved her mind, while Dr. J. R. Bascom softly descended to the sitting room in search of a book she had been reading.

There was Mr. Peebles, still uneasily asleep. She sat down quietly in a cane-seated rocker by the window and watched him awhile—first professionally, then with a deeper human interest.

Baldish, grayish, stoutish, with a face that wore a friendly smile for customers and showed grave, set lines that deepened about the corners of his mouth when there was no one to serve; very ordinary in dress, in carriage, in appearance was Arthur Peebles at fifty. He was not "the slave of love" of the Arab tale, but the slave of duty.

If ever a man had done his duty—as he saw it—he had done his, always.

His duty—as he saw it—was carrying women. First his mother, a comfortable competent person, who had run the farm after her husband's death, and added to their income by summer boarders until Arthur was old enough to "support her." Then she sold the old place and moved into the village to "make a home for Arthur," who incidentally provided a hired girl to perform the manual labor of that process.

He worked in the store. She sat on the piazza and chatted with her neighbors.

He took care of his mother until he was nearly thirty, when she left him finally; and then he installed another woman to make a home for him—also with the help of the hired girl. A pretty, careless, clinging little person he married, who had long made mute appeal to his strength and carefulness, and she had continued to cling uninterruptedly to this day.

Incidentally a sister had clung also. Both the daughters were married in due time, with sturdy young husbands to cling to in their turn; and now there remained only his wife to carry, a lighter load than he had ever known—at least numerically.

But either he was tired, very tired, or Mrs. Peebles' tendrils had grown tougher, tighter, more tenacious, with age. He did not complain of it. Never had it occurred to him in all these years that there was any other thing for a man to do than to carry whatsoever women came within range of lawful relationship.

Had Dr. Joan been—shall we say—carriageable—he would have cheerfully added her to the list, for he liked her extremely. She was different from any woman he had ever known, different from her sister as day from night, and, in lesser degree, from all the female inhabitants of Ellsworth.

She had left home at an early age, against her mother's will, absolutely run away; but when the whole countryside rocked with gossip and sought for the guilty man—it appeared that she had merely gone to college. She worked her way through, learning more, far more, than was taught in the curriculum, became a trained nurse, studied medicine, and had long since made good in her profession. There were even rumors that she must be "pretty well fixed" and about to "retire"; but others held that she must have failed, really, or she never would have come back home to settle.

Whatever the reason, she was there, a welcome visitor—a source of real pride to her sister, and of indefinable satisfaction to her brother-in-law. In her friendly atmosphere he felt a stirring of long unused powers; he remembered funny stories, and how to tell them; he felt a revival of interests he had thought quite outlived, early interests in the big world's movements.

"Of all unimpressive, unattractive, *good* little men—" she was thinking, as she watched, when one of his arms dropped off the slippery side of the sofa, the hand thumped on the floor, and he awoke and sat up hastily with an air of one caught off duty.

"Don't sit up as suddenly as that, Arthur, it's bad for your heart."

"Nothing the matter with my heart, is there?" he asked with his ready smile.

"I don't know—haven't examined it. Now—sit still—you know there's nobody in the store this afternoon—and if there is, Jake can attend to 'em."

"Where's Emma?"

"Oh, Emma's gone to her 'club' or something—wanted me to go, but I'd rather talk with you."

He looked pleased but incredulous, having a high opinion of that club, and a low one of himself.

"Look here," she pursued suddenly, after he had made himself comfortable with a drink from the swinging ice-pitcher, and another big cane rocker, "what would you like to do if you could?"

"Travel!" said Mr. Peebles, with equal suddenness. He saw her astonishment. "Yes, travel! I've always wanted to—since I was a kid. No use! We never could, you see. And now—even if we could—Emma hates it." He sighed resignedly.

"Do you like to keep store?" she asked sharply.

"*Like* it?" He smiled at her cheerfully, bravely, but with a queer blank hopeless background underneath. He shook his head gravely. "No, I do not, Joan. Not a little bit. But what of that?"

They were still for a little, and then she put another question. "What would you have chosen—for a profession —if you had been free to choose?"

His answer amazed her threefold: from its character, its sharp promptness, its deep feeling. It was in one word—"Music!"

"Music!" she repeated. "Music! Why I didn't know you played—or cared about it."

"When I was a youngster," he told her, his eyes looking far off through the vine-shaded window, "Father brought home a guitar—and said it was for the one that learned to play it first. He meant the girls of course. As a matter of fact I learned it first—but I didn't get it. That's all the music I ever had," he added. "And there's not much to listen to here, unless you count what's in church. I'd have a Victrola—but—" he laughed a little shame-facedly, "Emma says if I bring one into the house she'll smash it. She says they're worse than cats. Tastes differ, you know, Joan."

Again he smiled at her, a droll smile, a little pinched at the corners. "Well—I must be getting back to business."

She let him go, and turned her attention to her own business, with some seriousness.

"Emma," she proposed, a day or two later, "how would you like it if I should board here—live here, I mean, right along?"

"I should hope you would," her sister replied. "It would look nice to have you practicing in this town and not live with me—all the sister I've got."

"Do you think Arthur would like it?"

"Of course he would! Besides—even if he didn't— you're *my* sister—and this is my house. He put it in my name, long ago."

"I see," said Joan, "I see."

Then after a little—"Emma, are you contented?"

"Contented? Why, of course I am. It would be a sin not to be. The girls are well married—I'm happy about them both. This is a real comfortable house, and it runs itself—my Matilda is a jewel if ever there was one. And she doesn't mind company—likes to do for 'em. Yes— I've nothing to worry about."

"Your health's good—that I can see," her sister remarked, regarding with approval her clear complexion and bright eyes.

"Yes—I've nothing to complain about—that I know

of," Emma admitted, but among her causes for thankfulness she did not even mention Arthur, nor seem to think of him till Dr. Joan seriously inquired her opinion as to his state of health.

"His health? Arthur's? Why he's always well. Never had a sick day in his life—except now and then he's had a kind of a breakdown," she added as an afterthought.

Dr. Joan Bascom made acquaintances in the little town, both professional and social. She entered upon her practice, taking it over from the failing hands of old Dr. Braithwaite, her first friend, and feeling very much at home in the old place. Her sister's house furnished two comfortable rooms downstairs, and a large bedroom above. "There's plenty of room now the girls are gone," they both assured her.

Then, safely ensconced and established, Dr. Joan began a secret campaign to alienate the affections of her brother-in-law. Not for herself—oh no! If ever in earlier years she had felt the need of someone to cling to, it was long, long ago. What she sought was to free him from the tentacles—without reentanglement.

She bought a noble Gramophone with a set of first-class records, told her sister smilingly that she didn't have to listen, and Emma would sit sulkily in the back room on the other side of the house, while her husband and sister enjoyed the music. She grew used to it in time, she said, and drew nearer, sitting on the porch perhaps; but Arthur had his long-denied pleasure in peace.

It seemed to stir him strangely. He would rise and walk, a new fire in his eyes, a new firmness about the patient mouth, and Dr. Joan fed the fire with talk and books and pictures, with study of maps and sailing lists and accounts of economical tours.

"I don't see what you two find so interesting in all that stuff about music and those composers," Emma would say. "I never did care for foreign parts—musicians are all foreigners, anyway."

Arthur never quarrelled with her; he only grew quiet and lost that interested sparkle of the eye when she discussed the subject.

Then one day, Mrs. Peebles being once more at her club, content and yet aspiring, Dr. Joan made bold attack upon her brother-in-law's principles.

"Arthur," she said, "have you confidence in me as a physician?"

"I have," he said briskly. "Rather consult you than any doctor I ever saw."

"Will you let me prescribe for you if I tell you you need it?"

"I sure will."

"Will you take the prescription?"

"Of course I'll take it—no matter how it tastes."

"Very well. I prescribe two years in Europe."

He stared at her, startled.

"I mean it. You're in a more serious condition than you think. I want you to cut clear—and travel. For two years."

He still stared at her. "But Emma—"

"Never mind about Emma. She owns the house. She's got enough money to clothe herself—and I'm paying enough board to keep everything going. Emma doesn't need you."

"But the store—"

"Sell the store."

"Sell it! That's easy said. Who'll buy it?"

"I will. Yes—I mean it. You give me easy terms and I'll take the store off your hands. It ought to be worth seven or eight thousand dollars, oughtn't it—stock and all?"

He assented, dumbly.

"Well, I'll buy it. You can live abroad for two years, on a couple of thousand, or twenty-five hundred—a man of your tastes. You know those accounts we've read—it can be done easily. Then you'll have five thousand or so to come back to—and can invest it in something better than that shop. Will you do it?''

He was full of protests, of impossibilities.

She met them firmly. ''Nonsense! You can too. She doesn't need you, at all—she may later. No—the girls don't need you—and they may later. Now is your time—*now*. They say the Japanese sow their wild oats after they're fifty—suppose you do! You can't be so *very* wild on that much money, but you can spend a year in Germany—learn the language—go to the opera—take walking trips in the Tyrol—in Switzerland; see England, Scotland, Ireland, France, Belgium, Denmark—you can do a lot in two years.''

He stared at her fascinated.

''Why not? Why not be your own man for once in your life—do what *you* want to—not what other people want you to?''

He murmured something as to ''duty''—but she took him up sharply.

''If ever a man on earth has done his duty, Arthur Peebles, you have. You've taken care of your mother while she was perfectly able to take care of herself; of your sisters, long after they were; and of a wholly able-bodied wife. At present she does not need you the least bit in the world.''

''Now that's pretty strong,'' he protested. ''Emma'd miss me—I know she'd miss me—''

Dr. Bascom looked at him affectionately. ''There couldn't a better thing happen to Emma—or to you, for that matter—than to have her miss you, real hard.''

''I know she'd never consent to my going,'' he insisted, wistfully.

''That's the advantage of my interference,'' she replied serenely. ''You surely have a right to choose your doctor, and your doctor is seriously concerned about your health and orders foreign travel—rest—change—and music.''

''But Emma—''

''Now, Arthur Peebles, forget Emma for a while—I'll take care of her. And look here—let me tell you another thing—a change like this will do her good.''

He stared at her, puzzled.

''I mean it. Having you away will give her a chance to stand up. Your letters—about those places—will interest her. She may want to go, sometime. Try it.''

He wavered at this. Those who too patiently serve as props sometimes underrate the possibilities of the vine.

''Don't discuss it with her—that will make endless trouble. Fix up the papers for my taking over the store— I'll draw you a check, and you get the next boat for England, and make your plans from there. Here's a banking address that will take care of your letters and checks—''

The thing was done! Done before Emma had time to protest. Done, and she left gasping to upbraid her sister.

Joan was kind, patient, firm, and adamant.

''But how it *looks,* Joan—what will people think of me! To be left deserted—like this!''

''People will think according to what we tell them and to how you behave, Emma Peebles. If you simply say that Arthur was far from well and I advised him to take a foreign trip—and if you forget yourself for once, and show a little natural feeling for him—you'll find no trouble at all.''

For her own sake, the selfish woman, made more so by her husband's unselfishness, accepted the position. Yes— Arthur had gone abroad for his health—Dr. Bascom was much worried about him—chance of a complete breakdown, she said. Wasn't it pretty sudden? Yes—the doctor hurried him off. He was in England—going to take a walking trip—she did not know when he'd be back. The store? He'd sold it.

Dr. Bascom engaged a competent manager who ran that store successfully, more so than had the unenterprising Mr. Peebles. She made it a good paying business, which he ultimately bought back and found no longer a burden.

But Emma was the principal change. With talk, with books, with Arthur's letters followed carefully on maps, with trips to see the girls, trips in which traveling lost its terrors, with the care of the house, and the boarder or two they took "for company," she so ploughed and harrowed that long-fallow field of Emma's mind that at last it began to show signs of fruitfulness.

Arthur went away leaving a stout, dull woman who clung to him as if he was a necessary vehicle or beast of burden—and thought scarcely more of his constant service.

He returned younger, stronger, thinner, an alert vigorous man, with a mind enlarged, refreshed, and stimulated. He had found himself.

And he found her, also, most agreeably changed, having developed not merely tentacles, but feet of her own to stand on.

When next the thirst for travel seized him, she thought she'd go too, and proved unexpectedly pleasant as a companion.

But neither of them could ever wring from Dr. Bascom any definite diagnosis of Mr. Peebles' threatening disease. "A dangerous enlargement of the heart" was all she would commit herself to, and when he denied any such trouble now, she gravely wagged her head and said it had "responded to treatment."

# THE WIDOW'S MIGHT

James had come on to the funeral, but his wife had not; she could not leave the children—that is what he said. She said, privately, to him, that she would not go. She never was willing to leave New York except for Europe or for summer vacations; and a trip to Denver in November— to attend a funeral—was not a possibility to her mind.

Ellen and Adelaide were both there: they felt it a duty—but neither of their husbands had come. Mr. Jennings could not leave his classes in Cambridge, and Mr. Oswald could not leave his business in Pittsburgh—that is what they said.

The last services were over. They had had a cold, melancholy lunch and were all to take the night train home again. Meanwhile, the lawyer was coming at four to read the will.

"It is only a formality. There can't be much left," said James.

"No," agreed Adelaide, "I suppose not."

"A long illness eats up everything," said Ellen, and sighed. Her husband had come to Colorado for his lungs years before and was still delicate.

"Well," said James rather abruptly, "what are we going to do with Mother?"

"Why, of course—" Ellen began, "we *could* take her. It would depend a good deal on how much property there is—I mean, on where she'd want to go. Edward's salary is more than needed now." Ellen's mental processes seemed a little mixed.

"She can come to me if she prefers, of course," said Adelaide. "But I don't think it would be very pleasant for her. Mother never did like Pittsburgh."

James looked from one to the other.

"Let me see—how old is Mother?"

"Oh she's all of fifty," answered Ellen, "and much broken, I think. It's been a long strain, you know." She turned plaintively to her brother. "I should think you could make her more comfortable than either of us, James— with your big house."

"I think a woman is always happier living with a son than with a daughter's husband," said Adelaide. "I've always thought so."

"That is often true," her brother admitted. "But it depends." He stopped, and the sisters exchanged glances. They knew upon what it depended.

"Perhaps if she stayed with me, you could—help some," suggested Ellen.

"Of course, of course, I could do that," he agreed with evident relief. "She might visit between you—take turns—and I could pay her board. About how much ought it to amount to? We might as well arrange everything now."

"Things cost awfully in these days," Ellen said with a crisscross of fine wrinkles on her pale forehead. "But of course it would be only just *what* it costs. I shouldn't want to *make* anything."

"It's work and care, Ellen, and you may as well admit it. You need all your strength—with those sickly children and Edward on your hands. When she comes to me, there need be no expense, James, except for clothes. I have room enough and Mr. Oswald will never notice the difference in the house bills—but he does hate to pay out money for clothes."

"Mother must be provided for properly," her son declared. "How much ought it to cost—a year—for clothes?"

"You know what your wife's cost," suggested Adelaide, with a flicker of a smile about her lips.

"Oh, *no*," said Ellen. "That's no criterion! Maude is in society, you see. Mother wouldn't *dream* of having so much."

James looked at her gratefully. "Board—and clothes—all told; what should you say, Ellen?"

Ellen scrabbled in her small black handbag for a piece of paper, and found none. James handed her an envelope and a fountain pen.

"Food—just plain food materials—costs all of four dollars a week now—for one person," said she. "And heat—and light—and extra service. I should think six a week would be the *least*, James. And for clothes and carfare and small expenses—I should say—well, three hundred dollars!"

"That would make over six hundred a year," said James slowly. "How about Oswald sharing that, Adelaide?"

Adelaide flushed. "I do not think he would be willing, James. Of course, if it were absolutely necessary—"

"He has money enough," said her brother.

"Yes, but he never seems to have any outside of his business—and he has his own parents to carry now. No—I can give her a home, but that's all."

"You see, you'd have none of the care and trouble, James," said Ellen. "We—the girls—are each willing to have her with us, while perhaps Maude wouldn't care to, but if you could just pay the money—''

"Maybe there's some left, after all," suggested Adelaide. "And this place ought to sell for something."

"This place" was a piece of rolling land within ten miles of Denver. It had a bit of river bottom, and ran up towards the foothills. From the house the view ran north and south along the precipitous ranks of the "Big Rockies" to westward. To the east lay the vast stretches of sloping plain.

"There ought to be at least six or eight thousand dollars from it, I should say," he concluded.

"Speaking of clothes," Adelaide rather irrelevantly suggested, "I see Mother didn't get any new black. She's always worn it as long as I can remember."

"Mother's a long time," said Ellen. "I wonder if she wants anything. I'll go up and see."

"No," said Adelaide. "She said she wanted to be let alone—and rest. She said she'd be down by the time Mr. Frankland got here."

"She's bearing it pretty well," Ellen suggested, after a little silence.

"It's not like a broken heart," Adelaide explained. "Of course Father meant well—''

"He was a man who always did his duty," admitted Ellen. "But we none of us—loved him—very much."

"He is dead and buried," said James. "We can at least respect his memory."

"We've hardly seen Mother—under that black veil," Ellen went on. "It must have aged her. This long nursing."

"She had help toward the last—a man nurse," said Adelaide.

"Yes, but a long illness is an awful strain—and Mother never was good at nursing. She has surely done her duty," pursued Ellen.

"And now she's entitled to a rest," said James, rising and walking about the room. "I wonder how soon we can close up affairs here—and get rid of this place. There might be enough in it to give her almost a living—properly invested.''

Ellen looked out across the dusty stretches of land.

"How I did hate to live here!" she said.

"So did I," said Adelaide.

"So did I," said James.

And they all smiled rather grimly.

"We don't any of us seem to be very—affectionate, about Mother," Adelaide presently admitted. "I don't know why it is—we never were an affectionate family, I guess."

"Nobody could be affectionate with Father," Ellen suggested timidly.

"And Mother—poor Mother! She's had an awful life."

"Mother has always done her duty," said James in a determined voice, "and so did Father, as he saw it. Now we'll do ours."

"Ah," exclaimed Ellen, jumping to her feet, "here comes the lawyer. I'll call Mother."

She ran quickly upstairs and tapped at her mother's door.

"Mother, oh Mother," she cried. "Mr. Frankland's come."

"I know it," came back a voice from within. "Tell him to go ahead and read the will. I know what's in it. I'll be down in a few minutes."

Ellen went slowly back downstairs with the fine criss-cross of wrinkles showing on her pale forehead again, and delivered her mother's message.

The other two glanced at each other hesitatingly, but Mr. Frankland spoke up briskly.

"Quite natural, of course, under the circumstances. Sorry I couldn't get to the funeral. A case on this morning."

The will was short. The estate was left to be divided among the children in four equal parts, two to the son and one each to the daughters after the mother's legal share had been deducted, if she were still living. In such case they were furthermore directed to provide for their mother while she lived. The estate, as described, consisted of the ranch, the large, rambling house on it, with all the furniture, stock, and implements, and some five thousand dollars in mining stocks.

"That is less than I had supposed," said James.

"This will was made ten years ago," Mr. Frankland explained. "I have done business for your father since that time. He kept his faculties to the end, and I think that you will find that the property has appreciated. Mrs. McPherson has taken excellent care of the ranch, I understand—and has had some boarders."

Both the sisters exchanged pained glances.

"There's an end to all that now," said James.

At this moment, the door opened and a tall black figure, cloaked and veiled, came into the room.

"I'm glad to hear you say that Mr. McPherson kept his faculties to the last, Mr. Frankland," said the widow. "It's true. I didn't come down to hear that old will. It's no good now."

They all turned in their chairs.

"Is there a later will, madam?" inquired the lawyer.

"Not that I know of. Mr. McPherson had no property when he died."

"No property! My dear lady—four years ago he certainly had some."

"Yes, but three years and a half ago he gave it all to me. Here are the deeds."

There they were, in very truth—formal and correct, and quite simple and clear—for deeds. James R. McPherson, Sr., had assuredly given to his wife the whole estate.

"You remember that was the panic year," she continued. "There was pressure from some of Mr. McPherson's creditors; he thought it would be safer so."

"Why—yes," remarked Mr. Frankland. "I do re-

91

member now his advising with me about it. But I thought the step unnecessary.''

James cleared his throat.

"Well, Mother, this does complicate matters a little. We were hoping that we could settle up all the business this afternoon—with Mr. Frankland's help—and take you back with us.''

"We can't be spared any longer, you see, Mother,'' said Ellen.

"Can't you deed it back again, Mother,'' Adelaide suggested, "to James, or to—all of us, so we can get away?''

"Why should I?''

"Now, Mother,'' Ellen put in persuasively, "we know how badly you feel, and you are nervous and tired, but I told you this morning when we came, that we expected to take you back with us. You know you've been packing—''

"Yes, I've been packing,'' replied the voice behind the veil.

"I dare say it was safer—to have the property in your name—technically,'' James admitted, "but now I think it would be the simplest way for you to make it over to me in a lump, and I will see that Father's wishes are carried out to the letter.''

"Your father is dead,'' remarked the voice.

"Yes, Mother, we know—we know how you feel,'' Ellen ventured.

"I am alive,'' said Mrs. McPherson.

"Dear Mother, it's very trying to talk business to you at such a time. We all realize it,'' Adelaide explained with a touch of asperity. "But we told you we couldn't stay as soon as we got here.''

"And the business has to be settled,'' James added conclusively.

"It is settled.''

"Perhaps Mr. Frankland can make it clear to you," went on James with forced patience.

"I do not doubt that your mother understands perfectly," murmured the lawyer. "I have always found her a woman of remarkable intelligence."

"Thank you, Mr. Frankland. Possibly you may be able to make my children understand that this property—such as it is—is mine now."

"Why assuredly, assuredly, Mrs. McPherson. We all see that. But we assume, as a matter of course, that you will consider Mr. McPherson's wishes in regard to the disposition of the estate."

"I have considered Mr. McPherson's wishes for thirty years," she replied. "Now, I'll consider mine. I have done my duty since the day I married him. It is eleven thousand days—today." The last with sudden intensity.

"But madam, your children—"

"I have no children, Mr. Frankland. I have two daughters and a son. These two grown persons here, grown up, married, having children of their own—or ought to have—were my children. I did my duty by them, and they did their duty by me—and would yet, no doubt." The tone changed suddenly. "But they don't have to. I'm tired of duty."

The little group of listeners looked up, startled.

"You don't know how things have been going on here," the voice went on. "I didn't trouble you with my affairs. But I'll tell you now. When your father saw fit to make over the property to me—to save it—and when he knew that he hadn't many years to live, I took hold of things. I had to have a nurse for your father—and a doctor coming; the house was a sort of hospital, so I made it a little more so. I had half a dozen patients and nurses here—and made money by it. I ran the garden—kept cows—raised my own chickens—worked out-of-doors—slept out-of-doors. I'm a stronger woman today than I ever was in my life!"

She stood up, tall, strong, and straight, and drew a deep breath.

"Your father's property amounted to about eight thousand dollars when he died," she continued. "That would be two thousand dollars to James and one thousand dollars to each of the girls. That I'm willing to give you now—each of you—in your own name. But if my daughters will take my advice, they'd better let me send them the yearly income—in cash—to spend as they like. It is good for a woman to have some money of her own."

"I think you are right, Mother," said Adelaide.

"Yes indeed," murmured Ellen.

"Don't you need it yourself, Mother?" asked James, with a sudden feeling of tenderness for the stiff figure in black.

"No, James, I shall keep the ranch, you see. I have good reliable help. I've made two thousand dollars a year—clear—off it so far, and now I've rented it for that to a doctor friend of mine—woman doctor."

"I think you have done remarkably well, Mrs. McPherson—wonderfully well," said Mr. Frankland.

"And you'll have an income of two thousand dollars a year," said Adelaide incredulously.

"You'll come and live with me, won't you?" ventured Ellen.

"Thank you, my dear, I will not."

"You're more than welcome in my big house," said Adelaide.

"No thank you, my dear."

"I don't doubt Maude will be glad to have you," James rather hesitatingly offered.

"I do. I doubt it very much. No thank you, my dear."

"But what *are* you going to do?"

Ellen seemed genuinely concerned.

"I'm going to do what I never did before. I'm going to *live*!"

With a firm swift step, the tall figure moved to the windows and pulled up the lowered shades. The brilliant Colorado sunshine poured into the room. She threw off the long black veil.

"That's borrowed," she said. "I didn't want to hurt your feelings at the funeral."

She unbuttoned the long black cloak and dropped it at her feet, standing there in the full sunlight, a little flushed and smiling, dressed in a well-made traveling suit of dull mixed colors.

"If you want to know my plans, I'll tell you. I've got six thousand dollars of my own. I earned it in three years—off my little rancho-sanitarium. One thousand I have put in the savings bank—to bring me back from anywhere on earth, and to put me in an old lady's home if it is necessary. Here is an agreement with a cremation company. They'll import me, if necessary, and have me duly—expurgated—or they don't get the money. But I've got five thousand dollars to play with, and I'm going to play."

Her daughters looked shocked.

"Why, Mother—"

"At your age—"

James drew down his upper lip and looked like his father.

"I knew you wouldn't any of you understand," she continued more quietly. "But it doesn't matter any more. Thirty years I've given you—and your father. Now I'll have thirty years of my own."

"Are you—are you sure you're—well, Mother?" Ellen urged with real anxiety.

Her mother laughed outright.

"Well, really well, never was better, have been doing business up to today—good medical testimony that. No question of my sanity, my dears! I want you to grasp the fact that your mother is a Real Person with some interests of her own and half a lifetime yet. The first twenty didn't count for much—I was growing up and couldn't help myself. The last thirty have been—hard. James perhaps realizes that more than you girls, but you all know it. Now, I'm free.''

''Where *do* you mean to go, Mother?'' James asked.

She looked around the little circle with a serene air of decision and replied.

''To New Zealand. I've always wanted to go there,'' she pursued. ''Now I'm going. And to Australia—and Tasmania—and Madagascar—and Tierra del Fuego. I shall be gone some time.''

They separated that night—three going east, one west.

# Selections from
# HERLAND

Y ou see, their country was as neat
as a Dutch kitchen, and as to sanitation—but I might
as well start in now with as much as I can remember
of the history of this amazing country before further
description.

And I'll summarize here a bit as to our opportunities
for learning it. I will not try to repeat the careful, detailed
account I lost; I'll just say that we were kept in that
fortress a good six months all told, and after that, three in
a pleasant enough city where—to Terry's infinite disgust—
there were only "Colonels" and little children—no young
women whatever. Then we were under surveillance for
three more—always with a tutor or a guard or both. But
those months were pleasant because we were really getting
acquainted with the girls. That was a chapter!—or will
be—I will try to do justice to it.

We learned their language pretty thoroughly—had to;

and they learned ours much more quickly and used it to hasten our own studies.

Jeff, who was never without reading matter of some sort, had two little books with him, a novel and a little anthology of verse; and I had one of those pocket encyclopedias—a fat little thing, bursting with facts. These were used in our education—and theirs. Then as soon as we were up to it, they furnished us with plenty of their own books, and I went in for the history part—I wanted to understand the genesis of this miracle of theirs.

And this is what happened, according to their records:

As to geography—at about the time of the Christian era this land had a free passage to the sea. I'm not saying where, for good reasons. But there was a fairly easy pass through that wall of mountains behind us, and there is no doubt in my mind that these people were of Aryan stock, and were once in contact with the best civilization of the old world. They were "white," but somewhat darker than our northern races because of their constant exposure to sun and air.

The country was far larger then, including much land beyond the pass, and a strip of coast. They had ships, commerce, an army, a king—for at that time they were what they so calmly called us—a bi-sexual race.

What happened to them first was merely a succession of historic misfortunes such as have befallen other nations often enough. They were decimated by war, driven up from their coastline till finally the reduced population, with many of the men killed in battle, occupied this hinterland, and defended it for years, in the mountain passes. Where it was open to any possible attack from below they strengthened the natural defenses so that it became unscalably secure, as we found it.

They were a polygamous people, and a slave-holding people, like all of their time; and during the generation or two of this struggle to defend their mountain home they built the fortresses, such as the one we were held in, and other of their oldest buildings, some still in use. Nothing but earthquakes could destroy such architecture—huge solid blocks, holding by their own weight. They must have had efficient workmen and enough of them in those days.

They made a brave fight for their existence, but no nation can stand up against what the steamship companies call "an act of God." While the whole fighting force was doing its best to defend their mountain pathway, there occurred a volcanic outburst, with some local tremors, and the result was the complete filling up of the pass—their only outlet. Instead of a passage, a new ridge, sheer and high, stood between them and the sea; they were walled in, and beneath that wall lay their whole little army. Very few men were left alive, save the slaves; and these now seized their opportunity, rose in revolt, killed their remaining masters even to the youngest boy, killed the old women too, and the mothers, intending to take possession of the country with the remaining young women and girls.

But this succession of misfortunes was too much for those infuriated virgins. There were many of them, and but few of these would-be masters, so the young women, instead of submitting, rose in sheer desperation and slew their brutal conquerors.

This sounds like Titus Andronicus, I know, but that is their account. I suppose they were about crazy—can you blame them?

There was literally no one left on this beautiful high garden land but a bunch of hysterical girls and some older slave women.

That was about two thousand years ago.

At first there was a period of sheer despair. The mountains towered between them and their old enemies, but also between them and escape. There was no way up or down or out—they simply had to stay there. Some were for suicide, but not the majority. They must have been a plucky lot, as a whole, and they decided to live—as long as they did live. Of course they had hope, as youth must, that something would happen to change their fate.

So they set to work, to bury the dead, to plow and sow, to care for one another.

Speaking of burying the dead, I will set down while I think of it, that they had adopted cremation in about the thirteenth century, for the same reason that they had left off raising cattle—they could not spare the room. They were much surprised to learn that we were still burying—asked our reasons for it, and were much dissatisfied with what we gave. We told them of the belief in the resurrection of the body, and they asked if our God was not as well able to resurrect from ashes as from long corruption. We told them of how people thought it repugnant to have their loved ones burn, and they asked if it was less repugnant to have them decay. They were inconveniently reasonable, those women.

Well—that original bunch of girls set to work to clean up the place and make their living as best they could. Some of the remaining slave women rendered invaluable service, teaching such trades as they knew. They had such records as were then kept, all the tools and implements of the time, and a most fertile land to work in.

There were a handful of the younger matrons who had escaped slaughter, and a few babies were born after the cataclysm—but only two boys, and they both died.

For five or ten years they worked together, growing stronger and wiser and more and more mutually attached, and then the miracle happened—one of these young women bore a child. Of course they all thought there must be a man somewhere, but none was found. Then they decided it must be a direct gift from the gods, and placed the proud mother in the Temple of Maaia—their Goddess of Motherhood—under strict watch. And there, as years passed, this wonder-woman bore child after child, five of them—all girls.

I did my best, keenly interested as I have always been

in sociology and social psychology, to reconstruct in my mind the real position of these ancient women. There were some five or six hundred of them, and they were harem-bred; yet for the few preceding generations they had been reared in the atmosphere of such heroic struggle that the stock must have been toughened somewhat. Left alone in that terrific orphanhood, they had clung together, supporting one another and their little sisters, and developing unknown powers in the stress of new necessity. To this pain-hardened and work-strengthened group, who had lost not only the love and care of parents, but the hope of ever having children of their own, there now dawned the new hope.

Here at last was Motherhood, and though it was not for all of them personally, it might—if the power was inherited—found here a new race.

It may be imagined how those five Daughters of Maaia, Children of the Temple, Mothers of the Future—they had all the titles that love and hope and reverence could give—were reared. The whole little nation of women surrounded them with loving service, and waited, between a boundless hope and an equally boundless despair, to see if they, too, would be mothers.

And they were! As fast as they reached the age of twenty-five they began bearing. Each of them, like her mother, bore five daughters. Presently there were twenty-five New Women, Mothers in their own right, and the whole spirit of the country changed from mourning and mere courageous resignation to proud joy. The older women, those who remembered men, died off; the youngest of all the first lot of course died too, after a while, and by that time there were left one hundred and fifty-five parthenogenetic women, founding a new race.

They inherited all that the devoted care of that declining band of original ones could leave them. Their little country was quite safe. Their farms and gardens were all in full production. Such industries as they had were in

CHARLOTTE PERKINS GILMAN

careful order. The records of their past were all preserved, and for years the older women had spent their time in the best teaching they were capable of, that they might leave to the little group of sisters and mothers all they possessed of skill and knowledge.

There you have the start of Herland! One family, all descended from one mother! She lived to a hundred years old; lived to see her hundred and twenty-five great-granddaughters born; lived as Queen-Priestess-Mother of them all; and died with a nobler pride and a fuller joy than perhaps any human soul has ever known—she alone had founded a new race!

The first five daughters had grown up in an atmosphere of holy calm, of awed watchful waiting, of breathless prayer. To them the longed-for motherhood was not only a personal joy, but a nation's hope. Their twenty-five daughters in turn, with a stronger hope, a richer, wider outlook, with the devoted love and care of all the surviving population, grew up as a holy sisterhood, their whole ardent youth looking forward to their great office. And at last they were left alone; the white-haired First Mother was gone, and this one family, five sisters, twenty-five first cousins, and a hundred and twenty-five second cousins, began a new race.

Here you have human beings, unquestionably, but what we were slow in understanding was how these ultra-women, inheriting only from women, had eliminated not only certain masculine characteristics, which of course we did not look for, but so much of what we had always thought essentially feminine.

The tradition of men as guardians and protectors had quite died out. These stalwart virgins had no men to fear and therefore no need of protection. As to wild beasts—there were none in their sheltered land.

The power of mother-love, that maternal instinct we so highly laud, was theirs of course, raised to its highest

102

power; and a sister-love which, even while recognizing the actual relationship, we found it hard to credit.

Terry, incredulous, even contemptuous, when we were alone, refused to believe the story. "A lot of traditions as old as Herodotus—and about as trustworthy!" he said. "It's likely women—just a pack of women—would have hung together like that! We all know women can't organize—that they scrap like anything—are frightfully jealous."

"But these New Ladies didn't have anyone to be jealous of, remember," drawled Jeff.

"That's a likely story," Terry sneered.

"Why don't you invent a likelier one?" I asked him. "Here *are* the women—nothing but women, and you yourself admit there's no trace of a man in the country." This was after we had been about a good deal.

"I'll admit that," he growled. "And it's a big miss, too. There's not only no fun without 'em—no real sport—no competition; but these women aren't *womanly*. You know they aren't."

That kind of talk always set Jeff going; and I gradually grew to side with him. "Then you don't call a breed of women whose one concern is motherhood—womanly?" he asked.

"Indeed I don't," snapped Terry. "What does a man care for motherhood—when he hasn't a ghost of a chance at fatherhood? And besides—what's the good of talking sentiment when we are just men together? What a man wants of women is a good deal more than all this 'motherhood'!"

We were as patient as possible with Terry. He had lived about nine months among the "Colonels" when he made that outburst; and with no chance at any more strenuous excitement than our gymnastics gave us—save for our escape fiasco. I don't suppose Terry had ever lived so long with neither Love, Combat, nor Danger to employ his superabundant energies, and he was irritable. Neither Jeff nor I found it so wearing. I was so much interested intellectually that our confinement did not wear on me; and as for Jeff, bless his heart!—he enjoyed the society of that tutor of his almost as much as if she had been a girl—I don't know but more.

As to Terry's criticism, it was true. These women, whose essential distinction of motherhood was the dominant note of their whole culture, were strikingly deficient in what we call "femininity." This led me very promptly to the conviction that those "feminine charms" we are so fond of are not feminine at all, but mere reflected masculinity—developed to please us because they had to please us, and in no way essential to the real fulfillment of their great process. But Terry came to no such conclusion.

"Just you wait till I get out!" he muttered.

Then we both cautioned him. "Look here, Terry, my boy! You be careful! They've been mighty good to us—but do you remember the anesthesia? If you do any mischief in this virgin land, beware of the vengeance of the Maiden Aunts! Come, be a man! It won't be forever."

To return to the history:

They began at once to plan and build for their children, all the strength and intelligence of the whole of them devoted to that one thing. Each girl, of course, was reared in full knowledge of her Crowning Office, and they had, even then, very high ideas of the molding powers of the mother, as well as those of education.

Such high ideals as they had! Beauty, Health, Strength, Intellect, Goodness—for these they prayed and worked.

They had no enemies; they themselves were all sisters and friends. The land was fair before them, and a great future began to form itself in their minds.

The religion they had to begin with was much like that of old Greece—a number of gods and goddesses; but they lost all interest in deities of war and plunder, and gradually centered on their Mother Goddess altogether.

Then, as they grew more intelligent, this had turned into a sort of Maternal Pantheism.

Here was Mother Earth, bearing fruit. All that they ate was fruit of motherhood, from seed or egg or their product. By motherhood they were born and by motherhood they lived—life was, to them, just the long cycle of motherhood.

But very early they recognized the need of improvement as well as of mere repetition, and devoted their combined intelligence to that problem—how to make the best kind of people. First this was merely the hope of bearing better ones, and then they recognized that however the children differed at birth, the real growth lay later—through education.

Then things began to hum.

As I learned more and more to appreciate what these women had accomplished, the less proud I was of what we, with all our manhood, had done.

You see, they had had no wars. They had had no kings, and no priests, and no aristocracies. They were sisters, and as they grew, they grew together—not by competition, but by united action.

We tried to put in a good word for competition, and they were keenly interested. Indeed, we soon found from their earnest questions of us that they were prepared to believe our world must be better than theirs. They were not sure; they wanted to know; but there was no such arrogance about them as might have been expected.

We rather spread ourselves, telling of the advantages of competition: how it developed fine qualities; that without it there would be "no stimulus to industry." Terry was very strong on that point.

"No stimulus to industry," they repeated, with that puzzled look we had learned to know so well. "*Stimulus? To Industry?* But don't you *like* to work?"

"No man would work unless he had to," Terry declared.

"Oh, no *man*! You mean that is one of your sex distinctions?"

"No, indeed!" he said hastily. "No one, I mean, man or woman, would work without incentive. Competition is the—the motor power, you see."

"It is not with us," they explained gently, "so it is hard for us to understand. Do you mean, for instance, that with you no mother would work for her children without the stimulus of competition?"

No, he admitted that he did not mean that. Mothers, he supposed, would of course work for their children in the home; but the world's work was different—that had to be done by men, and required the competitive element.

All our teachers were eagerly interested.

"We want so much to know—you have the whole world to tell us of, and we have only our little land! And there are two of you—the two sexes—to love and help one another. It must be a rich and wonderful world. Tell us—what is the work of the world, that men do—which we have not here?"

"Oh, everything," Terry said grandly. "The men do everything, with us." He squared his broad shoulders and lifted his chest. "We do not allow our women to work. Women are loved—idolized—honored—kept in the home to care for the children."

"What is 'the home'?" asked Somel a little wistfully.

But Zava begged: "Tell me first, do *no* women work, really?"

"Why, yes," Terry admitted. "Some have to, of the poorer sort."

"About how many—in your country?"

"About seven or eight million," said Jeff, as mischievous as ever.

FROM

# Comparisons Are Odious

Do you mind telling what you intend to do with us?'' Terry burst forth one day, facing the calm and friendly Moadine with that funny half-blustering air of his. At first he used to storm and flourish quite a good deal, but nothing seemed to amuse them more; they would gather around and watch him as if it was an exhibition, politely, but with evident interest. So he learned to check himself, and was almost reasonable in his bearing—but not quite.

She announced smoothly and evenly: ''Not in the least. I thought it was quite plain. We are trying to learn of you all we can, and to teach you what you are willing to learn of our country.''

''Is that all?'' he insisted.

She smiled a quiet enigmatic smile. ''That depends.''

''Depends on what?''

''Mainly on yourselves,'' she replied.

''Why do you keep us shut up so closely?''

''Because we do not feel quite safe in allowing you at large where there are so many young women.''

Terry was really pleased at that. He had thought as much, inwardly; but he pushed the question. ''Why should you be afraid? We are gentlemen.''

She smiled that little smile again, and asked: ''Are 'gentlemen' always safe?''

''You surely do not think that any of us,'' he said it with a good deal of emphasis on the ''us,'' ''would hurt your young girls?''

''Oh no,'' she said quickly, in real surprise. ''The danger is quite the other way. They might hurt you. If, by any accident, you did harm any one of us, you would have to face a million mothers.''

He looked so amazed and outraged that Jeff and I laughed outright, but she went on gently.

''I do not think you quite understand yet. You are but men, three men, in a country where the whole population are mothers—or are going to be. Motherhood means to us something which I cannot yet discover in any of the countries of which you tell us. You have spoken''—she turned to Jeff, ''of Human Brotherhood as a great idea among you, but even that I judge is far from a practical expression?''

Jeff nodded rather sadly. ''Very far—'' he said.

''Here we have Human Motherhood—in full working use,'' she went on. ''Nothing else except the literal sisterhood of our origin, and the far higher and deeper union of our social growth.

''The children in this country are the one center and focus of all our thoughts. Every step of our advance is always considered in its effect on them—on the race. You see, we are *Mothers*,'' she repeated, as if in that she had said it all.

''I don't see how that fact—which is shared by all women—constitutes any risk to us,'' Terry persisted. ''You mean they would defend their children from attack. Of course. Any mothers would. But we are not savages, my dear lady; we are not going to hurt any mother's child.''

They looked at one another and shook their heads a little, but Zava turned to Jeff and urged him to make us see—said he seemed to understand more fully than we did. And he tried.

I can see it now, or at least much more of it, but it has taken me a long time, and a good deal of honest intellectual effort.

What they call Motherhood was like this:

They began with a really high degree of social development, something like that of Ancient Egypt or Greece.

Then they suffered the loss of everything masculine, and supposed at first that all human power and safety had gone too. Then they developed this virgin birth capacity. Then, since the prosperity of their children depended on it, the fullest and subtlest coordination began to be practiced.

I remember how long Terry balked at the evident unanimity of these women—the most conspicuous feature of their whole culture. "It's impossible!" he would insist. "Women cannot cooperate—it's against nature."

When we urged the obvious facts he would say: "Fiddlesticks!" or "Hang your facts—I tell you it can't be done!" And we never succeeded in shutting him up till Jeff dragged in the hymenoptera.

" 'Go to the ant, thou sluggard'—and learn something," he said triumphantly. "Don't they cooperate pretty well? You can't beat it. This place is just like an enormous anthill—you know an anthill is nothing but a nursery. And how about bees? Don't they manage to cooperate and love one another?

As the birds do love the Spring
Or the bees their careful king,

as that precious Constable had it. Just show me a combination of male creatures, bird, bug, or beast, that works as well, will you? Or one of our masculine countries where the people work together as well as they do here! I tell you, women are the natural cooperators, not men!"

Terry had to learn a good many things he did not want to.

To go back to my little analysis of what happened:

They developed all this close inter-service in the interests of their children. To do the best work they had to specialize, of course; the children needed spinners and weavers, farmers and gardeners, carpenters and masons, as well as mothers.

Then came the filling up of the place. When a population multiplies by five every thirty years it soon reaches the limits of a country, especially a small one like this. They very soon eliminated all the grazing cattle—sheep were the last to go, I believe. Also, they worked out a system of intensive agriculture surpassing anything I ever heard of, with the very forests all reset with fruit- or nut-bearing trees.

Do what they would, however, there soon came a time when they were confronted with the problem of "the pressure of population" in an acute form. There was really crowding, and with it, unavoidably, a decline in standards.

And how did those women meet it?

Not by a "struggle for existence" which would result in an everlasting writhing mass of underbred people trying to get ahead of one another—some few on top, temporarily, many constantly crushed out underneath, a hopeless substratum of paupers and degenerates, and no serenity or peace for anyone, no possibility for really noble qualities among the people at large.

Neither did they start off on predatory excursions to get more land from somebody else, or to get more food from somebody else, to maintain their struggling mass.

Not at all. They sat down in council together and thought it out. Very clear, strong thinkers they were. They said: "With our best endeavors this country will support about so many people, with the standard of peace, comfort, health, beauty, and progress we demand. Very well. That is all the people we will make."

There you have it. You see, they were Mothers, not in our sense of helpless involuntary fecundity, forced to fill and overfill the land, every land, and then see their children suffer, sin, and die, fighting horribly with one another; but in the sense of Conscious Makers of People. Mother-love with them was not a brute passion, a mere "instinct," a wholly personal feeling; it was—a religion.

It included that limitless feeling of sisterhood, that

wide unity in service which was so difficult for us to grasp. And it was National, Racial, Human—oh, I don't know how to say it.

We are used to seeing what we call "a mother" completely wrapped up in her own pink bundle of fascinating babyhood, and taking but the faintest theoretic interest in anybody else's bundle, to say nothing of the common needs of *all* the bundles. But these women were working all together at the grandest of tasks—they were Making People—and they made them well.

There followed a period of "negative eugenics" which must have been an appalling sacrifice. We are commonly willing to "lay down our lives" for our country, but they had to forego motherhood for their country—and it was precisely the hardest thing for them to do.

When I got this far in my reading I went to Somel for more light. We were as friendly by that time as I had ever been in my life with any woman. A mighty comfortable soul she was, giving one the nice smooth mother-feeling a man likes in a woman, and yet giving also the clear intelligence and dependableness I used to assume to be masculine qualities. We had talked volumes already.

"See here," said I. "Here was this dreadful period when they got far too thick, and decided to limit the population. We have a lot of talk about that among us, but your position is so different that I'd like to know a little more about it.

"I understand that you make Motherhood the highest social service—a sacrament, really; that it is only undertaken once, by the majority of the population; that those held unfit are not allowed even that; and that to be encouraged to bear more than one child is the very highest reward and honor in the power of the state."

(She interpolated here that the nearest approach to an aristocracy they had was to come of a line of "Over Mothers"—those who had been so honored.)

"But what I do not understand, naturally, is how you

*111*

prevent it. I gathered that each woman had five. You have no tyrannical husbands to hold in check—and you surely do not destroy the unborn—"

The look of ghastly horror she gave me I shall never forget. She started from her chair, pale, her eyes blazing.

"Destroy the unborn—!" she said in a hard whisper. "Do men do that in your country?"

"Men!" I began to answer, rather hotly, and then saw the gulf before me. None of us wanted these women to think that *our* women, of whom we boasted so proudly, were in any way inferior to them. I am ashamed to say that I equivocated. I told her of certain criminal types of women—perverts, or crazy, who had been known to commit infanticide. I told her, truly enough, that there was much in our land which was open to criticism, but that I hated to dwell on our defects until they understood us and our conditions better.

And, making a wide detour, I scrambled back to my question of how they limited the population.

As for Somel, she seemed sorry, a little ashamed even, of her too clearly expressed amazement. As I look back now, knowing them better, I am more and more and more amazed as I appreciate the exquisite courtesy with which they had received over and over again statements and admissions on our part which must have revolted them to the soul.

She explained to me, with sweet seriousness, that as I had supposed, at first each woman bore five children; and that, in their eager desire to build up a nation, they had gone on in that way for a few centuries, till they were confronted with the absolute need of a limit. This fact was equally plain to all—all were equally interested.

They were now as anxious to check their wonderful power as they had been to develop it; and for some generations gave the matter their most earnest thought and study.

"We were living on rations before we worked it out," she said. "But we did work it out. You see, before a child comes to one of us there is a period of utter exaltation—the whole being is uplifted and filled with a concentrated desire for that child. We learned to look forward to that period with the greatest caution. Often our young women, those to whom motherhood had not yet come, would voluntarily defer it. When that deep inner demand for a child began to be felt she would deliberately engage in the most active work, physical and mental; and even more important, would solace her longing by the direct care and service of the babies we already had.''

She paused. Her wise sweet face grew deeply, reverently tender.

"We soon grew to see that mother-love has more than one channel of expression. I think the reason our children are so—so fully loved, by all of us, is that we never—any of us—have enough of our own.''

This seemed to me infinitely pathetic, and I said so. "We have much that is bitter and hard in our life at home," I told her, "but this seems to me piteous beyond words—a whole nation of starving mothers!''

But she smiled her deep contented smile, and said I quite misunderstood.

"We each go without a certain range of personal joy," she said, "but remember—we each have a million children to love and serve—*our* children.''

It was beyond me. To hear a lot of women talk about "our children"! But I suppose that is the way the ants and bees would talk—do talk, maybe.

That was what they did, anyhow.

When a woman chose to be a mother, she allowed the child-longing to grow within her till it worked its natural miracle. When she did not so choose she put the whole thing out of her mind, and fed her heart with the other babies.

Let me see—with us, children—minors, that is—constitute about three-fifths of the population; with them only about one-third, or less. And precious—! No sole heir to an empire's throne, no solitary millionaire baby, no only child of middle-aged parents, could compare as an idol with these Herland children.

But before I start on that subject I must finish up that little analysis I was trying to make.

They did effectually and permanently limit the population in numbers, so that the country furnished plenty for the fullest, richest life for all of them: plenty of everything, including room, air, solitude even.

And then they set to work to improve that population in quality—since they were restricted in quantity. This they had been at work on, uninterruptedly, for some fifteen hundred years. Do you wonder they were nice people?

Physiology, hygiene, sanitation, physical culture—all that line of work had been perfected long since. Sickness was almost wholly unknown among them, so much so that a previously high development in what we call the "science of medicine" had become practically a lost art. They were a clean-bred, vigorous lot, having the best of care, the most perfect living conditions always.

When it came to psychology—there was no one thing which left us so dumbfounded, so really awed, as the everyday working knowledge—and practice—they had in this line. As we learned more and more of it, we learned to appreciate the exquisite mastery with which we ourselves, strangers of alien race, of unknown opposite sex, had been understood and provided for from the first.

With this wide, deep, thorough knowledge, they had met and solved the problems of education in ways some of which I hope to make clear later. Those nation-loved children of theirs compared with the average in our country as the most perfectly cultivated, richly developed roses compare with—tumbleweeds. Yet they did not *seem* "cultivated" at all—it had all become a natural condition.

And this people, steadily developing in mental capacity, in will power, in social devotion, had been playing with the arts and sciences—as far as they knew them—for a good many centuries now with inevitable success.

Into this quiet lovely land, among these wise, sweet, strong women, we, in our easy assumption of superiority, had suddenly arrived; and now, tamed and trained to a degree they considered safe, we were at last brought out to see the country, to know the people.

FROM

## The Girls of Herland

A still day—on the edge of the world, their world. The two of us, gazing out over the far dim forestland below, talking of heaven and earth and human life, and of my land and other lands and what they needed and what I hoped to do for them—

"If you will help me," I said.

She turned to me, with that high, sweet look of hers, and then, as her eyes rested in mine and her hands too—then suddenly there blazed out between us a farther glory, instant, overwhelming—quite beyond any words of mine to tell.

Celis was a blue-and-gold-and-rose person; Alma, black-and-white-and-red, a blazing beauty. Ellador was brown: hair dark and soft, like a seal coat; clear brown skin with a healthy red in it; brown eyes—all the way from topaz to black velvet they seemed to range—splendid girls, all of them.

They had seen us first of all, far down in the lake below, and flashed the tidings across the land even before our first exploring flight. They had watched our landing, flitted through the forest with us, hidden in that tree and—I shrewdly suspect—giggled on purpose.

They had kept watch over our hooded machine, taking turns at it; and when our escape was announced, had followed alongside for a day or two, and been there at the last, as described. They felt a special claim on us—called us "their men"—and when we were at liberty to study the land and people, and be studied by them, their claim was recognized by the wise leaders.

But I felt, we all did, that we should have chosen them among millions, unerringly.

And yet, "the path of true love never did run smooth"; this period of courtship was full of the most unsuspected pitfalls.

Writing this as late as I do, after manifold experiences both in Herland and, later, in my own land, I can now understand and philosophize about what was then a continual astonishment and often a temporary tragedy.

The "long suit" in most courtships is sex attraction, of course. Then gradually develops such comradeship as the two temperaments allow. Then, after marriage, there is either the establishment of a slow-growing, widely based friendship, the deepest, tenderest, sweetest of relations, all lit and warmed by the recurrent flame of love; or else that process is reversed, love cools and fades, no friendship grows, the whole relation turns from beauty to ashes.

Here everything was different. There was no sex-feeling to appeal to, or practically none. Two thousand years' disuse had left very little of the instinct; also we must remember that those who had at times manifested it as atavistic exceptions were often, by that very fact, denied motherhood.

Yet while the mother process remains, the inherent ground for sex-distinction remains also; and who shall say what long-forgotten feeling, vague and nameless, was stirred in some of these mother hearts by our arrival?

What left us even more at sea in our approach was the lack of any sex-tradition. There was no accepted standard of what was "manly" and what was "womanly."

When Jeff said, taking the fruit basket from his adored one, "A woman should not carry anything," Celis said, "Why?" with the frankest amazement. He could not look that fleet-footed, deep-chested young forester in the face and say, "Because she is weaker." She wasn't. One does not call a race horse weak because it is visibly not a cart horse.

He said, rather lamely, that women were not built for heavy work.

She looked out across the fields to where some women were working, building a new bit of wall out of large stones; looked back at the nearest town with its woman-built houses; down at the smooth, hard road we were walking on; and then at the little basket he had taken from her.

"I don't understand," she said quite sweetly. "Are the women in your country so weak that they could not carry such a thing as that?"

"It is a convention," he said. "We assume that motherhood is a sufficient burden—that men should carry all the others."

"What a beautiful feeling!" she said, her blue eyes shining.

"Does it work?" asked Alima, in her keen, swift way. "Do all men in all countries carry everything? Or is it only in yours?"

"Don't be so literal," Terry begged lazily. "Why aren't you willing to be worshipped and waited on? We like to do it."

"You don't like to have us do it to you," she answered.

"That's different," he said, annoyed; and when she said, "Why is it?" he quite sulked, referring her to me, saying, "Van's the philosopher."

Ellador and I talked it all out together, so that we had an easier experience of it when the real miracle time came. Also, between us, we made things clearer to Jeff and Celis. But Terry would not listen to reason.

He was madly in love with Alima. He wanted to take her by storm, and nearly lost her forever.

You see, if a man loves a girl who is in the first place young and inexperienced; who in the second place is educated with a background of caveman tradition, a middle-ground of poetry and romance, and a foreground of unspoken hope and interest all centering upon the one Event; and who has, furthermore, absolutely no other hope or interest worthy of the name—why, it is a comparatively easy matter to sweep her off her feet with a dashing attack. Terry was a past master in this process. He tried it here, and Alima was so affronted, so repelled, that it was weeks before he got near enough to try again.

The more coldly she denied him, the hotter his determination; he was not used to real refusal. The approach of flattery she dismissed with laughter, gifts and such "attentions" we could not bring to bear, pathos and complaint of cruelty stirred only a reasoning inquiry. It took Terry a long time.

I doubt if she ever accepted her strange lover as fully as did Celis and Ellador theirs. He had hurt and offended her too often; there were reservations.

But I think Alima retained some faint vestige of long-descended feeling which made Terry more possible to her than to others; and that she had made up her mind to the experiment and hated to renounce it.

However it came about, we all three at length achieved full understanding, and solemnly faced what was to them a step of measureless importance, a grave question as well as a great happiness; to us a strange, new joy.

Of marriage as a ceremony they knew nothing. Jeff was for bringing them to our country for the religious and the civil ceremony, but neither Celis nor the others would consent.

"We can't expect them to want to go with us—yet," said Terry sagely. "Wait a bit, boys. We've got to take 'em on their own terms—if at all.'' This, in rueful reminiscence of his repeated failures.

"But our time's coming," he added cheerfully. "These women have never been mastered, you see—" This, as one who had made a discovery.

"You'd better not try to do any mastering if you value your chances," I told him seriously; but he only laughed, and said, "Every man to his trade!"

We couldn't do anything with him. He had to take his own medicine.

If the lack of tradition of courtship left us much at sea in our wooing, we found ourselves still more bewildered by lack of tradition of matrimony.

And here again, I have to draw on later experience, and as deep an acquaintance with their culture as I could achieve, to explain the gulfs of difference between us.

Two thousand years of one continuous culture with no men. Back of that, only traditions of the harem. They had no exact analogue for our word *home,* any more than they had for our Roman-based *family.*

They loved one another with a practically universal affection, rising to exquisite and unbroken friendships, and broadening to a devotion to their country and people for which our word *patriotism* is no definition at all.

Patriotism, red hot, is compatible with the existence of a neglect of national interests, a dishonesty, a cold indifference to the suffering of millions. Patriotism is largely pride, and very largely combativeness. Patriotism generally has a chip on its shoulder.

This country had no other country to measure itself by—save the few poor savages far below, with whom they had no contact.

They loved their country because it was their nursery, playground, and workshop—theirs and their children's. They were proud of it as a workshop, proud of their record of ever-increasing efficiency; they had made a pleasant garden of it, a very practical little heaven; but most of all they valued it—and here it is hard for us to understand them—as a cultural environment for their children.

That, of course, is the keynote of the whole distinction—their children.

From those first breathlessly guarded, half-adored race mothers, all up the ascending line, they had this dominant thought of building up a great race through the children.

All the surrendering devotion our women have put into their private families, these women put into their country and race. All the loyalty and service men expect of wives, they gave, not singly to men, but collectively to one another.

And the mother instinct, with us so painfully intense, so thwarted by conditions, so concentrated in personal devotion to a few, so bitterly hurt by death, disease, or barrenness, and even by the mere growth of the children, leaving the mother alone in her empty nest—all this feeling with them flowed out in a strong, wide current, unbroken through the generations, deepening and widening through the years, including every child in all the land.

With their united power and wisdom, they had studied and overcome the "diseases of childhood"—their children had none.

They had faced the problems of education and so solved them that their children grew up as naturally as young trees; learning through every sense; taught continuously but unconsciously—never knowing they were being educated.

In fact, they did not use the word as we do. Their idea of education was the special training they took, when half grown up, under experts. Then the eager young minds fairly flung themselves on their chosen subjects, and acquired with an ease, a breadth, a grasp, at which I never ceased to wonder.

But the babies and little children never felt the pressure of that "forcible feeding" of the mind that we call "education." Of this, more later.

FROM

# Our Relations and Theirs

"There's nothing to smoke," complained Terry. He was in the midst of a prolonged quarrel with Alima, and needed a sedative. "There's nothing to drink. These blessed women have no pleasant vices. I wish we could get out of here!"

This wish was vain. We were always under a certain degree of watchfulness. When Terry burst forth to tramp the streets at night he always found a "Colonel" here or there; and when, on an occasion of fierce though temporary despair, he had plunged to the cliff edge with some vague view to escape, he found several of them close by. We were free—but there was a string to it.

"They've no unpleasant ones, either," Jeff reminded him.

"Wish they had!" Terry persisted. "They've neither the vices of men, nor the virtues of women—they're neuters!"

"You know better than that. Don't talk nonsense," said I, severely.

I was thinking of Ellador's eyes when they gave me a certain look, a look she did not at all realize.

Jeff was equally incensed. "I don't know what 'virtues of women' you miss. Seems to me they have all of them."

"They've no modesty," snapped Terry. "No patience, no submissiveness, none of that natural yielding which is woman's greatest charm."

I shook my head pityingly. "Go and apologize and make friends again, Terry. You've got a grouch, that's all. These women have the virtue of humanity, with less of its

121

faults than any folks I ever saw. As for patience—they'd
have pitched us over the cliffs the first day we lit among
'em, if they hadn't that.''

''There are no—distractions,'' he grumbled. ''Nowhere
a man can go and cut loose a bit. It's an everlasting parlor
and nursery.''

''And workshop,'' I added. ''And school, and office,
and laboratory, and studio, and theater, and—home.''

*''Home!''* he sneered. ''There isn't a home in the
whole pitiful place.''

''There isn't anything else, and you know it,'' Jeff
retorted hotly. ''I never saw, I never dreamed of, such
universal peace and good will and mutual affection.''

''Oh, well, of course, if you like a perpetual Sunday
school, it's all very well. But I like Something Doing. Here
it's all done.''

There was something to this criticism. The years of
pioneering lay far behind them. Theirs was a civilization in
which the initial difficulties had long since been overcome.
The untroubled peace, the unmeasured plenty, the steady
health, the large good will and smooth management which
ordered everything, left nothing to overcome. It was like a
pleasant family in an old established, perfectly run country
place.

I liked it because of my eager and continued interest
in the sociological achievements involved. Jeff liked it as
he would have liked such a family and such a place
anywhere.

Terry did not like it because he found nothing to
oppose, to struggle with, to conquer.

''Life is a struggle, has to be,'' he insisted. ''If there
is no struggle, there is no life—that's all.''

''You're talking nonsense—masculine nonsense,'' the
peaceful Jeff replied. He was certainly a warm defender of
Herland. ''Ants don't raise their myriads by a struggle, do
they? Or the bees?''

''Oh, if you go back to insects—and want to live in

an anthill—! I tell you the higher grades of life are reached only through struggle—combat. There's no Drama here. Look at their plays! They make me sick.''

He rather had us there. The drama of the country was—to our taste—rather flat. You see, they lacked the sex motive and, with it, jealousy. They had no interplay of warring nations, no aristocracy and its ambitions, no wealth and poverty opposition.

I see I have said little about the economics of the place; it should have come before, but I'll go on about the drama now.

They had their own kind. There was a most impressive array of pageantry, of processions, a sort of grand ritual, with their arts and their religion broadly blended. The very babies joined in it. To see one of their great annual festivals, with the massed and marching stateliness of those great mothers; the young women brave and noble, beautiful and strong; and then the children, taking part as naturally as ours would frolic round a Christmas tree—it was overpowering in the impression of joyous, triumphant life.

They had begun at a period when the drama, the dance, music, religion, and education were all very close together; and instead of developing them in detached lines, they had kept the connection. Let me try again to give, if I can, a faint sense of the difference in the life view—the background and basis on which their culture rested.

Ellador told me a lot about it. She took me to see the children, the growing girls, the special teachers. She picked out books for me to read. She always seemed to understand just what I wanted to know, and how to give it to me.

While Terry and Alima struck sparks and parted—he always madly drawn to her and she to him—she must have been, or she'd never have stood the way he behaved—Ellador and I had already a deep, restful feeling, as if we'd always had one another. Jeff and Celis were happy; there was no question of that; but it didn't seem to me as if they had the good times we did.

Well, here is the Herland child facing life—as Ellador tried to show it to me. From the first memory, they knew Peace, Beauty, Order, Safety, Love, Wisdom, Justice, Patience, and Plenty. By "plenty" I mean that the babies grew up in an environment which met their needs, just as young fawns might grow up in dewy forest glades and brook-fed meadows. And they enjoyed it as frankly and utterly as the fawns would.

They found themselves in a big bright lovely world, full of the most interesting and enchanting things to learn about and to do. The people everywhere were friendly and polite. No Herland child ever met the overbearing rudeness we so commonly show to children. They were People, too, from the first; the most precious part of the nation.

In each step of the rich experience of living, they found the instance they were studying widen out into contact with an endless range of common interests. The things they learned were *related*, from the first; related to one another, and to the national prosperity.

"It was a butterfly that made me a forester," said Ellador. "I was about eleven years old, and I found a big purple-and-green butterfly on a low flower. I caught it, very carefully, by the closed wings, as I had been told to do, and carried it to the nearest insect teacher"—I made a note there to ask her what on earth an insect teacher was—"to ask her its name. She took it from me with a little cry of delight. 'Oh, you blessed child,' she said. 'Do you like obernuts?' Of course I liked obernuts, and said so. It is our best food-nut, you know. 'This is a female of the obernut moth,' she told me. 'They are almost gone. We have been trying to exterminate them for centuries. If you had not caught this one, it might have laid eggs enough to raise worms enough to destroy thousands of our nut trees—thousands of bushels of nuts—and make years and years of trouble for us.'

"Everybody congratulated me. The children all over the country were told to watch for that moth, if there were any more. I was shown the history of the creature, and an account of the damage it used to do and of how long and hard our foremothers had worked to save that tree for us. I grew a foot, it seemed to me, and determined then and there to be a forester."

This is but an instance; she showed me many. The big difference was that whereas our children grow up in private homes and families, with every effort made to protect and seclude them from a dangerous world, here they grew up in a wide, friendly world, and knew it for theirs, from the first.

Their child-literature was a wonderful thing. I could have spent years following the delicate subtleties, the smooth simplicities with which they had bent that great art to the service of the child mind.

We have two life cycles: the man's and the woman's. To the man there is growth, struggle, conquest, the establishment of his family, and as much further success in gain or ambition as he can achieve.

To the woman, growth, the securing of a husband, the subordinate activities of family life, and afterward such "social" or charitable interests as her position allows.

Here was but one cycle, and that a large one.

The child entered upon a broad open field of life, in which motherhood was the one great personal contribution to the national life, and all the rest the individual share in their common activities. Every girl I talked to, at any age above babyhood, had her cheerful determination as to what she was going to be when she grew up.

What Terry meant by saying they had no "modesty" was that this great life-view had no shady places; they had a high sense of personal decorum, but no shame—no knowledge of anything to be ashamed of.

Even their shortcomings and misdeeds in childhood never were presented to them as sins; merely as errors and misplays—as in a game. Some of them, who were palpably less agreeable than others or who had a real weakness or fault, were treated with cheerful allowance, as a friendly group at whist would treat a poor player.

Their religion, you see, was maternal; and their ethics, based on the full perception of evolution, showed the principle of growth and the beauty of wise culture. They had no theory of the essential opposition of good and evil; life to them was growth; their pleasure was in growing, and their duty also.

With this background, with their sublimated mother-love, expressed in terms of widest social activity, every phase of their work was modified by its effect on the national growth. The language itself they had deliberately clarified, simplified, made easy and beautiful, for the sake of the children.

This seemed to us a wholly incredible thing: first, that any nation should have the foresight, the strength, and the persistence to plan and fulfill such a task; and second, that women should have had so much initiative. We have assumed, as a matter of course, that women had none; that only the man, with his natural energy and impatience of restriction, would ever invent anything.

Here we found that the pressure of life upon the environment develops in the human mind its inventive reactions, regardless of sex; and further, that a fully awakened motherhood plans and works without limit, for the good of the child.

That the children might be most nobly born, and reared in an environment calculated to allow the richest, freest growth, they had deliberately remodeled and improved the whole state.

I do not mean in the least that they stopped at that, any more than a child stops at childhood. The most impressive part of their whole culture beyond this perfect system of child-rearing was the range of interests and associations open to them all, for life. But in the field of literature I was most struck, at first, by the child-motive.

They had the same gradation of simple repetitive verse and story that we are familiar with, and the most exquisite, imaginative tales; but where, with us, these are the dribbled remnants of ancient folk myths and primitive lullabies, theirs were the exquisite work of great artists; not only simple and unfailing in appeal to the child-mind, but *true*, true to the living world about them.

To sit in one of their nurseries for a day was to change one's views forever as to babyhood. The youngest ones, rosy fatlings in their mothers' arms, or sleeping lightly in the flower-sweet air, seemed natural enough, save that they never cried. I never heard a child cry in Herland, save once or twice at a bad fall; and then people ran to help, as we would at a scream of agony from a grown person.

Each mother had her year of glory; the time to love and learn, living closely with her child, nursing it proudly, often for two years or more. This perhaps was one reason for their wonderful vigor.

But after the baby-year the mother was not so constantly in attendance, unless, indeed, her work was among the little ones. She was never far off, however, and her attitude toward the co-mothers, whose proud child-service was direct and continuous, was lovely to see.

As for the babies—a group of those naked darlings playing on short velvet grass, clean-swept; or rugs as soft; or in shallow pools of bright water; tumbling over with bubbling joyous baby laughter—it was a view of infant happiness such as I had never dreamed.

The babies were reared in the warmer part of the country, and gradually acclimated to the cooler heights as they grew older.

Sturdy children of ten and twelve played in the snow as joyfully as ours do; there were continuous excursions of them, from one part of the land to another, so that to each child the whole country might be home.

It was all theirs, waiting for them to learn, to love, to use, to serve; as our own little boys plan to be "a big soldier," or "a cowboy," or whatever pleases their fancy; and our little girls plan for the kind of home they mean to have, or how many children; these planned, freely and gaily with much happy chattering, of what they would do for the country when they were grown.

It was the eager happiness of the children and young people which first made me see the folly of that common notion of ours—that if life was smooth and happy, people would not enjoy it. As I studied these youngsters, vigorous, joyous, eager little creatures, and their voracious appetite for life, it shook my previous ideas so thoroughly that they have never been re-established. The steady level of good health gave them all that natural stimulus we used to call "animal spirits"—an odd contradiction in terms. They found themselves in an immediate environment which was agreeable and interesting, and before them stretched the years of learning and discovery, the fascinating, endless process of education.

As I looked into these methods and compared them with our own, my strange uncomfortable sense of race-humility grew apace.

Ellador could not understand my astonishment. She explained things kindly and sweetly, but with some amazement that they needed explaining, and with sudden questions as to how we did it that left me meeker than ever.

I betook myself to Somel one day, carefully not taking Ellador. I did not mind seeming foolish to Somel—she was used to it.

"I want a chapter of explanation," I told her. "You know my stupidities by heart, and I do not want to show them to Ellador—she thinks me so wise!"

She smiled delightedly. "It is beautiful to see," she told me, "this new wonderful love between you. The whole country is interested, you know—how can we help it!''

I had not thought of that. We say: "All the world loves a lover," but to have a couple of million people watching one's courtship—and that a difficult one—was rather embarrassing.

"Tell me about your theory of education," I said. "Make it short and easy. And, to show you what puzzles me, I'll tell you that in our theory great stress is laid on the forced exertion of the child's mind; we think it is good for him to overcome obstacles."

"Of course it is," she unexpectedly agreed. "All our children do that—they love to.''

That puzzled me again. If they loved to do it, how could it be educational?

"Our theory is this," she went on carefully. "Here is a young human being. The mind is as natural a thing as the body, a thing that grows, a thing to use and to enjoy. We seek to nourish, to stimulate, to exercise the mind of a child as we do the body. There are the two main divisions in education—you have those of course?—the things it is necessary to know, and the things it is necessary to do."

"To do? Mental exercises, you mean?''

"Yes. Our general plan is this: In the matter of feeding the mind, of furnishing information, we use our best powers to meet the natural appetite of a healthy young brain; not to overfeed it, to provide such amount and variety of impressions as seem most welcome to each child. That is the easiest part. The other division is in arranging a properly graduated series of exercises which will best develop each mind; the common faculties we all have, and most carefully, the especial faculties some of us have. You do this also, do you not?''

"In a way," I said rather lamely. "We have not so subtle and highly developed a system as you, not approaching it; but tell me more. As to the information—

how do you manage? It appears that all of you know pretty much everything—is that right?"

This she laughingly disclaimed. "By no means. We are, as you soon found out, extremely limited in knowledge. I wish you could realize what a ferment the country is in over the new things you have told us; the passionate eagerness among thousands of us to go to your country and learn—learn—learn! But what we do know is readily divisible into common knowledge and special knowledge. The common knowledge we have long since learned to feed into the minds of our little ones with no waste of time or strength; the special knowledge is open to all, as they desire it. Some of us specialize in one line only. But most take up several—some for their regular work, some to grow with."

"To grow with?"

"Yes. When one settles too close in one kind of work there is a tendency to atrophy in the disused portions of the brain. We like to keep on learning, always."

"What do you study?"

"As much as we know of the different sciences. We have, within our limits, a good deal of knowledge of anatomy, physiology, nutrition—all that pertains to a full and beautiful personal life. We have our botany and chemistry, and so on—very rudimentary, but interesting; our own history, with its accumulating psychology."

"You put psychology with history—not with personal life?"

"Of course. It is ours; it is among and between us, and it changes with the succeeding and improving generations. We are at work, slowly and carefully, developing our whole people along these lines. It is glorious work— splendid! To see the thousands of babies improving, showing stronger clearer minds, sweeter dispositions, higher capacities—don't you find it so in your country?"

This I evaded flatly. I remembered the cheerless claim that the human mind was no better than in its earliest period of savagery, only better informed—a statement I had never believed.

"We try most earnestly for two powers," Somel continued. "The two that seem to us basically necessary for all noble life: a clear, far-reaching judgment, and a strong well-used will. We spend our best efforts, all through childhood and youth, in developing these faculties, individual judgment and will."

"As part of your system of education, you mean?"

"Exactly. As the most valuable part. With the babies, as you may have noticed, we first provide an environment which feeds the mind without tiring it; all manner of simple and interesting things to do, as soon as they are old enough to do them; physical properties, of course, come first. But as early as possible, going very carefully, not to tax the mind, we provide choices, simple choices, with very obvious causes and consequences. You've noticed the games?"

I had. The children seemed always playing something; or else, sometimes, engaged in peaceful researches of their own. I had wondered at first when they went to school, but soon found that they never did—to their knowledge. It was all education but no schooling.

"We have been working for some sixteen hundred years, devising better and better games for children," continued Somel.

I sat aghast. "Devising games?" I protested. "Making up new ones, you mean?"

"Exactly," she answered. "Don't you?"

Then I remembered the kindergarten, and the "material" devised by Signora Montessori, and guardedly replied: "To some extent." But most of our games, I told her, were very old—came down from child to child, along the ages, from the remote past.

"And what is their effect?" she asked. "Do they develop the faculties you wish to encourage?"

Again I remembered the claims made by the advocates of "sports," and again replied guardedly that that was, in part, the theory.

"But do the children *like* it?" I asked. "Having things made up and set before them that way? Don't they want the old games?"

"You can see the children," she answered. "Are yours more contented—more interested—happier?"

Then I thought, as in truth I never had thought before, of the dull, bored children I had seen, whining: "What can I do now?"; of the little groups and gangs hanging about; of the value of some one strong spirit who possessed initiative and would "start something"; of the children's parties and the onerous duties of the older people set to "amuse the children"; also of that troubled ocean of misdirected activity we call "mischief," the foolish, destructive, sometimes evil things done by unoccupied children.

"No," said I grimly. "I don't think they are."

The Herland child was born not only into a world carefully prepared, full of the most fascinating materials and opportunities to learn, but into the society of plentiful numbers of teachers, teachers born and trained, whose business it was to accompany the children along that, to us, impossible thing—the royal road to learning.

There was no mystery in their methods. Being adapted to children it was at least comprehensible to adults. I spent many days with the little ones, sometimes with Ellador, sometimes without, and began to feel a crushing pity for my own childhood, and for all others that I had known.

The houses and gardens planned for babies had in them nothing to hurt—no stairs, no corners, no small loose objects to swallow, no fire—just a babies' paradise. They were taught, as rapidly as feasible, to use and control their own bodies, and never did I see such sure-footed, steady-handed, clear-headed little things. It was a joy to watch a row of toddlers learning to walk, not only on a level floor, but, a little later, on a sort of rubber rail raised an inch or two above the soft turf or heavy rugs, and falling off with shrieks of infant joy, to rush back to the end of the line and try again. Surely we have noticed how children love to get up on something and walk along it! But we have never thought to provide that simple and inexhaustible form of amusement and physical education for the young.

Water they had, of course, and could swim even before they walked. If I feared at first the effects of a too intensive system of culture, that fear was dissipated by seeing the long sunny days of pure physical merriment and natural sleep in which these heavenly babies passed their first years. They never knew they were being educated. They did not dream that in this association of hilarious experiment and achievement they were laying the foundation for that close beautiful group feeling into which they grew so firmly with the years. This was education for citizenship.

Selections from

# WOMEN AND ECONOMICS:
## A Study of the Economic Relation Between Men and Women

FROM

*The Economic Relations of the Sexes*

We are the only animal species in which the female depends on the male for food, the only animal species in which the sex-relation is also an economic relation. With us an entire sex lives in a relation of economic dependence upon the other sex, and the economic relation is combined with the sex-relation. The economic status of the human female is relative to the sex-relation.

It is commonly assumed that this condition also obtains among other animals, but such is not the case. There are many birds among which, during the nesting season, the male helps the female feed the young, and partially feeds her; and, with certain of the higher carnivora, the male helps the female feed the young, and partially feeds her. In no case does she depend on him absolutely, even during this season, save in that of the hornbill, where the female, sitting on her nest in a hollow tree, is walled in with clay by the male, so that only her beak projects; and then he feeds her while the eggs are developing. But even the female hornbill does not expect to be fed at any other time. The female bee and ant are economically dependent, but not on the male. The workers are females, too, specialized to economic functions solely. And with the carnivora, if the young are to lose one parent, it might far better be the father: the mother is quite competent to take care of them herself. With many species, as in the case of the common cat, she not only feeds herself and her young, but has to defend the young against the male as well. In no case is the female throughout her life supported by the male.

In the human species the condition is permanent and general, though there are exceptions, and though the present century is witnessing the beginnings of a great change in this respect. We have not been accustomed to face this fact beyond our loose generalization that it was "natural," and that other animals did so, too.

To many this view will not seem clear at first; and the case of working peasant women or females of savage tribes, and the general household industry of women, will be instanced against it. Some careful and honest discrimination is needed to make plain to ourselves the essential facts of the relation, even in these cases. The horse, in his free natural condition, is economically independent. He gets his living by his own exertions, irrespective of any other creature. The horse, in his present condition of slavery, is economically dependent. He gets his living at the hands of his master; and his exertions, though strenuous, bear no direct relation to his living. In fact, the horses who are the best fed and cared for and the horses who are the hardest worked are quite different animals. The horse works, it is true; but what he gets to eat depends on the power and will of his master. His living comes through another. He is economically dependent. So with the hard-worked savage or peasant women. Their labor is the property of another: they work under another will; and what they receive depends not on their labor, but on the power and will of another. They are economically dependent. This is true of the human female both individually and collectively.

In studying the economic position of the sexes collectively, the difference is most marked. As a social animal, the economic status of man rests on the combined and exchanged services of vast numbers of progressively specialized individuals. The economic progress of the race, its maintenance at any period, its continued advance, involve the collective activities of all the trades, crafts, arts, manufactures, inventions, discoveries, and all the civil and military institutions that go to maintain them. The economic status of any race at any time, with its involved effect on all the constituent individuals, depends on their world-wide labors and their free exchange. Economic progress, however, is almost exclusively masculine. Such economic processes as women have been allowed to exercise are of the earliest and most primitive kind. Were men to perform no economic services save such as are still performed by women, our racial status in economics would be reduced to most painful limitations.

To take from any community its male workers would paralyze it economically to a far greater degree than to remove its female workers. The labor now performed by the women could be performed by the men, requiring only the setting back of many advanced workers into earlier forms of industry; but the labor now performed by the men could not be performed by the women without generations of effort and adaptation. Men can cook, clean, and sew as well as women; but the making and managing of the great engines of modern industry, the threading of earth and sea in our vast systems of transportation, the handling of our elaborate machinery of trade, commerce, government, —these things could not be done so well by women in their present degree of economic development.

This is not owing to lack of the essential human faculties necessary to such achievements, nor to any inherent disability of sex, but to the present condition of woman, forbidding the development of this degree of economic ability. The male human being is thousands of years in advance of the female in economic status. Speaking collectively, men produce and distribute wealth; and women receive it at their hands. As men hunt, fish, keep cattle, or raise corn, so do women eat game, fish, beef, or corn. As men go down to the sea in ships, and bring coffee and spices and silks and gems from far away, so do women partake of the coffee and spices and silks and gems the men bring.

The economic status of the human race in any nation, at any time, is governed mainly by the activities of the male: the female obtains her share in the racial advance only through him.

Studied individually, the facts are even more plainly visible, more open and familiar. From the day laborer to the millionaire, the wife's worn dress or flashing jewels, her low roof or her lordly one, her weary feet or her rich equipage,—these speak of the economic ability of the husband. The comfort, the luxury, the necessities of life itself, which the woman receives, are obtained by the husband, and given her by him. And, when the woman, left alone with no man to "support" her, tries to meet her own economic necessities, the difficulties which confront her prove conclusively what the general economic status of the woman is. None can deny these patent facts—that the economic status of women generally depends upon that of men generally, and that the economic status of women individually depends upon that of men individually, those men to whom they are related. But we are instantly confronted by the commonly received opinion that, although it must be admitted that men make and distribute the wealth of the world, yet women earn their share of it as wives. This assumes either that the husband is in the position of employer and the wife as employee, or that marriage is a "partnership," and the wife an equal factor with the husband in producing wealth.

Economic independence is a relative condition at best. In the broadest sense, all living things are economically dependent upon others—the animals upon the vegetables, and man upon both. In a narrower sense, all social life is economically interdependent, man producing collectively what he could by no possibility produce separately. But, in the closest interpretation, individual economic independence among human beings means that the individual pays for what he gets, works for what he gets, gives to the other an equivalent for what the other gives him. I depend on the shoemaker for shoes, and the tailor for coats; but, if I give the shoemaker and the tailor enough of my own labor as a house-builder to pay for the shoes and coats they give me, I retain my personal independence. I have not taken of their product, and given nothing of mine. As long as what I get is obtained by what I give, I am economically independent.

Women consume economic goods. What economic product do they give in exchange for what they consume? The claim that marriage is a partnership, in which the two persons married produce wealth which neither of them, separately, could produce, will not bear examination. A man happy and comfortable can produce more than one unhappy and uncomfortable, but this is as true of a father or son as of a husband. To take from a man any of the conditions which make him happy and strong is to cripple his industry, generally speaking. But those relatives who make him happy are not therefore his business partners, and entitled to share his income.

Grateful return for happiness conferred is not the method of exchange in a partnership. The comfort a man takes with his wife is not in the nature of a business partnership, nor are her frugality and industry. A house-keeper, in her place, might be as frugal, as industrious, but would not therefore be a partner. Man and wife are part-ners truly in their mutual obligation to their children—their common love, duty, and service. But a manufacturer who marries, or a doctor, or a lawyer, does not take a partner in his business, when he takes a partner in parenthood, unless his wife is also a manufacturer, a doctor, or a lawyer. In his business, she cannot even advise wisely without training and experience. To love her husband, the composer, does not enable her to compose; and the loss of a man's wife, though it may break his heart, does not cripple his business, unless his mind is affected by grief. She is in no sense a business partner, unless she contrib-utes capital or experience or labor, as a man would in like relation. Most men would hesitate very seriously before entering a business partnership with any woman, wife or not.

If the wife is not, then, truly a business partner, in what way does she earn from her husband the food, cloth-ing, and shelter she receives at his hands? By house ser-vice, it will be instantly replied. This is the general misty idea upon the subject—that women earn all they get, and more, by house service. Here we come to a very practical and definite economic ground. Although not producers of wealth, women serve in the final processes of preparation and distribution. Their labor in the household has a genu-ine economic value.

For a certain percentage of persons to serve other persons, in order that the ones so served may produce more, is a contribution not to be overlooked. The labor of women in the house, certainly, enables men to produce more wealth than they otherwise could; and in this way women are economic factors in society. But so are horses. The labor of horses enables men to produce more wealth than they otherwise could. The horse is an economic factor in society. But the horse is not economically independent, nor is the woman. If a man plus a valet can perform more useful service than he could minus a valet, then the valet is performing useful service. But, if the valet is the property of the man, is obliged to perform this service, and is not paid for it, he is not economically independent.

The labor which the wife performs in the household is given as part of her functional duty, not as employment. The wife of the poor man, who works hard in a small house, doing all the work for the family, or the wife of the rich man, who wisely and gracefully manages a large house and administers its functions, each is entitled to fair pay for services rendered.

To take this ground and hold it honestly, wives, as earners through domestic service, are entitled to the wages of cooks, housemaids, nursemaids, seamstresses, or housekeepers, and to no more. This would of course reduce the spending money of the wives of the rich, and put it out of the power of the poor man to "support" a wife at all, unless, indeed, the poor man faced the situation fully, paid his wife her wages as house servant, and then she and he combined their funds in the support of their children. He would be keeping a servant: she would be helping keep the family. But nowhere on earth would there be "a rich iwoman" by these means. Even the highest class of private housekeeper, useful as her services are, does not accumulate a fortune. She does not buy diamonds and sables and keep a carriage. Things like these are not earned by house service.

But the salient fact in this discussion is that, whatever the economic value of the domestic industry of women is, they do not get it. The women who do the most work get the least money, and the women who have the most money do the least work. Their labor is neither given nor taken as a factor in economic exchange. It is held to be their duty as women to do this work; and their economic status bears no relation to their domestic labors, unless an inverse one. Moreover, if they were thus fairly paid—given what they earned, and no more—all women working in this way would be reduced to the economic status of the house servant. Few women—or men either—care to face this condition. The ground that women earn their living by domestic labor is instantly forsaken, and we are told that they obtain their livelihood as mothers. This is a peculiar position. We speak of it commonly enough, and often with deep feeling, but without due analysis.

In treating of an economic exchange, asking what return in goods or labor women make for the goods and labor given them—either to the race collectively or to their husbands individually—what payment women make for their clothes and shoes and furniture and food and shelter, we are told that the duties and services of the mother entitle her to support.

If this is so, if motherhood is an exchangeable commodity given by women in payment for clothes and food, then we must of course find some relation between the quantity or quality of the motherhood and the quantity and quality of the pay. This being true, then the women who are not mothers have no economic status at all; and the economic status of those who are must be shown to be relative to their motherhood. This is obviously absurd. The childless wife has as much money as the mother of many—more, for the children of the latter consume what would otherwise be hers, and the inefficient mother is no less provided for than the efficient one. Visibly, and upon the face of it, women are not maintained in economic prosperity proportioned to their motherhood. Motherhood bears no relation to their economic status. Among primitive races, it is true—in the patriarchal period, for instance—there was some truth in this position. Women being of no value whatever save as bearers of children, their favor and indulgence did bear direct relation to maternity; and they had reason to exult on more grounds than one when they could boast a son. Today, however, the maintenance of the woman is not conditioned upon this. A man is not allowed to discard his wife because she is barren. The claim of motherhood as a factor in economic exchange is false today. But suppose it were true. Are we willing to hold this ground, even in theory? Are we willing to consider motherhood as a business, a form of commercial exchange? Are the cares and duties of the mother, her travail and her love, commodities to be exchanged for bread?

It is revolting so to consider them; and, if we dare face our own thoughts, and force them to their logical conclusion, we shall see that nothing could be more repugnant to human feeling, or more socially and individually injurious, than to make motherhood a trade. Driven off these alleged grounds of women's economic independence; shown that women, as a class, neither produce nor distribute wealth; that women, as individuals, labor mainly as house servants, are not paid as such, and would not be satisfied with such an economic status if they were so paid; that wives are not business partners or co-producers of wealth with their husbands, unless they actually practice the same profession; that they are not salaried as mothers, and that it would be unspeakably degrading if they were. What remains to those who deny that women are supported by men? This (and a most amusing position it is)—that the function of maternity unfits a woman for economic production, and, therefore, it is right that she should be supported by her husband.

The ground is taken that the human female is not economically independent, that she is fed by the male of her species. In denial of this, it is first alleged that she is economically independent—that she does support herself by her own industry in the house. It being shown that there is no relation between the economic status of woman and the labor she performs in the home, it is then alleged that not as house servant, but as mother, does woman earn her living. It being shown that the economic status of woman bears no relation to her motherhood, either in quantity or quality, it is then alleged that motherhood renders a woman unfit for economic production, and that, therefore, it is right that she be supported by her husband. Before going farther, let us seize upon this admission—that she *is* supported by her husband.

Without going into either the ethics or the necessities of the case, we have reached so much common ground: the female of genus homo is supported by the male. Whereas, in other species of animals, male and female alike graze and browse, hunt and kill, climb, swim, dig, run, and fly for their livings, in our species the female does not seek her own living in the specific activities of our race, but is fed by the male.

Now as to the alleged necessity. Because of her maternal duties, the human female is said to be unable to get her own living. As the maternal duties of other females do not unfit them for getting their own living and also the livings of their young, it would seem that the human maternal duties require the segregation of the entire energies of the mother to the service of the child during her entire adult life, or so large a proportion of them that not enough remains to devote to the individual interests of the mother.

Such a condition, did it exist, would of course excuse and justify the pitiful dependence of the human female, and her support by the male. As the queen bee, modified entirely to maternity, is supported, not by the male, to be sure, but by her co-workers, the "old maids," the barren working bees, who labor so patiently and lovingly in their branch of the maternal duties of the hive, so would the human female, modified entirely to maternity, become unfit for any other exertion, and a helpless dependent.

Is this the condition of human motherhood? Does the human mother, by her motherhood, thereby lose control of brain and body, lose power and skill and desire for any other work? Do we see before us the human race, with all its females segregated entirely to the uses of motherhood, consecrated, set apart, specially developed, spending every power of their nature on the service of their children?

We do not. We see the human mother worked far harder than a mare, laboring her life long in the service, not of her children only, but of men; husbands, brothers, fathers, whatever male relatives she has; for mother and sister also; for the church a little, if she is allowed; for society, if she is able; for charity and education and reform—working in many ways that are not the ways of motherhood.

It is not motherhood that keeps the housewife on her feet from dawn till dark; it is house service, not child service. Women work longer and harder than most men, and not solely in maternal duties. The savage mother carries the burdens, and does all menial service for the tribe. The peasant mother toils in the fields, and the workingman's wife in the home. Many mothers, even now, are wage-earners for the family, as well as bearers and rearers of it. And the women who are not so occupied, the women who belong to rich men—here perhaps is the exhaustive devotion to maternity which is supposed to justify an admitted economic dependence. But we do not find it even among these. Women of ease and wealth provide for their children better care than the poor woman can; but they do not spend more time upon it themselves, nor more care and effort. They have other occupation.

In spite of her supposed segregation to maternal duties, the human female, the world over, works at extra-maternal duties for hours enough to provide her with an independent living, and then is denied independence on the ground that motherhood prevents her working!

If this ground were tenable, we should find a world full of women who never lifted a finger save in the service of their children, and of men who did *all* the work besides, and waited on the women whom motherhood prevented from waiting on themselves. The ground is not tenable. A human female, healthy, sound, has twenty-five years of life before she is a mother, and should have twenty-five years more after the period of such maternal service as is expected of her has been given. The duties of grandmotherhood are surely not alleged as preventing economic independence.

The working power of the mother has always been a prominent factor in human life. She is the worker *par excellence,* but her work is not such as to affect her economic status. Her living, all that she gets—food, clothing, ornaments, amusements, luxuries—these bear no relation to her power to produce wealth, to her services in the house, or to her motherhood. These things bear relation only to the man she marries, the man she depends on—to how much he has and how much he is willing to give her. The women whose splendid extravagance dazzles the world, whose economic goods are the greatest, are often neither houseworkers nor mothers, but simply the women who hold most power over the men who have the most money. The female of genus homo is economically dependent on the male. He is her food supply.

# Sex Distinctions

In its psychic manifestation this intense sex-distinction is equally apparent. The primal instinct of sex-attraction has developed under social forces into a conscious passion of enormous power, a deep and lifelong devotion, overwhelming in its force. This is excessive in both sexes, but more so in women than in men—not so commonly in its simple physical form, but in the unreasoning intensity of emotion that refuses all guidance, and drives those possessed by it to risk every other good for this one end. It is not at first sight easy, and it may seem an irreverent and thankless task, to discriminate here between what is good in the "master passion" and what is evil, and especially to claim for one sex more of this feeling than for the other; but such discrimination can be made.

It is good for the individual and for the race to have developed such a degree of passionate and permanent love as shall best promote the happiness of individuals and the reproduction of species. It is not good for the race or for the individual that this feeling should have become so intense as to override all other human faculties, to make a mock of the accumulated wisdom of the ages, the stored power of the will; to drive the individual—against his own plain conviction—into a union sure to result in evil, or to hold the individual helpless in such an evil union, when made.

Such is the condition of humanity, involving most evil results to its offspring and to its own happiness. And, while in men the immediate dominating force of the passion may be more conspicuous, it is in women that it holds more universal sway. For the man has other powers and faculties in full use, whereby to break loose from the force of this; and the woman, specially modified to sex and denied racial activity, pours her whole life into her love, and, if injured here, she is injured irretrievably. With him it is frequently light and transient, and, when most intense, often most transient. With her it is a deep, all-absorbing force, under the action of which she will renounce all that life offers, take any risk, face any hardships, bear any pain. It is maintained in her in the face of a lifetime of neglect and abuse. The common instance of the police court trials—the woman cruelly abused who will not testify against her husband—shows this. This devotion, carried to such a degree as to lead to the mismating of individuals with its personal and social injury, is an excessive sex-distinction.

But it is in our common social relations that the predominance of sex-distinction in women is made most manifest. The fact that, speaking broadly, women have, from the very beginning, been spoken of expressively enough as "the sex," demonstrates clearly that this is the main impression which they have made upon observers and recorders. Here one need attempt no farther proof than to turn the mind of the reader to an unbroken record of facts and feelings perfectly patent to every one, but not hitherto looked at as other than perfectly natural and right. So utterly has the status of woman been accepted as a sexual one that it has remained for the woman's movement of the nineteenth century to devote much contention to the claim that women are persons! That women are persons as well as females—an unheard of proposition!

In a "Handbook of Proverbs of All Nations," a collection comprising many thousands, these facts are to be observed: first, that the proverbs concerning women are an insignificant minority compared to those concerning men; second, that the proverbs concerning women almost invariably apply to them in general—to the sex. Those concerning men qualify, limit, describe, specialize. It is "a lazy man," "a violent man," "a man in his cups." Qualities and actions are predicated of man individually, and not as a sex, unless he is flatly contrasted with woman, as in "A man of straw is worth a woman of gold," "Men are deeds, women are words," or "Man, woman, and the devil are the three degrees of comparison." But of woman it is always and only "a woman," meaning simply a female, and recognizing no personal distinction: "As much pity to see a woman weep as to see a goose go barefoot." "He that hath an eel by the tail and a woman by her word hath a slippery handle." "A woman, a span-iel, and a walnut-tree—the more you beat 'em, the better

147

they be.'' Occasionally a distinction is made between "a fair woman" and "a black woman"; and Solomon's "virtuous woman," who commanded such a high price, is familiar to us all. But in common thought it is simply "a woman" always. The boast of the profligate that he knows "the sex," so recently expressed by a new poet—"The things you will learn from the Yellow and Brown, they'll 'elp you an' 'eap with the White''; the complaint of the angry rejected that "all women are just alike!''—the consensus of public opinion of all time goes to show that the characteristics common to the sex have predominated over the characteristics distinctive of the individual, a marked excess in sex-distinction.

From the time our children are born, we use every means known to accentuate sex-distinction in both boy and girl; and the reason that the boy is not so hopelessly marked by it as the girl is that he has the whole field of human expression open to him besides. In our steady insistence on proclaiming sex-distinction we have grown to consider most human attributes as masculine attributes, for the simple reason that they were allowed to men and forbidden to women.

A clear and definite understanding of the difference between race-attributes and sex-attributes should be established. Life consists of action. The action of a living thing is along two main lines—self-preservation and race-preservation. The processes that keep the individual alive, from the involuntary action of his internal organs to the voluntary action of his external organs—every act, from breathing to hunting his food, which contributes to the maintenance of the individual life—these are the processes of self-preservation. Whatever activities tend to keep the race alive, to reproduce the individual, from the involuntary action of the internal organs to the voluntary action of the external organs; every act from the development of germ-cells to the taking care of children, which contributes to the maintenance of the racial life—these are the processes of race-preservation. In race-preservation, male and female have distinctive organs, distinctive functions, distinctive lines of action. In self-preservation, male and female have the same organs, the same functions, the same lines of action. In the human species our processes of race-preservation have reached a certain degree of elaboration; but our processes of self-preservation have gone farther, much farther.

All the varied activities of economic production and distribution, all our arts and industries, crafts and trades, all our growth in science, discovery, government, religion—these are along the line of self-preservation. These are, or should be, common to both sexes. To teach, to rule, to make, to decorate, to distribute—these are not sex-functions: they are race-functions. Yet so inordinate is the sex-distinction of the human race that the whole field of human progress has been considered a masculine prerogative. What could more absolutely prove the excessive sex-distinction of the human race? That this difference should surge over all its natural boundaries and blazon itself across every act of life, so that every step of the human creature is marked "male" or "female"—surely, this is enough to show our over-sexed condition.

Little by little, very slowly, and with most unjust and cruel opposition, at cost of all life holds most dear, it is being gradually established by many martyrdoms that human work is woman's as well as man's. Harriet Martineau must conceal her writing under her sewing when callers came, because "to sew" was a feminine verb, and "to write" a masculine one. Mary Somerville must struggle to hide her work from even relatives, because mathematics was a "masculine" pursuit. Sex has been made to dominate the whole human world—all the main avenues of life marked "male," and the female left to be a female, and nothing else.

But while with the male the things he fondly imagined to be "masculine" were merely human, and very good for him, with the female the few things marked "feminine" were feminine, indeed; and her ceaseless reiterance of one short song, however sweet, has given it a conspicuous monotony. In garments whose main purpose is unmistakably to announce her sex; with a tendency to ornament which marks exuberance of sex-energy, with a body so modified to sex as to be grievously deprived of its natural activities; with a manner and behavior wholly attuned to sex-advantage, and frequently most disadvantageous to any human gain; with a field of action most rigidly confined to sex-relations; with her overcharged sensibility, her prominent modesty, her "eternal femininity"— the female of genus homo is undeniably over-sexed.

This excessive distinction shows itself again in a marked precocity of development. Our little children, our very babies, show signs of it when the young of other creatures are serenely asexual in general appearance and habit. We eagerly note this precocity. We are proud of it. We carefully encourage it by precept and example, taking pains to develop the sex-instinct in little children, and think no harm. One of the first things we force upon the child's dawning consciousness is the fact that he is a boy or that she is a girl, and that, therefore, each must regard everything from a different point of view. They must be dressed differently, not on account of their personal needs, which are exactly similar at this period, but so that neither they, nor any one beholding them, may for a moment forget the distinction of sex.

Our peculiar inversion of the usual habit of species, in which the male carries ornament and the female is dark and plain, is not so much a proof of excess indeed, as a proof of the peculiar reversal of our position in the matter of sex-selection. With the other species the males compete in ornament, and the females select. With us the females compete in ornament, and the males select. If this theory of sex-ornament is disregarded, and we prefer rather to see in masculine decoration merely a form of exuberant sex-energy, expending itself in non-productive excess, then, indeed, the fact that with us the females manifest such a display of gorgeous adornment is another sign of excessive sex-distinction. In either case the forcing upon girl-children of an elaborate ornamentation which interferes with their physical activity and unconscious freedom, and fosters a premature sex-consciousness, is as clear and menacing a proof of our condition as could be mentioned. That the girl-child should be so dressed as to require a difference in care and behavior, resting wholly on the fact that she is a girl—a fact not otherwise present to her thought at that age—is a precocious insistence upon sex-distinction, most unwholesome in its results. Boys and girls are expected, also, to behave differently to each other, and to people in general—a behavior to be briefly described in two words. To the boy we say, "Do"; to the girl, "Don't." The little boy must "take care" of the little girl, even if she is larger than he is. "Why?" he asks. Because he is a boy. Because of sex. Surely, if she is the stronger, she ought to take care of him, especially as the protective instinct is purely feminine in a normal race. It is not long before the boy learns his lesson. He is a boy, going to be a man; and that means all. "I thank the Lord that I was not born a woman," runs the Hebrew prayer. She is a girl, "only a girl," "nothing but a girl," and going to be a woman—only a woman. Boys are encouraged from the beginning to show the feelings supposed to be proper to their sex. When our infant son bangs about, roars, and smashes things, we say proudly that he is "a regular boy!" When our infant daughter coquettes with visitors, or wails in maternal agony because her brother has broken her doll, whose sawdust remains she nurses with piteous care, we say proudly that "she is a perfect little mother already!" What business has a little girl with the instincts of maternity? No more than the little boy should have with the instincts of paternity. They are sex-instincts, and should not appear till the period of adolescence. The most normal girl is the "tom-boy"—whose numbers increase among us in these wiser days—a healthy young creature, who is human through and through, not feminine till it is time to be. The most normal boy has calmness and gentleness as well as vigor and courage. He is a human creature as well as a male creature, and not aggressively masculine till it is time to be. Childhood is not the period for these marked manifestations of sex. That we exhibit them, that we admire and encourage them, shows our over-sexed condition.

# The Evolution of the Women's Sphere

Primitive man and his female were animals, like other animals. They were strong, fierce, lively beasts; and she was as nimble and ferocious as he, save for the added belligerence of the males in their sex-competition. In this competition, he, like the other male creatures, fought savagely with his hairy rivals; and she, like the other female creatures, complacently viewed their struggles and mated with the victor. At other times she ran about in the forest, and helped herself to what there was to eat as freely as he did.

There seems to have come a time when it occurred to the dawning intelligence of this amiable savage that it was cheaper and easier to fight a little female, and have it done with, than to fight a big male every time. So he instituted the custom of enslaving the female; and she, losing freedom, could no longer get her own food nor that of her young. The mother ape, with her maternal function well fulfilled, flees leaping through the forest—plucks her fruit and nuts, keeps up with the movement of the tribe, her young one on her back or held in one strong arm. But the mother woman, enslaved, could not do this. Then man, the father, found that slavery had its obligations: he must care for what he forbade to care for itself, else it died on his hands. So he slowly and reluctantly shouldered the duties of his new position. He began to feed her, and not only that, but to express in his own person the thwarted uses of maternity: he had to feed the children, too. It seems a simple arrangement. When we have thought of it at all, we have thought of it with admiration. The naturalist defends it on the ground of advantage to the species through the freeing of the mother from all other cares and confining her unreservedly to the duties of maternity. The poet and novelist, the painter and sculptor, the priest and teacher, have all extolled this lovely relation. It remains for the sociologist, from a biological point of view, to note its effects on the constitution of the human race, both in the individual and in society.

When man began to feed and defend woman, she ceased proportionately to feed and defend herself. When he stood between her and her physical environment, she ceased proportionately to feel the influence of that environment and respond to it. When he became her immediate and all-important environment, she began proportionately to respond to this new influence, and to be modified accordingly. In a free state, speed was of as great advantage to the female as to the male, both in enabling her to catch prey and in preventing her from being caught by enemies; but, in her new condition, speed was a disadvantage. She was not allowed to do the catching, and it profited her to be caught by her new master. Free creatures, getting their own food and maintaining their own lives, develop an active capacity for attaining their ends. Parasitic creatures, whose living is obtained by the exertions of others, develop powers of absorption and of tenacity—the powers by which they profit most. The human female was cut off from the direct action of natural selection, that mighty force which heretofore had acted on male and female alike with inexorable and beneficial effect, developing strength, developing skill, developing endurance, developing courage—developing species. She now met the influence of natural selection acting indirectly through the male, and developing, of course, the faculties required to secure and obtain a hold on him. Needless to state that these faculties were those of sex-attraction, the one power that has made him cheerfully maintain, in what luxury he could, the being in whom he delighted. For many, many centuries she had no other hold, no other assurance of being fed. The young girl had a prospective value, and was maintained for what should follow; but the old woman, in more primitive times, had but a poor hold on life. She who could best please her lord was the favorite slave or favorite wife, and she obtained the best economic conditions.

With the growth of civilization, we have gradually crystallized into law the visible necessity for feeding the helpless female; and even old women are maintained by their male relatives with a comfortable assurance. But to this day—save, indeed, for the increasing army of women wage-earners, who are changing the face of the world by their steady advance toward economic independence—the personal profit of women bears but too close a relation to their power to win and hold the other sex. From the odalisque with the most bracelets to the débutante with the most bouquets, the relation still holds good—woman's economic profit comes through the power of sex-attraction.

When we confront this fact boldly and plainly in the open market of vice, we are sick with horror. When we see the same economic relation made permanent, established by law, sanctioned and sanctified by religion, covered with flowers and incense and all accumulated sentiment, we think it innocent, lovely, and right. The transient trade we think evil. The bargain for life we think good. But the biological effect remains the same. In both cases the female gets her food from the male by virtue of her sex-relationship to him. In both cases, perhaps even more in marriage because of its perfect acceptance of the situation, the female of genus homo, still living under natural law, is inexorably modified to sex in an increasing degree.

Followed in specific detail, the action of the changed environment upon women has been in given instances as follows: In the matter of mere passive surroundings she has been immediately restricted in her range. This one factor has an immense effect on man and animal alike. An absolutely uniform environment, one shape, one size, one color, one sound, would render life, if any life could be, one helpless, changeless thing. As the environment increases and varies, the development of the creature must increase and vary with it; for he acquires knowledge and power, as the material for knowledge and the need for power appear. In migratory species the female is free to acquire the same knowledge as the male by the same means, the same development by the same experiences. The human female has been restricted in range from the earliest beginning. Even among savages, she has a much more restricted knowledge of the land she lives in. She moves with the camp, of course, and follows her primitive industries in its vicinity; but the war-path and the hunt are the man's. He has a far larger habitat. The life of the female savage is freedom itself, however, compared with the increasing constriction of custom closing in upon the woman, as civilization advanced, like the iron torture chamber of romance. Its culmination is expressed in the proverb: "A woman should leave her home but three times —when she is christened, when she is married, and when she is buried." Or this: "The woman, the cat, and the chimney should never leave the house." The absolutely stationary female and the wide-ranging male are distinctly human institutions, after we leave behind such low forms of life as the gypsy moth, whose female seldom moves more than a few feet from the pupa moth. She has aborted wings, and cannot fly. She waits humbly for the winged male, lays her myriad eggs, and dies—a fine instance of modification to sex.

To reduce so largely the mere area of environment is a great check to race-development; but it is not to be compared in its effects with the reduction in voluntary activity to which the human female has been subjected. Her restricted impression, her confinement to the four walls of the home, have done great execution, of course, in limiting her ideas, her information, her thought-processes, and power of judgment; and in giving a disproportionate prominence and intensity to the few things she knows about; but this is innocent in action compared with her restricted expression, the denial of freedom to act. A living organism is modified far less through the action of external circumstances upon it and its reaction thereto, than through the effect of its own exertions. Skin may be thickened gradually by exposure to the weather; but it is thickened far more quickly by being rubbed against something, as the handle of an oar or of a broom. To be surrounded by beautiful things has much influence upon the human creature: to make beautiful things has more. To live among beautiful surroundings and make ugly things is more directly lowering than to live among ugly surroundings and make beautiful things. What we do modifies us more than what is done to us. The freedom of expression has been more restricted in women than the freedom of impression, if that be possible. Something of the world she lived in she has seen from her barred windows. Some air has come through the purdah's folds, some knowledge has filtered to her eager ears from the talk of men. Desdemona learned somewhat of Othello. Had she known more, she might have lived longer. But in the ever-growing human impulse to create, the power and will to make, to do, to express one's new spirit in new forms—here she has been utterly debarred. She might work as she had worked from the beginning—at the primitive labors of the household; but in the inevitable expansion of even those industries to professional levels we have striven to hold her back. To work with her own hands, for nothing, in direct body-service to her own family—this has been permitted—yes, compelled. But to be and do anything further from this she has been forbidden. Her labor has not only been limited in kind, but in degree. Whatever she has been allowed to do must be done in private and alone, the first-hand industries of savage times.

Our growth in industry has been not only in kind, but in class. The baker is not in the same industrial grade with the house-cook, though both make bread. To specialize any form of labor is a step up: to organize it is another step. Specialization and organization are the basis of human progress, the organic methods of social life. They have been forbidden to women almost absolutely. The greatest and most beneficent change of this century is the progress of women in these two lines of advance. The effect of this check in industrial development, accompanied as it was by the constant inheritance of increased racial power, has been to intensify the sensations and emotions of women, and to develop great activity in the lines allowed. The nervous energy that up to present memory has impelled women to labor incessantly at something, be it the veriest folly of fancy work, is one mark of the effect.

In religious development the same dead-line has held back the growth of women through all the races and ages. In dim early times she was sharer in the mysteries and rites; but, as religion developed, her place receded, until Paul commanded her to be silent in the churches. And she has been silent until to-day. Even now, with all the ground gained, we have but the beginnings—the slowly forced and disapproved beginnings—of religious equality for the sexes. In some nations, religion is held to be a masculine attribute exclusively, it being even questioned whether women have souls. An early Christian council settled that important question by vote, fortunately deciding that they had. In a church whose main strength has always been derived from the adherence of women, it would have been an uncomfortable reflection not to have allowed them souls. Ancient family worship ran in the male line. It was the son who kept the sacred grandfathers in due respect, and poured libations to their shades. When the woman married, she changed her ancestors, and had to worship her husband's progenitors instead of her own. This is why the Hindu and the Chinaman and many others of like stamp must have a son to keep them in countenance—a deep-seated sex-prejudice, coming to slow extinction as women rise in economic importance.

It is painfully interesting to trace the gradual cumulative effect of these conditions upon women: first, the action of large natural laws, acting on her as they would act on any other animal; then the evolution of social customs and laws (with her position as the active cause), following the direction of mere physical forces, and adding heavily to them; then, with increasing civilization, the unbroken accumulation of precedent, burnt into each generation by the growing force of education, made lovely by art, holy by religion, desirable by habit; and, steadily acting from beneath, the unswerving pressure of economic necessity upon which the whole structure rested. These are strong modifying conditions, indeed.

To the young man confronting life the world lies wide. Such powers as he has he may use, must use. If he chooses wrong at first, he may choose again, and yet again. Not effective or successful in one channel, he may do better in another. The growing, varied needs of all mankind call on him for the varied service in which he finds his growth. What he wants to be, he may strive to be. What he wants to get, he may strive to get. Wealth, power, social distinction, fame—what he wants he can try for.

To the young woman confronting life there is the same world beyond, there are the same human energies and human desires and ambition within. But all that she may wish to have, all that she may wish to do, must come through a single channel and a single choice. Wealth, power, social distinction, fame—not only these, but home and happiness, reputation, ease and pleasure, her bread and butter—all, must come to her through a small gold ring.

## The Institution of Marriage

The girl must marry: else how live? The prospective husband prefers the girl to know nothing. He is the market, the demand. She is the supply. And with the best intentions the mother serves her child's economic advantage by preparing her for the market. This is an excellent instance. It is common. It is most evil. It is plainly traceable to our sexuo-economic relation.

Another instance of so grossly unjust, so palpable, so general an evil that it has occasionally aroused some protest even from our dull consciousness is this: the enforced attitude of the woman toward marriage. To the young girl, as has been previously stated, marriage is the one road to fortune, to life. She is born highly specialized as a female: she is carefully educated and trained to realize in all ways her sex-limitations and her sex-advantages. What she has to gain even as a child is largely gained by feminine tricks and charms. Her reading, both in history and fiction, treats of the same position for women; and romance and poetry give it absolute predominance. Pictorial art, music, the drama, society, everything, tells her that she is *she,* and that all depends on whom she marries. Where young boys plan for what they will achieve and attain, young girls plan for whom they will achieve and attain. Little Ellie and her swan's nest among the reeds is a familiar illustration. It is the lover on the red roan steed she planned for. It is Lancelot riding through the sheaves that called the Lady from her loom at Shalott: "he" is the coming world.

With such a prospect as this before her; with an organization specially developed to this end; with an education adding every weight of precept and example, of wisdom and virtue, to the natural instincts; with a social environment the whole machinery of which is planned to give the girl a chance to see and to be seen, to provide her with "opportunities"; and with all the pressure of personal advantage and self-interest added to the sex-instinct—what one would logically expect is a society full of desperate and eager husband-hunters, regarded with popular approval.

Not at all! Marriage is the woman's proper sphere, her divinely ordered place, her natural end. It is what she is born for, what she is trained for, what she is exhibited for. It is, moreover, her means of honorable livelihood and advancement. *But*—she must not even look as if she wanted it! She must not turn her hand over to get it. She must sit passive as the seasons go by, and her "chances" lessen with each year. Think of the strain on a highly sensitive nervous organism to have so much hang on one thing, to see the possibility of attaining it grow less and less yearly, and to be forbidden to take any step toward securing it! This she must bear with dignity and grace to the end.

To what end? To the end that, if she does not succeed in being chosen, she becomes a thing of mild popular contempt, a human being with no further place in life save as an attachée, a dependent upon more fortunate relatives, an old maid. The open derision and scorn with which unmarried women used to be treated is lessening each year in proportion to their advance in economic independence. But it is not very long since the popular proverb, "Old maids lead apes in hell," was in common use; since unwelcome lovers urged their suit with the awful argument that they might be the last askers; since the hapless lady in the wood prayed for a husband, and, when the owl an-

swered, "Who? who?" cried, "Anybody, good Lord!"
There is still a pleasant ditty afloat as to the "Three Old
Maids of Lynn," who did not marry when they could, and
could not when they would.

The cruel and absurd injustice of blaming the girl for
not getting what she is allowed no effort to obtain seems
unaccountable; but it becomes clear when viewed in connection with the sexuo-economic relation. Although marriage is a means of livelihood, it is not honest employment
where one can offer one's labor without shame, but a
relation where the support is given outright, and enforced
by law in return for the functional service of the woman,
the "duties of wife and mother." Therefore no honorable
woman can ask for it. It is not only that the natural
feminine instinct is to retire, as that of the male is to
advance, but that, because marriage means support, a woman
must not ask a man to support her. It is economic beggary
as well as a false attitude from a sex point of view.

Observe the ingenious cruelty of the arrangement. It
is just as humanly natural for a woman as for a man to
want wealth. But, when her wealth is made to come
through the same channels as her love, she is forbidden to
ask for it by her own sex-nature and by business honor.
Hence the millions of mismade marriages with "anybody,
good Lord!" Hence the million broken hearts which must
let all life pass, unable to make any attempt to stop it.
Hence the many "maiden aunts," elderly sisters and daughters, unattached women everywhere, who are a burden on
their male relatives and society at large. This is changing
for the better, to be sure, but changing only through the
advance of economic independence for women. A "bachelor maid" is a very different thing from "an old maid."

This, then, is the reason for the Andromeda position
of the possibly-to-be-married young woman, and for the
ridicule and reproach meted out to her. Since women are
viewed wholly as creatures of sex even by one another,
and since everything is done to add to their young powers

of sex-attraction; since they are marriageable solely on this ground, unless, indeed, "a fortune" has been added to their charms—failure to marry is held a clear proof of failure to attract, a lack of sex-value. And, since they have no other value, save in a low order of domestic service, they are quite naturally despised. What else is the creature good for, failing in the functions for which it was created? The scorn of male and female alike falls on this sexless thing: she is a human failure.

It is not strange, therefore, though just as pitiful—this long chapter of patient, voiceless, dreary misery in the lives of women; and it is not strange, either, to see the marked and steady change in opinion that follows the development of other faculties in woman besides those of sex. Now that she is a person as well as a female, filling economic relation to society, she is welcomed and accepted as a human creature, and need not marry the wrong man for her bread and butter. So sharp is the reaction from this unlovely yoke that there is a limited field of life today wherein women choose not to marry, preferring what they call "their independence"—a new-born, hard-won, dear-bought independence. That any living woman should prefer it to home and husband, to love and motherhood, throws a fierce light on what women must have suffered for lack of freedom before.

# Production, Consumption, and Sex Roles

In the industrial evolution of the human race, that marvellous and subtle drawing out and interlocking of special functions which constitute the organic life of society, we find that production and consumption go hand in hand; and production comes first. One cannot consume what has not been produced. Economic production is the natural expression of human energy—not sex-energy at all, but race-energy—the unconscious functioning of the social organism. Socially organized human beings tend to produce, as a gland to secrete: it is the essential nature of the relation. The creative impulse, the desire to make, to express the inner thought in outer form, "just for the work's sake, no use at all i' the work!" this is the distinguishing character of humanity. "I want to mark!" cries the child, demanding the pencil. He does not want to eat. He wants to mark. He is not seeking to get something into himself, but to put something out of himself. He generally wants to do whatever he sees done—to make pie-crust or to make shavings, as it happens. The pie he may eat, the shavings not; but he likes to make both. This is the natural process of production, and is followed by the natural process of consumption, where practicable. But consumption is not the main end, the governing force. Under this organic social law, working naturally, we have the evolution of those arts and crafts in the exercise of which consists our human living, and on the product of which we live. So does society evolve within itself—secrete as it were—the social structure with all its complex machinery; and we function therein as naturally as so many glands, other things being equal.

But other things are not equal. Half the human race is denied free productive expression, is forced to confine its productive human energies to the same channels as its reproductive sex-energies. Its creative skill is confined to the level of immediate personal bodily service, to the making of clothes and preparing of food for individuals. No social service is possible. While its power of production is checked, its power of consumption is inordinately increased by the showering upon it of the "unearned increment" of masculine gifts. For the woman there is, first, no free production allowed; and, second, no relation maintained between what she does produce and what she consumes. She is forbidden to make, but encouraged to take. Her industry is not the natural output of creative energy, not the work she does because she has the inner power and strength to do it; nor is her industry even the measure of her gain. She has, of course, the natural desire to consume; and to that is set no bar save the capacity or the will of her husband.

Thus we have painfully and laboriously evolved and carefully maintain among us an enormous class of non-productive consumers—a class which is half the world, and mother of the other half. We have built into the constitution of the human race the habit and desire of taking, as divorced from its natural precursor and concomitant of making. We have made for ourselves this endless array of horse-leech's daughters, crying, "Give! give!" To consume food, to consume clothes, to consume houses and furniture and decorations and ornaments and amusements, to take and take and take forever—from one man if they are virtuous, from many if they are vicious, but always to take and never to think of giving anything in return except their womanhood—this is the enforced condition of the mothers of the race. What wonder that their sons go into business "for what there is in it"! What wonder that the world is full of the desire to get as much as possible and to give as little as possible! What wonder, either, that the glory and sweetness of love are but a name among us, with here and there a strange and beautiful exception, of which our admiration proves the rarity!

Between the brutal ferocity of excessive male energy struggling in the market-place as in a battlefield and the unnatural greed generated by the perverted condition of female energy, it is not remarkable that the industrial evolution of humanity has shown peculiar symptoms. One of the minor effects of this last condition—this limiting of female industry to close personal necessities, and this tendency of her over-developed sex-nature to overestimate the so-called "duties of her position"—has been to produce an elaborate devotion to individuals and their personal needs—not to the understanding and developing of their higher natures, but to the intensification of their bodily tastes and pleasure. The wife and mother, pouring the rising tide of racial power into the same old channels that were allowed her primitive ancestors, constantly ministers to the physical needs of her family with a ceaseless and concentrated intensity. They like it, of course. But it maintains in the individuals of the race an exaggerated sense of the importance of food and clothes and ornaments to themselves, without at all including a knowledge of their right use and value to us all. It develops personal selfishness.

Again, the consuming female, debarred from any free production, unable to estimate the labor involved in the making of what she so lightly destroys, and her consumption limited mainly to those things which minister to physical pleasure, creates a market for sensuous decoration and personal ornament, for all that is luxurious and enervating, and for a false and capricious variety in such supplies, which operates as a most deadly check to true industry and true art. As the priestess of the temple of consumption, as the limitless demander of things to use up, her economic influence is reactionary and injurious. Much, very much, of the current of useless production in which our economic energies run waste—man's strength poured out like water on the sand—depends on the creation and careful maintenance of this false market, this sink into which human labor vanishes with no return. Woman, in her false economic position, reacts injuriously upon industry, upon art, upon science, discovery, and progress. The sexuo-economic relation in its effect on the constitution of the individual keeps alive in us the instincts of savage individualism which we should otherwise have well outgrown. It sexualizes our industrial relation and commercializes our sex-relation. And, in the external effect upon the market, the over-sexed woman, in her unintelligent and ceaseless demands, hinders and perverts the economic development of the world.

## Motherhood

The more absolutely woman is segregated to sex-functions only, cut off from all economic use and made wholly dependent on the sex-relation as means of livelihood, the more pathological does her motherhood become. The over-development of sex caused by her economic dependence on the male reacts unfavorably upon her essential duties. She is too female for perfect motherhood! Her excessive specialization in the secondary sexual characteristics is a detrimental element in heredity. Small, weak, soft, ill-proportioned women do not tend to produce large, strong, sturdy, well-made men or women. When Frederic the Great wanted grenadiers of great size, he married big men to big women—not to little ones. The female segregated to the uses of sex alone naturally deteriorates in racial development, and naturally transmits that deterioration to her offspring. The human mother, in the processes of reproduction, shows no gain in efficiency over the lower animals, but rather a loss, and so far presents no evidence to prove that her specialization to sex is of any advantage to her young. The mother of a dead baby or the baby of a dead mother; the sick baby, the crooked baby, the idiot baby; the exhausted, nervous, prematurely aged mother— these are not uncommon among us; and they do not show much progress in our motherhood.

Since we cannot justify the human method of maternity in the physical processes of reproduction, can we prove its advantages in the other branch, education? Though the mother be sickly and the child the same, will not her loving care more than make up for it? Will not the tender devotion of the mother, and her unflagging attendance upon the child, render human motherhood sufficiently successful in comparison with that of other species to justify our peculiar method? We must now show that our motherhood, in its usually accepted sense, the "care" of the child (more accurately described as education), is of a superior nature.

Here, again, we lack the benefit of comparison. No other animal species is required to care for its young so long, to teach it so much. So far as they have it to do, they do it well. The hen with her brood is an accepted model of motherhood in this respect. She not only lays eggs and hatches them, but educates and protects her young so far as it is necessary. But beyond such simple uses as this we have no standard of comparison for educative motherhood. We can only study it among ourselves, comparing the child left motherless with the child mothered, the child with a mother and nothing else with the child whose mother is helped by servants and teachers, the child with what we recognize as a superior mother to the child with an inferior mother. This last distinction, a comparison between mothers, is of great value. We have tacitly formulated a certain vague standard of human motherhood, and loosely apply it, especially in the epithets "natural" and "unnatural" mother.

But these terms again show how prone we still are to consider the whole field of maternal action as one of instinct rather than of reason, as a function rather than a service. We do have a standard, however, loose and vague as it is; and even by that standard it is painful to see how many human mothers fail. Ask yourselves honestly how many of the mothers whose action toward their children confronts you in street and shop and car and boat, in hotel and boarding-house and neighboring yard—how many call forth favorable comment compared with those you judge unfavorably? Consider not the rosy ideal of motherhood you have in your mind, but the coarse, hard facts of motherhood as you see them, and hear them, in daily life.

Motherhood in its fulfilment of educational duty can be measured only by its effects. If we take for a standard the noble men and women whose fine physique and character we so fondly attribute to "a devoted mother," what are we to say of the motherhood which has filled the world with the ignoble men and women, of depraved physique and character? If the good mother makes the good man, how about the bad ones? When we see great men and women, we give credit to their mothers. When we see inferior men and women—and that is a common circumstance —no one presumes to question the motherhood which has produced them. When it comes to congenital criminality, we are beginning to murmur something about "heredity"; and, to meet gross national ignorance, we do demand a better system of education. But no one presumes to suggest that the mothering of mankind could be improved upon; and yet there is where the responsibility really lies. If our human method of reproduction is defective, let the mother answer. She is the main factor in reproduction. If our human method of education is defective, let the mother answer. She is the main factor in education.

To this it is bitterly objected that such a claim omits the father and his responsibility. When the mother of the world is in her right place and doing her full duty, she will have no ground of complaint against the father. In the first place, she will make better men. In the second, she will hold herself socially responsible for the choice of a right father for her children. In the third place, as an economic free agent, she will do half duty in providing for the child. Men who are not equal to good fatherhood under such conditions will have no chance to become fathers, and will die with general pity instead of living with general condemnation. In his position, doing all the world's work, all the father's, and half the mother's, man has made better shift to achieve the impossible than woman has in hers. She has been supposed to have no work or care on earth save as mother. She has really had the work of the mother and that of the world's house service besides. But she has surely had as much time and strength to give to motherhood as man to fatherhood; and not until she can show that the children of the world are as well mothered as they are well fed can she cast on him the blame for our general deficiency.

There is no personal blame to be laid on either party. The sexuo-economic relation has its inevitable ill-effects on both motherhood and fatherhood. But it is to the mother that the appeal must be made to change this injurious relation. Having the deeper sense of duty to the young, the larger love, she must come to feel how her false position hurts her motherhood, and for her children's sake break away from it. Of man and his fatherhood she can make what she will.

The duty of the mother is first to produce children as good as or better than herself; to hand down the constitution and character of those behind her the better for her stewardship; to build up and improve the human race through her enormous power as mother; to make better people. This being done, it is then the duty of the mother, the human mother, so to educate her children as to complete what bearing and nursing have only begun. She carries the child nine months in her body, two years in her arms, and as long as she lives in her heart and mind. The education of the young is a tremendous factor in human reproduction. A right motherhood should be able to fulfil this great function perfectly. It should understand with an ever-growing power the best methods of developing, strengthening, and directing the child's faculties of body and mind, so that each generation, reaching maturity, would start clear of the last, and show a finer, fuller growth, both physically and mentally, than the preceding. That humanity does slowly improve is not here denied; but, granting our gradual improvement, is it all that we could make? And is the gain due to a commensurate improvement in motherhood?

To both we must say no. When we see how some families improve, while others deteriorate, and how uncertain and irregular is such improvement as appears, we know that we could make better progress if all children had the same rich endowment and wise care that some receive. And, when we see how much of our improvement is due to gains made in hygienic knowledge, in public provision for education and sanitary regulation, none of which has been accomplished by mothers, we are forced to see that whatever advance the race has made is not exclusively attributable to motherhood. The human mother does less for her young, both absolutely and proportionately, than any kind of mother on earth. She does not obtain food for them, nor covering, nor shelter, nor protection, nor defense. She does not educate them beyond the personal habits required in the family circle and in her limited range of social life. The necessary knowledge of the world, so indispensable to every human being, she cannot give, because she does not possess it. All this provision and education are given by other hands and brains than hers. Neither does the amount of physical care and labor bestowed on the child by its mother warrant her claims to superiority in motherhood: this is but a part of our idealism of the subject.

The poor man's wife has far too much of other work to do to spend all her time in waiting on her children. The rich man's wife could do it, but does not, partly because she hires some one to do it for her, and partly because she, too, has other duties to occupy her time. Only in isolated cases do we find a mother deputing all other service to others, and concentrating her energies on feeding, clothing, washing, dressing, and, as far as may be, educating her own child. When such cases are found, it remains to be shown that the child so reared is proportionately benefited by this unremittent devotion of its mother. On the contrary, the best service and education a child can receive involve the accumulated knowledge and exchanged activities of thousands upon thousands besides his mother—the fathers of the race.

There does not appear, in the care and education of the child as given by the mother, any special superiority in human maternity. Measuring woman first in direct comparison of her reproductive processes with those of other animals, she does not fulfil this function so easily or so well as they. Measuring her educative processes by interpersonal comparison, the few admittedly able mothers with the many painfully unable ones, she seems more lacking, if possible, than in the other branch. The gain in human education thus far has not been acquired or distributed through the mother, but through men and single women; and there is nothing in the achievements of human motherhood to prove that it is for the advantage of the race to have women give all their time to it. Giving all their time to it does not improve it either in quantity or quality. The woman who works is usually a better reproducer than the woman who does not. And the woman who does not work is not proportionately a better educator.

An extra-terrestrial sociologist, studying human life and hearing for the first time of our so-called "maternal sacrifice" as a means of benefiting the species, might be touched and impressed by the idea. "How beautiful!" he would say. "How exquisitely pathetic and tender! One-half of humanity surrendering all other human interests and activities to concentrate its time, strength, and devotion upon the functions of maternity! To bear and rear the majestic race to which they can never fully belong! To live vicariously forever, through their sons, the daughters being only another vicarious link! What a supreme and magnificent martyrdom!" And he would direct his researches toward discovering what system was used to develop and perfect this sublime consecration of half the race to the perpetuation of the other half. He would view with intense and pathetic interest the endless procession of girls, born human as their brothers were, but marked down at once as "female—abortive type—only use to produce males." He would expect to see this "sex sacrificed to reproductive necessities," yet gifted with human consciousness and intelligence, rise grandly to the occasion, and strive to fit itself in every way for its high office. He would expect to find society commiserating the sacrifice, and honoring above all the glorious creature whose life was to be sunk utterly in the lives of others, and using every force properly to rear and fully to fit these functionaries for their noble office. Alas for the extra-terrestrial sociologist and his natural expectations! After exhaustive study, finding nothing of these things, he would return to Mars or Saturn to wherever he came from, marvelling within himself at the vastness of the human paradox.

If the position of woman is to be justified by the doctrine of maternal sacrifice, surely society, or the individual, or both, would make some preparation for it. No such preparation is made. Society recognizes no such function. Premiums have been sometimes paid for large numbers of children, but they were paid to the fathers of them. The elaborate social machinery which constitutes our universal marriage market has no department to assist or advance motherhood. On the contrary, it is directly inimical to it, so that in our society life motherhood means direct loss, and is avoided by the social devotee. And the individual? Surely here right provision will be made. Young women, glorying in their prospective duties, their sacred and inalienable office, their great sex-martyrdom to race-advantage, will be found solemnly preparing for this work. What do we find? We find our young women reared in an attitude which is absolutely unconscious of and often injurious to their coming motherhood—an irresponsible, indifferent, ignorant class of beings, so far as motherhood is concerned. They are fitted to attract the other sex for economic uses or, at most, for mutual gratification, but not for motherhood. They are reared in unbroken ignorance of their supposed principal duties, knowing nothing of these duties till they enter upon them.

This is as though all men were to be soldiers with the fate of nations in their hands; and no man told or taught a word of war or military service until he entered the battle-field!

The education of young women has no department of maternity. It is considered indelicate to give this conse-crated functionary any previous knowledge of her sacred duties. This most important and wonderful of human func-tions is left from age to age in the hands of absolutely untaught women. It is tacitly supposed to be fulfilled by the mysterious working of what we call "the divine in-stinct of maternity." Maternal instinct is a very respectable and useful instinct common to most animals. It is "di-vine" and "holy" only as all the laws of nature are divine and holy; and it is such only when it works to the right fulfilment of its use. If the race-preservative processes are to be held more sacred than the self-preservative pro-cesses, we must admit all the functions and faculties of reproduction to the same degree of reverence—the passion of the male for the female as well as the passion of the mother for her young. And if, still further, we are to honor the race-preservative processes most in their highest and latest development, which is the only comparison to be made on a natural basis, we should place the great, disin-terested, social function of education far above the second-selfishness of individual maternal functions. Maternal instinct, merely as an instinct, is unworthy of our supersti-tious reverence. It should be measured only as a means to an end, and valued in proportion to its efficacy.

Among animals, which have but a low degree of intelligence, instinct is at its height, and works well. Among savages, still incapable of much intellectual development, instinct holds large place. The mother beast can and does take all the care of her young by instinct; the mother savage, nearly all, supplemented by the tribal traditions, the educative influences of association, and some direct instruction. As humanity advances, growing more complex and varied, and as human intelligence advances to keep pace with new functions and new needs, instinct decreases in value. The human creature prospers and progresses not by virtue of his animal instinct, but by the wisdom and force of a cultivated intelligence and will, with which to guide his action and to control and modify the very instincts which used to govern him.

The human female, denied the enlarged activities which have developed intelligence in man, denied the education of the will which only comes by freedom and power, has maintained the rudimentary forces of instinct to the present day. With her extreme modification to sex, this faculty of instinct runs mainly along sex-lines, and finds fullest vent in the processes of maternity, where it has held unbroken sway. So the children of humanity are born into the arms of an endless succession of untrained mothers, who bring to the care and teaching of their children neither education for that wonderful work nor experience therein: they bring merely the intense accumulated force of a brute instinct— the blind devoted passion of the mother for the child. Maternal love is an enormous force, but force needs direction. Simply to love the child does not serve him unless specific acts of service express this love. What these acts of service are and how they are performed make or mar his life forever.

Observe the futility of unaided maternal love and instinct in the simple act of feeding the child. Belonging to order mammalia, the human mother has an instinctive desire to suckle her young. (Some ultra-civilized have lost even that.) But this instinct has not taught her such habits of life as insure her ability to fulfil this natural function. Failing in the natural method, of what further use is instinct in the nourishment of the child? Can maternal instinct discriminate between Marrow's Food and Bridge's Food, Hayrick's Food and Pestle's Food, Pennywhistle's Sterilized Milk, and all the other infants' foods which are prepared and put upon the market by—men! These are not prepared by instinct, maternal or paternal, but by chemical analysis and physiological study; and their effect is observed and the diet varied by physicians, who do not do their work by instinct, either.

If the bottle-baby survive the loss of mother's milk, when he comes to the table, does maternal instinct suffice then to administer a proper diet for young children? Let the doctor and the undertaker answer. The wide and varied field of masculine activity in the interests of little children, from the peculiar human phenomenon of masculine assistance in parturition (there is one animal, the obstetric frog, where it also appears) to the manufacture of articles for feeding, clothing, protecting, amusing, and educating the baby, goes to show the utter inadequacy of maternal instinct in the human female. Another thing it shows is the criminal failure of that human female to supply by intelligent effort what instinct can no longer accomplish. For a reasoning, conscious being to deliberately undertake the responsibility of maintaining human life without making due preparation for the task is more than carelessness.

# Family and Home
# as Institutions

Marriage and "the family" are two institutions, not one, as is commonly supposed. We confuse the natural result of marriage in children, common to all forms of sex-union, with the family—a purely social phenomenon. Marriage is a form of sex-union recognized and sanctioned by society. It is a relation between two or more persons, according to the custom of the country, and involves mutual obligations. Although made by us an economic relation, it is not essentially so, and will exist in much higher fulfilment after the economic phase is outgrown.

The family is a social group, an entity, a little state. It holds an important place in the evolution of society quite aside from its connection with marriage. There was a time when the family was the highest form of social relation— indeed, the only form of social relation—when to the minds of pastoral, patriarchal tribes there was no conception so large as "my country," no State, no nation. There was only a great land spotted with families, each family its own little world, of which Grandpa was priest and king. The family was a social unit. Its interests were common to its members, and inimical to those of other families. It moved over the earth, following its food supply, and fighting occasionally with stranger families for the grass or water on which it depended. Indissoluble common interests are what make organic union, and those interests long rested on blood relationship.

While the human individual was best fed and guarded by the family, and so required the prompt, correlative action of all the members of that family, naturally the family must have a head; and that form of government known as the patriarchal was produced. The natural family relation, as seen in parents and young of other species, or in ourselves in later forms, involves no such governmental development: that is a feature of the family as a social entity alone.

One of the essentials of the patriarchal family life was polygamy, and not only polygamy, but open concubinage, and a woman slavery which was almost the same thing. The highest period of the family as a social institution was a very low period for marriage as a social institution—a period, in fact, when marriage was but partially evolved from the early promiscuity of the primitive savage. The family seems indeed to be a gradually disappearing survival of the still looser unit of the horde, which again is more closely allied to the band or pack of gregarious carnivora than to an organic social relation. A loose, promiscuous group of animals is not a tribe; and the most primitive savage groups seem to have been no more than this.

The tribe in its true form follows the family—is a natural extension of it, and derives its essential ties from the same relationship. These social forms, too, are closely related to economic conditions. The horde was the hunting unit; the family, and later the tribe, the pastoral unit. Agriculture and its resultant, commerce and manufacture, gradually weaken these crude blood ties, and establish the social relationship which constitutes the State. Before the pastoral era the family held no important position, and since that era it has gradually declined. With social progress we find human relations resting less and less on a personal and sex basis, and more and more on general economic independence. As individuals have become more highly specialized, they have made possible a higher form of marriage.

The family is a decreasing survival of the earliest grouping known to man. Marriage is an increasing development of high social life, not fully evolved. So far from being identical with the family, it improves and strengthens in inverse ratio to the family, as is easily seen by the broad contrast between the marriage relations of Jacob and the unquenchable demand for lifelong single mating that grows in our hearts today. There was no conception of marriage as a personal union for life of two well-matched individuals during the patriarchal era. Wives were valued merely for child-bearing. The family needed numbers of its own blood, especially males; and the man-child was the price of favor to women then. It was but a few degrees beyond the horde, not yet become a tribe in the full sense. Its bonds of union were of the loosest—merely common paternity, with a miscellaneous maternity of inimical interests. Such a basis forever forbade any high individualization, and high individualization with its demands for a higher marriage forbids any numerical importance to the family. Marriage has risen and developed in social importance as the family has sunk and decreased.

It is most interesting to note that, under the comparatively similar conditions of the settlement of Utah, the numerical strength and easily handled common interests of many people under one head, which distinguish the polygamous family, were found useful factors in that great pioneering enterprise. In the further development of society a relation of individuals more fluent, subtle, and extensive was needed. The family as a social unit makes a ponderous body of somewhat irreconcilable constituents, requiring a sort of military rule to make it work at all; and it is only useful while the ends to be attained are of a simple nature, and allow of the slowest accomplishment. It is easy to see the family extending to the tribe by its own physical increase; and, similarly, the father hardening into the chief, under the necessities of larger growth. Then, as the steadily enlarging forces of national unity make the chief an outgrown name and the tribe an outgrown form, the family dwindles to a monogamic basis, as the higher needs of the sex-relation become differentiated from the more primitive economic necessities of the family.

And now, further, when our still developing social needs call for an ever-increasing delicacy and freedom in the inter-service and common service of individuals, we find that even what economic unity remains to the family is being rapidly eliminated. As the economic relation becomes rudimentary and disappears, the sex-relation asserts itself more purely; and the demand in the world today for a higher and nobler sex-union is as sharply defined as the growing objection to the existing economic union. Strange as it may seem to us, so long accustomed to confound the two, it is precisely the outgrown relics of a previously valuable family relation which so painfully retard the higher development of the monogamic marriage relation.

Each generation of young men and women comes to the formation of sex-union with higher and higher demands for a true marriage, with ever-growing needs for companionship. Each generation of men and women need and ask more of each other. A woman is no longer content and grateful to have "a kind husband": a man is no longer content with a patient Griselda; and, as all men and women, in marrying, revert to the economic status of the earlier family, they come under conditions which steadily tend to lower the standard of their mutual love, and make of the average marriage only a sort of compromise, borne with varying ease or difficulty according to the good breeding and loving-kindness of the parties concerned. This is not necessarily, to their conscious knowledge, an "unhappy marriage." It is as happy as those they see about them, as happy perhaps as we resignedly expect "on earth"; and in heaven we do not expect marriages. But it is not what they looked forward to when they were young.

When two young people love each other, in the long hours which are never long enough for them to be together in, do they dwell in ecstatic forecast on the duties of housekeeping? They do not. They dwell on the pleasure of having a home, in which they can be "at last alone"; on the opportunity of enjoying each other's society; and, always, on what they will *do* together. To act with those we love—to walk together, work together, read together, paint, write, sing, anything you please, so that it be together—that is what love looks forward to.

Human love, as it rises to an ever higher grade, looks more and more for such companionship. But the economic status of marriage rudely breaks in upon love's young dream. On the economic side, apart from all the sweetness and truth of the sex-relation, the woman in marrying becomes the house-servant, or at least the housekeeper, of the man. Of the world we may say that the intimate personal necessities of the human animal are ministered to by woman. Married lovers do not work together. They may, if they have time, rest together; they may, if they can, play together; but they do not make beds and sweep and cook together, and they do not go down town to the office together. They are economically on entirely different social planes, and these constitute a bar to any higher, truer union than such as we see about us. Marriage is not perfect unless it is between class equals. There is no equality in class between those who do their share in the world's work in the largest, newest, highest ways and those who do theirs in the smallest, oldest, lowest ways.

Granting squarely that it is the business of women to make the home life of the world true, healthful, and beautiful, the economically dependent woman does not do this, and never can. The economically independent woman can and will. As the family is by no means identical with marriage, so is the home by no means identical with either.

A home is a permanent dwelling-place, whether for one, two, forty, or a thousand, for a pair, a flock, or a swarm. The hive is the home of the bees as literally and absolutely as the nest is the home of mating birds in their season. Home and the love of it may dwindle to the one chamber of the bachelor or spread to the span of a continent, when the returning traveller sees land and calls it "home." There is no sweeter word, there is no dearer fact, no feeling closer to the human heart than this.

On close analysis, what are the bases of our feelings in this connection? and what are their supporting facts? Far down below humanity, where "the foxes have holes, and the birds of the air have nests," there begins the deep home feeling. Maternal instinct seeks a place to shelter the defenseless young, while the mother goes abroad to search for food. The first sharp impressions of infancy are associated with the sheltering walls of home, be it the swinging cradle in the branches, the soft dark hollow in the trunk of a tree, or the cave with its hidden lair. A place to be safe in; a place to be warm and dry in; a place to eat in peace and sleep in quiet; a place whose close, familiar limits rest the nerves from the continuous hail of impressions in the changing world outside; the same place over and over—the restful repetition, rousing no keen response, but healing and soothing each weary sense—that "feels like home." All this from our first consciousness. All this for millions and millions of years. No wonder we love it.

Then comes the gradual addition of tenderer associations, family ties of the earliest. Then, still primitive, but not yet outgrown, the groping religious sentiment of early ancestor-worship, adding sanctity to safety, and driving deep our sentiment for home. It was the place in which to pray, to keep alight the sacred fire, and pour libations to departed grandfathers. Following this, the slow-dying era of paternal government gave a new sense of honor to the place of comfort and the place of prayer. It became the seat of government also—the palace and the throne. Upon this deep foundation we have built a towering superstructure of habit, custom, law; and in it dwell together every deepest, oldest, closest, and tenderest emotion of the human individual. No wonder we are blind and deaf to any suggested improvement in our lordly pleasure-house.

But look farther. Without contradicting any word of the above, it is equally true that the highest emotions of humanity arise and live outside the home and apart from it. While religion stayed at home, in dogma and ceremony, in spirit and expression, it was a low and narrow religion. It could never rise till it found a new spirit and a new expression in human life outside the home, until it found a common place of worship, a ceremonial and a morality on a human basis, not a family basis. Science, art, government, education, industry—the home is the cradle of them all, and their grave, if they stay in it. Only as we live, think, feel, and work outside the home, do we become humanly developed, civilized, socialized.

The exquisite development of modern home life is made possible only as an accompaniment and result of modern social life. If the reverse were true, as is popularly supposed, all nations that have homes would continue to evolve a noble civilization. But they do not. On the contrary, those nations in which home and family worship most prevail, as in China, present a melancholy proof of the result of the domestic virtues without the social. A noble home life is the product of a noble social life. The home does not produce the virtues needed in society. But society does produce the virtues needed in such homes as we desire today. The members of the freest, most highly civilized and individualized nations, make the most delightful members of the home and family. The members of the closest and most highly venerated homes do not necessarily make the most delightful members of society.

In social evolution as in all evolution the tendency is from "indefinite, incoherent homogeneity to definite, coherent heterogeneity"; and the home, in its rigid maintenance of a permanent homogeneity, constitutes a definite limit to social progress. What we need is not less home, but more; not a lessening of the love of human beings for a home, but its extension through new and more effective expression. And, above all, we need the complete disentanglement in our thoughts of the varied and often radically opposed interests and industries so long supposed to be component parts of the home and family.

The change in the economic position of woman from dependence to independence must bring with it a rearrangement of these home interests and industries, to our great gain.

Besides comparatively external conditions, there are psychic effects produced upon the family by the sexuo-economic relation not altogether favorable to our best growth. One is the levelling effect of the group upon its members, under pressure of this relation. Such privacy as we do have in our homes is family privacy, an aggregate privacy; and this does not insure—indeed, it prevents—individual privacy. This is another of the lingering rudiments of methods of living belonging to ages long since outgrown, and maintained among us by the careful preservation of primitive customs in the unchanged position of women. In very early times a crude and undifferentiated people could flock in family groups in one small tent without serious inconvenience or injury. The effects of such grouping on modern people is known in the tenement districts of large cities, where families live in single rooms; and these effects are of a distinctly degrading nature.

The progressive individuation of human beings requires a personal home, one room at least for each person. This need forces some recognition for itself in family life, and is met so far as private purses in private houses can meet it; but for the vast majority of the population no such provision is possible. To women, especially, a private room is the luxury of the rich alone. Even where a partial provision for personal needs is made under pressure of social development, the other pressure of undeveloped family life is constantly against it. The home is the one place on earth where no one of the component individuals can have any privacy. A family is a crude aggregate of persons of different ages, sizes, sexes, and temperaments, held together by sex-ties and economic necessity; and the affection which should exist between the members of a family is not increased in the least by the economic pressure, rather it is lessened. Such affection as is maintained by economic forces is not the kind which humanity most needs.

At present any tendency to withdraw and live one's own life on any plane of separate interest or industry is naturally resented, or at least regretted, by the other members of the family. This affects women more than men, because men live very little in the family and very much in the world. The man has his individual life, his personal expression and its rights, his office, studio, shop: the women and children live in the home—because they must. For a woman to wish to spend much time elsewhere is considered wrong, and the children have no choice. The historic tendency of women to "gad abroad," of children to run away, to be forever teasing for permission to go and play somewhere else; the ceaseless, futile, well-meant efforts to "keep the boys at home"—these facts, together with the definite absence of the man of the home for so much of the time, constitute a curious commentary upon our patient belief that we live at home, and like it. Yet the home ties bind us with a gentle dragging hold that few can resist. Those who do resist, and who insist upon living their individual lives, find that this costs them loneliness and privation; and they lose so much in daily comfort and affection that others are deterred from following them.

There is no reason why this painful choice should be forced upon us, no reason why the home life of the human race should not be such as to allow—yes, to promote—the highest development of personality. We need the society of those dear to us, their love and their companionship. These will endure. But the common cook-shops of our industrially undeveloped homes, and all the allied evils, are not essential, and need not endure.

To our general thought the home just as it stands is held to be what is best for us. We imagine that it is at home that we learn the higher traits, the nobler emotions—that the home teaches us how to live. The truth beneath this popular concept is this: the love of the mother for the child is at the base of all our higher love for one another. Indeed, even behind that lies the generous giving impulse of sex-love, the out-going force of sex-energy. The family relations ensuing do underlie our higher, wider social relations. The "home comforts" are essential to the preservation of individual life. And the bearing and forbearing of home life, with the dominant, ceaseless influence of conservative femininity, is a most useful check to the irregular flying impulses of masculine energy. While the world lasts, we shall need not only the individual home, but the family home, the common sheath for the budded leaflets of each new branch, held close to the parent stem before they finally diverge.

Granting all this, there remains the steadily increasing ill effect, not of home life *per se,* but of the kind of home life based on the sexuo-economic relation. A home in which the rightly dominant feminine force is held at a primitive plane of development, and denied free participation in the swift, wide, upward movement of the world, reacts upon those who hold it down by holding them down in turn. A home in which the inordinate love of receiving things, so long bred into one sex, and the fierce hunger for procuring things, so carefully trained into the other, continually act upon the child, keeps ever before his eyes the fact that life consists in getting dinner and in getting the money to pay for it, getting the food from the market, working forever and ever to cook and serve it. These are the prominent facts of the home as we have made it. The kind of care in which our lives are spent, the things that wear and worry us, are things that should have been outgrown long, long ago if the human race had advanced evenly. Man has advanced, but woman has been kept behind. By inheritance she advances, by experience she is retarded, being always forced back to the economic grade of many thousand years ago.

If a modern man, with all his intellect and energy and resource, were forced to spend all his days hunting with a bow and arrow, fishing with a bone-pointed spear, waiting hungrily on his traps and snares in hope of prey, he could not bring to his children or to his wife the uplifting influences of the true manhood of our time. Even if he started with a college education, even if he had large books to read (when he had time to read them) and improving conversation, still the economic efforts of his life, the steady daily pressure of what he had to do for his living, would check the growth of higher powers. If all men had to be hunters from day to day, the world would be savage still. While all women have to be house servants from day to day, we are still a servile world.

A home life with a dependent mother, a servant-wife, is not an ennobling influence. We all feel this at times. The man, spreading and growing with the world's great growth, comes home, and settles into the tiny talk and fret, or the alluring animal comfort of the place, with a distinct sense of coming down. It is pleasant, it is gratifying to every sense, it is kept warm and soft and pretty to suit the needs of the feebler and smaller creature who is forced to stay in it. It is even considered a virtue for the man to stay in it and to prize it, to value his slippers and his newspaper, his hearth fire and his supper table, his spring bed, and his clean clothes above any other interests.

The harm does not lie in loving home and in staying there as one can, but in the kind of a home and in the kind of womanhood that it fosters, in the grade of industrial development on which it rests. And here, without prophesying, it is easy to look along the line of present progress, and see whither our home life tends. From the cave and tent and hovel up to a graded, differentiated home, with as much room for the individual as the family can afford; from the surly dominance of the absolute patriarch, with his silent servile women and chattel children, to the comparative freedom, equality, and finely diversified lives of a well-bred family of today; from the bottom grade of industry in the savage camp, where all things are cooked together by the same person in the same pot—without neatness, without delicacy, without specialization—to the million widely separated hands that serve the home today in a thousand wide-spread industries—the man and the mill have achieved it all; the woman has but gone shopping outside, and stayed at the base of the pyramid within.

And, more important and suggestive yet, mark this: whereas, in historic beginnings, nothing but the home of the family existed; slowly, as we have grown, has developed the home of the individual. The first wider movement of social life meant a freer flux of population—trade, commerce, exchange, communication. Along river courses and sea margins, from canoe to steamship, along paths and roads as they made them, from "shank's mare to the iron horse," faster and freer, wider and oftener, the individual human beings have flowed and mingled in the life that is humanity. At first the traveller's only help was hospitality—the right of the stranger; but his increasing functional use brought with it, of necessity, the organic structure which made it easy, the transitory individual home. From the most primitive caravansary up to the square miles of floorspace in our grand hotels, the public house has met the needs of social evolution as no private house could have done.

To man, so far the only fully human being of his age, the bachelor apartment of some sort has been a temporary home for that part of his life wherein he had escaped from one family and not yet entered another. To woman this possibility is opening today. More and more we see women presuming to live and have a home, even though they have not a family. The family home itself is more and more yielding to the influence of progress. Once it was stationary and permanent, occupied from generation to generation. Now we move, even in families—move with reluctance and painful objection and with bitter sacrifice of household gods; but move we must under the increasing irritation of irreconcilable conditions. And so has sprung up and grown to vast proportions that startling portent of our times, the "family hotel."

Consider it. Here is the inn, once a mere makeshift stopping-place for weary travellers. Yet even so the weary traveller long since noted the difference between his individual freedom there and his home restrictions, and cheerfully remarked, "I take mine ease in mine inn." Here is this temporary stopping-place for single men become a permanent dwelling-place for families! Not from financial necessity. These are inhabited by people who could well afford to "keep house." But they do not want to keep house. They are tired of keeping house. It is so difficult to keep house, the servant problem is so trying. The health of their wives is not equal to keeping house. These are the things they say.

But under these vague perceptions and expressions is heaving and stirring a slow, uprising social tide. The primitive home, based on the economic dependence of women, with its unorganized industries, its servile labors, its smothering drag on individual development, is becoming increasingly unsuitable to the men and women of today. Of course, they hark back to it, of necessity, so long as marriage and childbearing are supposed to require it, so long as our fondest sentiments and our earliest memories so closely cling to it. But in its practical results, as shown by the ever-rising draught upon the man's purse and the woman's strength, it is fast wearing out.

We have watched the approach of this condition, and have laid it to every cause but the real one. We have blamed men for not staying at home as they once did. We have blamed women for not being as good housekeepers as they once were. We have blamed the children for their discontent, the servants for their inefficiency, the very brick and mortar for their poor construction. But we have never thought to blame the institution itself, and see whether it could not be improved upon.

On wide Western prairies, or anywhere in lonely farm houses, the women of today, confined absolutely to this strangling cradle of the race, go mad by scores and hundreds. Our asylums show a greater proportion of insane women among farmers' wives than in any other class. In the cities, where there is less "home life," people seem to stand it better. There are more distractions, the men say, and seek them. There is more excitement, amusement, variety, the women say, and seek them. What is really felt is the larger social interests and the pressure of forces newer than those of the home circle.

Many fear this movement, and vainly strive to check it. There is no cause for alarm. We are not going to lose our homes nor our families, nor any of the sweetness and happiness that go with them. But we are going to lose our kitchens, as we have lost our laundries and bakeries. The cook-stove will follow the loom and wheel, the wool-carder and shears. We shall have homes that are places to live in and love in, to rest in and play in, to be alone in and to be together in; and they will not be confused and declassed by admixture with any industry whatever.

In homes like these the family life will have all its finer, truer spirit well maintained; and the cares and labors that now mar its beauty will have passed out into fields of higher fulfilment. The relation of wife to husband and mother to child is changing for the better with this outward alteration. All the personal relations of the family will be open to a far purer and fuller growth.

Nothing in the exquisite pathos of woman's long subjection goes deeper to the heart than the degradation of motherhood by the very conditions we supposed were essential to it. To see the mother's heart and mind longing to go with the child, to help it all the way, and yet to see it year by year pass farther from her, learn things she never was allowed to know, do things she never was allowed to do, go out into "the world"—their world, not hers—alone, and

"To bear, to nurse, to rear, to love, and then to lose!"

this not by the natural separation of growth and personal divergence, but by the unnatural separation of falsely divided classes—rudimentary women and more highly developed men. It is the fissure that opens before the boy is ten years old, and it widens with each year.

A mother economically free, a world-servant instead of a house-servant; a mother knowing the world and living in it—can be to her children far more than has ever been possible before. Motherhood in the world will make that world a different place for her child.

# Toward a Wider Sense of Love and Duty

In reconstructing in our minds the position of woman under conditions of economic independence, it is most difficult to think of her as a mother.

We are so unbrokenly accustomed to the old methods of motherhood, so convinced that all its processes are inter-relative and indispensable, and that to alter one of them is to endanger the whole relation, that we cannot conceive of any desirable change.

When definite plans for such change are suggested—ways in which babies might be better cared for than at present—we either deny the advantages of the change proposed or insist that these advantages can be reached under our present system. Just as in cooking we seek to train the private cook and to exalt and purify the private taste, so in baby-culture we seek to train the individual mother, and to call for better conditions in the private home; in both cases ignoring the relation between our general system and its particular phenomena. Though it may be shown, with clearness, that in physical conditions the private house, as a place in which to raise children, may be improved upon, yet all the more stoutly do we protest that the mental life, the emotional life, of the home is the best possible environment for the young.

There was a time in human history when this was

true. While progress derived its main impetus from the sex-passion, and the highest emotions were those that held us together in the family relation, such education and such surroundings as fostered and intensified these emotions were naturally the best. But in the stage into which we are now growing, when the family relation is only a part of life, and our highest duties lie between individuals in social relation, the child has new needs.

This does not mean, as the scared rush of the unreasoning mind to an immediate opposite would suggest, a disruption of the family circle or the destruction of the home. It does not mean the separation of mother and child—that instant dread of the crude instinct of animal maternity. But it does mean a change of basis in the family relation by the removal of its previous economic foundation, and a change of method in our child-culture. We are no more bound to maintain forever our early methods in baby-raising than we are bound to maintain them in the education of older children, or in floriculture. All human life is in its very nature open to improvement, and motherhood is not excepted. The relation between men and women, between husband and wife, between parent and child, changes inevitably with social advance; but we are loath to admit it. We think a change here must be wrong, because we are so convinced that the present condition is right.

On examination, however, we find that the existing relation between parents and children in the home is by no means what we unquestioningly assume. We all hold certain ideals of home life, of family life. When we see around us, or read of, scores and hundreds of cases of family unhappiness and open revolt, we lay it to the individual misbehavior of the parties concerned, and go on implicitly believing in the intrinsic perfection of the institution. When, on the other hand, we find people living together in this relation, in peace and love and courtesy, we do not conversely attribute this to individual superiority and virtue; but we point to it as instancing the innate beauty of the relation.

To the careful sociological observer what really appears is this: when individual and racial progress was best served by the close associations of family life, people were very largely developed in capacity for family affection. They were insensitive to the essential limitations and incessant friction of the relation. They assented to the absolute authority of the head of the family and to the minor despotism of lower functionaries, manifesting none of those sharply defined individual characteristics which are so inimical to the family relation.

But we have reached a stage where individual and racial progress is best served by the higher specialization of individuals and by a far wider sense of love and duty. This change renders the psychic condition of home life increasingly disadvantageous. We constantly hear of the inferior manners of the children of today, of the restlessness of the young, of the flat treason of deserting parents. It is visibly not so easy to live at home as it used to be. Our children are not more perversely constituted than the children of earlier ages, but the conditions in which they are reared are not suited to develop the qualities now needed in human beings.

This increasing friction between members of families should not be viewed with condemnation from a moral point of view, but studied with scientific interest. If our families are so relatively uncomfortable under present conditions, are there not conditions wherein the same families could be far more comfortable? No: we are afraid not. We think it is right to have things as they are, wrong to wish to change them. We think that virtue lies largely in being uncomfortable, and that there is special virtue in the existing family relation.

Virtue is a relative term. Human virtues change from age to age with the change in conditions. Consider the great virtue of loyalty—our highest name for duty. This is a quality that became valuable in human life the moment we began to do things which were not instantly and visibly profitable to ourselves. The permanent application of the individual to a task not directly attractive was an indispensable social quality, and therefore a virtue. Steadfastness, faithfulness, loyalty, duty, that conscious, voluntary attitude of the individual which holds him to a previously assumed relation, even to his extreme personal injury—to death itself—from this results the cohesion of the social body: it is a first principle of social existence.

To the personal conscience a social necessity must express itself in a recognized and accepted pressure—a force to which we bow, a duty, a virtue. So the virtue of loyalty came into early and lasting esteem, whether in the form of loyalty to one's own spoken word or vow—"He that sweareth to his hurt, and doeth it"—to a friend or group of friends in temporary union for some common purpose, or to a larger and more permanent relation. The highest form is, of course, loyalty to the largest common interest.

# Toward a New Concept of Home

What the human race requires is permanent provision for the needs of individuals, disconnected from the sex-relation. Our assumption that only married people and their immediate relatives have any right to live in comfort and health is erroneous. Every human being needs a home—bachelor, husband, or widower, girl, wife, or widow, young or old. They need it from the cradle to the grave, and without regard to sex-connections. We should so build and arrange for the shelter and comfort of humanity as not to interfere with marriage, and yet not to make that comfort dependent upon marriage. With the industries of home life managed professionally, with rooms and suites of rooms and houses obtainable by any person or persons desiring them, we could live singly without losing home comfort and general companionship, we could meet bereavement without being robbed of the common conveniences of living as well as of the heart's love, and we could marry in ease and freedom without involving any change in the economic base of either party concerned.

Married people will always prefer a home together, and can have it; but groups of women or groups of men can also have a home together if they like, or contiguous rooms. And individuals even could have a house to themselves, without having, also, the business of a home upon their shoulders.

Take the kitchens out of the houses, and you leave rooms which are open to any form of arrangement and extension; and the occupancy of them does not mean "housekeeping." In such living, personal character and taste would flower as never before; the home of each individual would be at last a true personal expression; and the union of individuals in marriage would not compel the jumbling together of all the external machinery of their lives—a process in which much of the delicacy and freshness of love, to say nothing of the power of mutual rest and refreshment, is constantly lost. The sense of lifelong freedom and self-respect and of the peace and permanence of one's own home will do much to purify and uplift the personal relations of life, and more to strengthen and extend the social relations. The individual will learn to feel himself an integral part of the social structure, in close, direct, permanent connection with the needs and uses of society.

This is especially needed for women, who are generally considered, and who consider themselves, mere fractions of families, and incapable of any wholesome life of their own. The knowledge that peace and comfort may be theirs for life, even if they do not marry—and may be still theirs for life, even if they do—will develop a serenity and strength most beneficial to them and to the world. It is a glaring proof of the insufficient and irritating character of our existing form of marriage that women must be forced to it by the need of food and clothes, and men by the need of cooks and housekeepers. We are absurdly afraid that, if men or women can meet these needs of life by other means, they will cheerfully renounce the marriage relation. And yet we sing adoringly of the power of love!

In reality, we may hope that the most valuable effect of this change in the basis of living will be the cleansing of love and marriage from this base admixture of pecuniary interest and creature comfort, and that men and women, eternally drawn together by the deepest force in nature, will be able at last to meet on a plane of pure and perfect love. We shame our own ideals, our deepest instincts, our highest knowledge, by this gross assumption that the noblest race on earth will not mate, or, at least, not mate monogamously, unless bought and bribed through the common animal necessities of food and shelter, and chained by law and custom.

The depth and purity and permanence of the marriage relation rest on the necessity for the prolonged care of children by both parents—a law of racial development which we can never escape. When parents are less occupied in getting food and cooking it, in getting furniture and dusting it, they may find time to give new thought and new effort to the care of their children. The necessities of the child are far deeper than for bread and bed: those are his mere racial needs, held in common with all his kind. What he needs far more and receives far less is the companionship, the association, the personal touch, of his father and mother. When the common labors of life are removed from the home, we shall have the time, and perhaps the inclination, to make the personal acquaintance of our children. They will seem to us not so much creatures to be waited on as people to be understood.

# Toward a New Concept of Social Life

The present economic basis of family life holds our friendly and familiar intercourse in narrow grooves. Such visiting and mingling as is possible to us is between families rather than between individuals; and the growing specialization of individuals renders it increasingly unlikely that all the members of a given family shall please a given visitor or he please them. This, on our present basis, either checks the intercourse or painfully strains the family relation. The change of economic relation in families from a sex-basis to a social basis will make possible wide individual intercourse without this accompanying strain on the family ties.

This outgoing impulse among members of families, their growing desire for general and personal social intercourse, has been considered as a mere thirst for amusement, and deprecated by the moralist. He has so far maintained that the highest form of association was association with one's own family, and that a desire for a wider and more fluent relationship was distinctly unworthy. "He is a good family man," we say admiringly of him who asks only for his newspaper and slippers in the evening; and for the woman who dares admit that she wishes further society than that of her husband we have but one name. With the children, too, our constant effort is to "keep the

boys at home,'' to ''make home attractive,'' so that our
ancient ideal, the patriarchal ideal, of a world of families
and nothing else, may be maintained.

But this is a world of persons as well as of families.
We are persons as soon as we are born, though born into
families. We are persons when we step out of families,
and persons still, even when we step into new families of
our own. As persons, we need more and more, in each
generation, to associate with other persons. It is most
interesting to watch this need making itself felt, and getting itself supplied, by fair means or foul, through all these
stupid centuries. In our besotted exaggeration of the sex-
relation, we have crudely supposed that a wish for wider
human relationship was a wish for wider sex-relationship,
and was therefore to be discouraged, as in Spain it was
held unwise to teach women to write, lest they become
better able to communicate with their lovers, and so shake
the foundations of society.

But, when our sex-relation is made pure and orderly
by the economic independence of women, when sex-
attraction is no longer a consuming fever, forever convuls-
ing the social surface, under all its bars and chains, we
shall not be content to sit down forever with half a dozen
blood relations for our whole social arena. We shall need
each other more, not less, and shall recognize that social
need of one another as the highest faculty of this the
highest race on earth.

The force which draws friends together is a higher one
than that which draws the sexes together—higher in the
sense of belonging to a later race-development. ''Passing
the love of women'' is no unmeaning phrase. Children
need one another; young people need one another. Middle-
aged people need one another: old people need one another. We all need one another, much and often. Just as
every human creature needs a place to be alone in, a
sacred, private ''home'' of his own, so all human creatures
need a place to be together in, from the two who can show

each other their souls uninterruptedly, to the largest throng that can throb and stir in unison.

Humanity means being together, and our unutterably outgrown way of living keeps us apart. How many people, if they dare face the fact, have often hopelessly longed for some better way of seeing their friends, their own true friends, relatives by soul, if not by body!

Acting always under the heated misconceptions of our over-sexed minds, we have pictured mankind as a race of beasts whose only desire to be together was based on one great, overworked passion, and who were only kept from universal orgies of promiscuity by being confined in homes. This is not true. It is not true even now in our over-sexed condition. It will be still less true when we are released from the artificial pressure of the sexuo-economic relation and grow natural again.

Men, women, and children need freedom to mingle on a human basis; and that means to mingle in their daily lives and occupations, not to go laboriously to see each other, with no common purpose. We all know the pleasant acquaintance and deep friendship that springs up when people are thrown together naturally, at school, at college, on shipboard, in the cars, in a camping trip, in business. The social need of one another rests at bottom on a common, functional development; and the common, functional service is its natural opportunity.

The reason why friendship means more to men than to women, and why they associate so much more easily and freely, is that they are further developed in race-functions, and that they *work together*. In the natural association of common effort and common relaxation is the true opening for human companionship. Just to put a number of human beings in the same room, to relate their bodies as to cubic space, does not relate their souls. Our present methods of association, especially for women, are most unsatisfactory. They arise, and go to "call" on one another. They solemnly "return" these calls. They prepare much food, and invite many people to come and eat it; or some dance, music, or entertainment is made the temporary ground of union. But these people do not really meet one another. They pass whole lifetimes in going through the steps of these elaborate games, and never become acquainted. There is a constant thirst among us for fuller and truer social intercourse; but our social machinery provides no means for quenching it.

Men have satisfied this desire in large measure; but between women, or between men and women, it is yet far from accomplishment. Men meet one another freely in their work, while women work alone. But the difference is sharpest in their play. "Girls don't have any fun!" say boys, scornfully; and they don't have very much. What they do have must come, like their bread and butter, on lines of sex. Some man must give them what amusement they have, as he must give them everything else. Men have filled the world with games and sports, from the noble contests of the Olympic plain to the brain and body training sports of today, good, bad, and indifferent. Through all the ages the men have played; and the women have looked on, when they were asked. Even the amusing occupation of seeing other people do things was denied them, unless they were invited by the real participants. The "queen of the ball-room" is but a wall-flower, unless she is asked to dance by the real king.

Even today, when athletics are fast opening to women, when tennis and golf and all the rest are possible to them, the two sexes are far from even in chances to play. To want a good time is not the same thing as to want the society of the other sex, and to make a girl's desire for a good time hang so largely on her power of sex-attraction is another of the grievous strains we put upon that faculty. That people want to see each other is construed by us to mean that "he" wants to see "her," and "she" wants to see "him." The fun and pleasure of the world are so interwound with the sex-dependence of women upon men that women are forced to court "attentions," when not really desirous of anything but amusement; and, as we force the association of the sexes on this plane, so we restrict it on a more wholesome one.

Selections from

# THE MAN-MADE WORLD: *Our Androcentric Culture*

## *As to Human-ness*

Human life of any sort is dependent upon what Kropotkin calls "mutual aid," and human progress keeps step absolutely with that interchange of specialized services which makes society organic. The nomad, living on cattle as ants live on theirs, is less human than the farmer, raising food by intelligently applied labor; and the extension of trade and commerce, from mere village market-places to the world-exchanges of today, is extension of human-ness as well.

Humanity, thus considered, is not a thing made at once and unchangeable, but a stage of development; and is still, as Wells describes it, "in the making." Our humanness is seen to lie not so much in what we are individually, as in our relations to one another; and even that individuality is but the result of our relations to one another. It is in what we do and how we do it, rather than in what we are. Some, philosophically inclined, exalt "being" over "doing."

To them this question may be put: "Can you mention any forms of life that merely 'is,' without doing anything?"

Taken separately and physically, we are animals, *genus homo;*taken socially and psychically, we are, in varying degree, human; and our real history lies in the development of this human-ness.

Our historic period is not very long. Real written history only goes back a few thousand years, beginning with the stone records of ancient Egypt. During this period we have had almost universally what is here called an Androcentric Culture. The history, such as it was, was made and written by men.

The mental, the mechanical, the social development, was almost wholly theirs. We have, so far, lived and suffered and died in a man-made world. So general, so unbroken, has been this condition, that to mention it arouses no more remark than the statement of a natural law. We have taken it for granted, since the dawn of civilization, that "mankind" meant men-kind, and the world was theirs.

Women we have sharply delimited. Women were a sex; "the sex," according to chivalrous toasts; they were set apart for special services peculiar to femininity. As one English scientist put it, in 1888, "Women are not only not the race—they are not even half the race, but a sub-species told off for reproduction only."

This mental attitude toward women is even more clearly expressed by Mr. H. B. Marriot-Watson in his article on "The American Woman" in the "Nineteenth Century" for June, 1904, where he says: "Her constitutional restlessness has caused her to abdicate those functions which alone excuse or explain her existence." This is a peculiarly happy and condensed expression of the relative position of women during our androcentric culture. The man was accepted as the race type without one dissentient voice; and the woman—a strange, diverse creature, quite disharmonious in the accepted scheme of things— was excused and explained only as a female.

She has needed volumes of such excuse and explanation; also, apparently, volumes of abuse and condemnation. In any library catalogue we may find books upon books about women: physiological, sentimental, didactic, religious—all manner of books about women, as such. Even today in the works of Marholm—poor young Weininger, Moebius, and others, we find the same perpetual discussion of women—as such.

This is a book about men—as such. It differentiates between the human nature and the sex nature. It will not go so far as to allege man's masculine traits to be all that excuse or explain his existence; but it will point out what are masculine traits as distinct from human ones, and what has been the effect on our human life of the unbridled dominance of one sex.

We can see at once, glaringly, what would have been the result of giving all human affairs into female hands. Such an extraordinary and deplorable situation would have "feminized" the world. We should have all become "effeminate."

See how in our use of language the case is clearly shown. The adjectives and derivatives based on woman's distinctions are alien and derogatory when applied to human affairs; "effeminate"—too female, connotes contempt, but has no masculine analogue; whereas "emasculate"—not enough male, is a term of reproach, and has no feminine analogue. "Virile"—manly, we oppose to "puerile"—childish, and the very word "virtue" is derived from "vir"—a man.

Even in the naming of other animals we have taken the male as the race type, and put on a special termination to indicate "his female," as in lion, lioness; leopard, leopardess; while all our human scheme of things rests on the same tacit assumption; man being held the human type; woman a sort of accompaniment and subordinate assistant, merely essential to the making of people.

She has held always the place of a preposition in

relation to man. She has been considered above him or below
him, before him, behind him, beside him, a wholly relative
existence—"Sydney's sister," "Pembroke's mother"—
but never by any chance Sydney or Pembroke herself.

Acting on this assumption, all human standards have
been based on male characteristics, and when we wish to
praise the work of a woman, we say she has "a masculine
mind."

It is no easy matter to deny or reverse a universal
assumption. The human mind has had a good many jolts
since it began to think, but after each upheaval it settles
down as peacefully as the vine-growers on Vesuvius, accepting the last lava crust as permanent ground.

What we see immediately around us, what we are
born into and grow up with, be it mental furniture or
physical, we assume to be the order of nature.

If a given idea has been held in the human mind for
many generations, as almost all our common ideas have, it
takes sincere and continued effort to remove it; and if it is
one of the oldest we have in stock, one of the big, common, unquestioned world ideas, vast is the labor of those
who seek to change it.

Nevertheless, if the matter is one of importance, if the
previous idea was a palpable error, of large and evil effect,
and if the new one is true and widely important, the effort
is worth making.

The task here undertaken is of this sort. It seeks to
show that what we have all this time called "human
nature" and deprecated, was in great part only male nature, and good enough in its place; that what we have
called "masculine" and admired as such, was in large part
human, and should be applied to both sexes; that what we
have called "feminine" and condemned, was also largely
human and applicable to both. Our androcentric culture is
so shown to have been, and still to be, a masculine culture
in excess, and therefore undesirable.

In the preliminary work of approaching these facts it

will be well to explain how it can be that so wide and serious an error should have been made by practically all men. The reason is simply that they were men. They were males, and saw women as females—and not otherwise.

So absolute is this conviction that the man who reads will say, "Of course! How else are we to look at women except as females? They are females, aren't they?" Yes, they are, as men are males unquestionably; but there is possible the frame of mind of the old marquise who was asked by an English friend how she could bear to have the footman serve her breakfast in bed—to have a man in her bed-chamber—and replied sincerely, "Call you that thing there a man?"

The world is full of men, but their principal occupation is human work of some sort; and women see in them the human distinction preponderantly. Occasionally some unhappy lady marries her coachman—long contemplation of broad shoulders having an effect, apparently; but in general women see the human creature most; the male creature only when they love.

To the man, the whole world was his world; his because he was male; and the whole world of woman was the home; because she was female. She had her prescribed sphere, strictly limited to her feminine occupations and interests; he had all the rest of his life; and not only so, but, having it, insisted on calling it male.

This accounts for the general attitude of men toward the now rapid humanization of women. From her first faint struggles toward freedom and justice, to her present valiant efforts toward full economic and political equality, each step has been termed "unfeminine," and resented as an intrusion upon man's place and power. Here shows the need of our new classification, of the three distinct fields of life—masculine, feminine and human.

As a matter of fact, there is a "woman's sphere," sharply defined and quite different from his; there is also a "man's sphere," as sharply defined and even more limited; but there remains a common sphere—that of humanity, which belongs to both alike.

In the earlier part of what is known as "the woman's movement," it was sharply opposed on the ground that women would become "unsexed." Let us note in passing that they have become unsexed in one particular, most glaringly so, and that no one has noticed or objected to it.

As part of our androcentric culture, we may point to the peculiar reversal of sex characteristics which makes the human female carry the burden of ornament. She alone, of all human creatures, has adopted the essentially masculine attribute of special sex-decoration; she does not fight for her mate, as yet, but she blooms forth as the peacock and bird of paradise, in poignant reversal of nature's laws, even wearing masculine feathers to further her feminine ends.

Woman's natural work as a female is that of the mother; man's natural work as a male is that of the father; their mutual relation to this end being a source of joy and well-being when rightly held; but human work covers all our life outside of these specialities. Every handicraft, every profession, every science, every art, all normal amusements and recreations, all government, education, religion; the whole living world of human achievement: all this is human.

That one sex should have monopolized all human activities, called them "man's work," and managed them as such, is what is meant by the phrase "Androcentric Culture."

# The Man-Made Family

The family is older than humanity, and therefore cannot be called a human institution. A postoffice, now, is *wholly* human; no other creature has a post office, but there are families in plenty among birds and beasts; all kinds permanent and transient; monogamous, polygamous and polyandrous.

We are now to consider the growth of the family in humanity; what is its rational development in humanness; in mechanical, mental and social lines; in the extension of love and service; and the effect upon it of this strange new arrangement—a masculine proprietor.

Like all natural institutions the family has a purpose; and is to be measured primarily as it serves that purpose; which is, the care and nurture of the young. To protect the helpless little ones, to feed and shelter them, to ensure them the benefits of an ever longer period of immaturity, and so to improve the race—this is the original purpose of the family.

When a natural institution becomes human it enters the plane of consciousness. We think about it; and, in our strange new power of voluntary action, do things to it. We have done strange things to the family; or, more specifically, men have.

Balsac, at his bitterest, observed, "Woman's virtue is man's best invention." Balsac was wrong. Virtue—the unswerving devotion to one mate—is common among birds and some of the higher mammals. If Balzac meant celibacy when he said virtue, why that is one of man's inventions—though hardly his best.

What man has done to the family, speaking broadly, is to change it from an institution for the best service of the

207

child to one modified to his own service, the vehicle of his comfort, power and pride.

Among the heavy millions of the unstirred East, a child—necessarily a male child—is desired for the credit and glory of the father, and his fathers; in place of seeing that all a parent is for is the best service of the child. Ancestor worship, that gross reversal of all natural law, is of wholly androcentric origin. It is strongest among old patriarchal races; lingers on in feudal Europe; is to be traced even in America today in a few sporadic efforts to magnify the deeds of our ancestors.

The best thing any of us can do for our ancestors is to be better than they were; and we ought to give our minds to it. When we use our past merely as a guide-book, and concentrate our noble emotions on the present and future, we shall improve more rapidly.

The peculiar changes brought about in family life by the predominance of the male are easily traced. In these studies we must keep clearly in mind the basic masculine characteristics: desire, combat, self-expression; all legitimate and right in proper use, only mischievous when excessive or out of place. Through them the male is led to strenuous competition for the favor of the female; in the overflowing ardour of song, as in nightingale and tom-cat; in wasteful splendor of personal decoration, from the pheasant's breast to an embroidered waistcoat; and in direct struggle for the prize, from the stag's locked horns to the clashing spears of the tournament.

It is earnestly hoped that no reader will take offense at the necessarily frequent reference to these essential features of maleness. In the many books about women it is, naturally, their femaleness that has been studied and enlarged upon. And though women, after thousands of years of such discussion, have become a little restive under the constant use of the word female: men, as rational beings, should not object to an analogous study—at least not for some time—a few centuries or so.

How, then, do we find these masculine tendencies, desire, combat and self-expression, affect the home and family when given too much power?

First comes the effect in the preliminary work of selection. One of the most uplifting forces of nature is that of sex selection. The males, numerous, varied, pouring a flood of energy into wide modifications, compete for the female, and she selects the victor; thus securing to the race the new improvements.

In forming the proprietary family there is no such competition, no such selection. The man, by violence or by purchase, does the choosing—he selects the kind of woman that pleases him. Nature did not intend him to select; he is not good at it. Neither was the female intended to compete—she is not good at it.

If there is a race between males for a mate—the swiftest gets her first; but if one male is chasing a number of females he gets the slowest first. The one method improves our speed: the other does not. If males struggle and fight with one another for a mate, the strongest secures her; if the male struggles and fights with the female (a peculiar and unnatural horror, known only among human beings), he most readily secures the weakest. The one method improves our strength—the other does not.

When women became the property of men; sold and bartered; "given away" by their paternal owner to their marital owner; they lost this prerogative of the female, this primal duty of selection. The males were no longer improved by their natural competition for the female; and the females were not improved; because the male did not select for points of racial superiority, but for such qualities as pleased him.

There is a locality in northern Africa, where young girls are deliberately fed with a certain oily seed, to make them fat—that they may be the more readily married—as the men like fat wives. Among certain more savage African tribes the chief's wives are prepared for him by being kept in small dark huts and fed on "mealies" and molasses; precisely as a Strasbourg goose is fattened for the gourmand. Now fatness is not a desirable race characteristic; it does not add to the woman's happiness of efficiency; or to the child's; it is merely an accessory pleasant to the master; his attitude being much as the amorous monad ecstatically puts it, in Sill's quaint poem, "Five Lives,"

> "O the little female monad's lips!
> O the little female monad's eyes!
> O the little, little, female, female monad!"

This ultra littleness and ultra femaleness has been demanded and produced by our Androcentric Culture.

Following this, and part of it, comes the effect on motherhood. This function was the original and legitimate base of family life; and its ample sustaining power throughout the long early period of "the mother-right"; or as we call it, the matriarchate; the father being her assistant in the great work. The patriarchate, with its proprietary family, changed this altogether; the woman, as the property of the man, was considered first and foremost as a means of pleasure to him; and while she was still valued as a mother, it was in a tributary capacity. Her children were now his; his property, as she was; the whole enginery of the family was turned from its true use to this new one, hitherto unknown, the service of the adult male.

To this day we are living under the influence of the proprietary family. The duty of the wife is held to involve man-service as well as child-service; and indeed far more; as the duty of the wife to the husband quite transcends the duty of the mother to the child.

See for instance the English wife staying with her husband in India and sending the children home to be brought up; because India is bad for children. See our common law that the man decides the place of residence; if the wife refuses to go with him to howsoever unfit a place for her and for the little ones, such refusal on her part constitutes "desertion" and is ground for divorce.

See again the idea that the wife must remain with the husband though a drunkard, or diseased; regardless of the sin against the child involved in such a relation. Public feeling on these matters is indeed changing; but as a whole the ideals of the man-made family still obtain.

The effect of this on the woman has been inevitably to weaken and over-shadow her sense of the real purpose of the family; of the relentless responsibilities of her duty as a mother. She is first taught duty to her parents, with heavy religious sanction; and then duty to her husband, similarly buttressed; but her duty to her children has been left to instinct. She is not taught in girlhood as to her preëminent power and duty as a mother; her young ideals are all of devotion to the lover and husband, with only the vaguest sense of results.

The young girl is reared in what we call "innocence"; poetically described as "bloom"; and this condition is held to be one of her chief "charms." The requisite is wholly androcentric. This "innocence" does not enable her to choose a husband wisely; she does not even know the dangers that possibly confront her. We vaguely imagine that her father or brother, who do know, will protect her. Unfortunately the father and brother, under our current "double standard" of morality, do not judge the applicants as she would if she knew the nature of their offenses.

Furthermore, if her heart is set on one of them, no amount of general advice and opposition serves to prevent her marrying him. "I love him!" she says, sublimely. "I do not care what he has done. I will forgive him. I will save him!"

This state of mind serves to forward the interests of the lover, but is of no advantage to the children. We have magnified the duties of the wife, and minified the duties of the mother; and this is inevitable in a family relation every law and custom of which is arranged from the masculine viewpoint.

From this same viewpoint, equally essential to the proprietary family, comes the requirement that the woman shall serve the man. Her service is not that of the associate and equal, as when she joins him in his business. It is not that of a beneficial combination, as when she practices another business and they share the profits; it is not even that of the specialist, as the service of a tailor or barber; it is personal service—the work of a servant.

In large generalization, the women of the world cook and wash, sweep and dust, sew and mend, for the men.

We are so accustomed to this relation; have held it for so long to be the "natural" relation, that it is difficult indeed to show it to be distinctly unnatural and injurious. The father expects to be served by the daughter, a service quite different from what he expects of the son. This shows at once that such service is no integral part of motherhood, or even of marriage; but is supposed to be the proper industrial position of women, as such.

Why is this so? Why, on the face of it, given a daughter and a son, should a form of service be expected of the one, which would be considered ignominious by the other?

The underlying reason is this. Industry, at its base, is a feminine function. The surplus energy of the mother does not manifest itself in noise, or combat, or display, but in productive industry. Because of her mother-power she became the first inventor and laborer; being in truth the mother of all industry as well as all people.

Man's entrance upon industry is late and reluctant; as will be shown later in treating his effect on economics. In this field of family life, his effect was as follows:

Establishing the proprietary family at an age when the industry was primitive and domestic; and thereafter confining the woman solely to the domestic area, he thereby confined her to primitive industry. The domestic industries, in the hands of women, constitute a survival of our remotest past. Such work was "woman's work" as was all the work then known; such work is still considered woman's work because they have been prevented from doing any other.

The term "domestic industry" does not define a certain kind of labor, but a certain grade of labor. Architecture was a domestic industry once—when every savage mother set up her own tepee. To be confined to domestic industry is no proper distinction of womanhood; it is an historic distinction, an economic distinction, it sets a date and limit to woman's industrial progress.

In this respect the man-made family has resulted in arresting the development of half the world. We have a world wherein men, industrially, live in the twentieth century; and women, industrially, live in the first—and back of it.

To the same source we trace the social and educational limitations set about women. The dominant male, holding his women as property, and fiercely jealous of them, considering them always as *his,* not belonging to themselves, their children, or the world; has hedged them in with restrictions of a thousand sorts; physical, as in the crippled Chinese lady or the imprisoned odalisque; moral, as in the oppressive doctrines of submission taught by all our androcentric religions; mental, as in the enforced ignorance from which women are now so swiftly emerging.

This abnormal restriction of women has necessarily injured motherhood. The man, free, growing in the world's growth, has mounted with the centuries, filling an ever wider range of world activities. The woman, bound, has not so grown; and the child is born to a progressive fatherhood and a stationary motherhood. Thus the man-made family reacts unfavorably upon the child. We rob our children of half their social heredity by keeping the mother in an inferior position; however legalized, hallowed, or ossified by time, the position of domestic servant is inferior.

It is for this reason that child culture is at so low a level, and for the most part utterly unknown. Today, when the forces of education are steadily working nearer to the cradle, a new sense is wakening of the importance of the period of infancy, and its wiser treatment; yet those who know of such a movement are few, and of them some are content to earn easy praise—and pay—by belittling right progress to gratify the prejudices of the ignorant.

The whole position is simple and clear; and easily traceable to its root. Given a proprietary family, where the man holds the woman primarily for his satisfaction and service—then necessarily he shuts her up and keeps her for these purposes. Being so kept, she cannot develop humanly, as he has, through social contact, social service, true social life. (We may note in passing, her passionate fondness for the child-game called "society" she has been allowed to entertain herself withal; that poor simulacrum of real social life, in which people decorate themselves and madly crowd together, chattering, for what is called "entertainment.") Thus checked in social development, we have but a low grade motherhood to offer our children; and the children, reared in the primitive conditions thus artificially maintained, enter life with a false perspective, not only toward men and women, but toward life as a whole.

The child should receive in the family, full preparation for his relation to the world at large. His whole life must be spent in the world, serving it well or ill; and youth is the time to learn how. But the androcentric home cannot teach him. We live today in a democracy—the man-made family is a despotism. It may be a weak one; the despot may be dethroned and overmastered by his little harem of one; but in that case she becomes the despot—that is all. The male is esteemed "the head of the family"; it belongs to him; he maintains it; and the rest of the world is a wide hunting ground and battlefield wherein he competes with other males as of old.

The girl-child, peering out, sees this forbidden field as belonging wholly to menkind; and her relation to it is to secure one for herself—not only that she may love, but that she may live. He will feed, clothe and adorn her—she will serve him; from the subjection of the daughter to that of the wife she steps; from one home to the other, and never enters the world at all—man's world.

The boy, on the other hand, considers the home as a place of women, an inferior place, and longs to grow up and leave it—for the real world. He is quite right. The error is that this great social instinct, calling for full social exercise, exchange, service, is considered masculine, whereas it is human, and belongs to boy and girl alike.

The child is affected first through the retarded development of his mother, then through the arrested conditions of home industry; and further through the wrong ideals which have arisen from these conditions. A normal home, where there was human equality between mother and father, would have a better influence.

We must not overlook the effect of the proprietary family on the proprietor himself.

He, too, has been held back somewhat by this reactionary force. In the process of becoming human we must learn to recognize justice, freedom, human rights; we must learn self-control and to think of others; have minds that grow and broaden rationally; we must learn the broad mutual interservice and unbounded joy of social intercourse and service. The pretty despot of the man-made home is hindered in his humanness by too much manness.

For each man to have one whole woman to cook for and wait upon him is a poor education for democracy. The boy with a servile mother, the man with a servile wife, cannot reach the sense of equal rights we need today. Too constant consideration of the master's tastes makes the master selfish; and the assault upon his heart direct, or through that proverbial side-avenue, the stomach, which the dependent woman needs must make when she wants anything, is bad for the man, as well as for her.

We are slowly forming a nobler type of family; the union of two, based on love and recognized by law, maintained because of its happiness and use. We are even now approaching a tenderness and permanence of love, high pure enduring love; combined with the broad deep-rooted friendliness and comradeship of equals; which promises us more happiness in marriage than we have yet known. It will be good for all the parties concerned—man, woman and child; and promote our general social progress admirably.

If it needs "a head" it will elect a chairman pro tem. Friendship does not need "a head." Love does not need "a head." Why should a family?

## Masculine Literature

History is, or should be, the story of our racial life. What have men made it? The story of warfare and conquest. Begin at the very beginning with the carven stones of Egypt, the clay records of Chaldea, what do we find of history?

"I, Pharaoh, King of Kings! Lord of Lords!" (etc. etc.), "went down into the miserable land of Kush, and slew of the inhabitants thereof an hundred and forty and two thousands!" That, or something like it, is the kind of record early history gives us.

The story of Conquering Kings, whom and how many they killed and enslaved, the grovelling adulation of the abased, the unlimited jubilation of the victor, from the primitive state of most ancient kings, and the Roman triumphs where queens walked in chains, down to our omnipresent soldier's monuments; the story of war and conquest—war and conquest—over and over, with such boasting and triumph, such cock-crow and flapping of wings as show most unmistakably the natural source.

All this will strike the reader at first as biased and unfair. "That was the way people lived in those days!" says the reader.

No—it was not the way women lived.

"Oh, women!" says the reader, "Of course not! Women are different!"

Yes, women are different; and *men are different!* Both of them, as sexes, differ from the human norm, which is social life and all social development. Society was slowly growing in all those black, blind years. The arts, the sciences, the trades and crafts and professions, religion, philosophy, government, law, commerce, agriculture—all the human processes were going on as well as they were able, between wars.

The male naturally fights, and naturally crows, triumphs over his rival and takes the prize—therefore was he made male. Maleness means war.

Not only so; but as a male, he cares only for male interests. Men, being the sole arbiters of what should be done and said and written, have given us not only a social growth scarred and thwarted from the beginning by continual destruction; but a history which is one unbroken record of courage and red cruelty, of triumph and black shame.

As to what went on that was of real consequence, the great slow steps of the working world, the discoveries and inventions, the real progress of humanity—that was not worth recording, from a masculine point of view. Within this last century, "the woman's century," the century of the great awakening, the rising demand for freedom, political, economic, and domestic, we are beginning to write real history, human history, and not merely masculine history. But that great branch of literature—Hebrew, Greek,

Roman, and all down later times, shows beyond all question, the influence of our androcentric culture.

Literature is the most powerful and necessary of the arts, and fiction is its broadest form. If art "holds the mirror up to nature" this art's mirror is the largest of all, the most used. Since our very life depends on some communication, and our progress is in proportion to our fullness and freedom of communication, since real communication requires mutual understanding; so in the growth of the social consciousness, we note from the beginning a passionate interest in other people's lives.

The art which gives humanity consciousness is the most vital art. Our greatest dramatists are lauded for their breadth of knowledge of "human nature," their range of emotion and understanding; our greatest poets are those who most deeply and widely experience and reveal the feelings of the human heart; and the power of fiction is that it can reach and express this great field of human life with no limits but those of the author.

When fiction began it was the legitimate child of oral tradition, a product of natural brain activity; the legend constructed instead of remembered. (This stage is with us yet as seen in the constant changes in repetition of popular jokes and stories.)

Fiction today has a much wider range; yet it is still restricted, heavily and most mischievously restricted.

What is the preferred subject matter of fiction?

There are two main branches found everywhere, from the Romaunt of the Rose to the Purplish Magazine; the Story of Adventure, and the Love Story.

The Story-of-Adventure branch is not so thick as the other by any means, but it is a sturdy bough for all that. Stevenson and Kipling have proved its immense popularity, with the whole brood of detective stories and the tales of successful rascality we call "picturesque." Our most popular weekly shows the broad appeal of this class of fiction.

All these tales of adventure, of struggle and difficulty, of hunting and fishing and fighting, of robbing and murdering, catching and punishing, are distinctly and essentially masculine. They do not touch on human processes, social processes, but on the special field of predatory excitement so long the sole province of men.

It is to be noted here that even in the overwhelming rise of industrial interests today, these, when used as the basis for a story, are forced into line with one, or both, of these two main branches of fiction—conflict or love. Unless the story has one of these "interests" in it, there is no story—so holds the editor; the dictum being, put plainly, "life has no interests except conflict and love!"

It is surely something more than a coincidence that these are the two essential features of masculinity—Desire and Combat—Love and War.

As a matter of fact the major interests of life are in line with its major processes; and these—in our stage of human development—are more varied than our fiction would have us believe. Half the world consists of women, we should remember, who are types of human life as well as men, and their major processes are not those of conflict and adventure, their love means more than mating. Even on so poor a line of distinction as the "woman's column" offers, if women are to be kept to their four K's, there should be a "men's column" also, and all the "sporting news" and fish stories be put in that; they are not world interests, they are male interests.

Now for the main branch—the Love Story. Ninety per cent of fiction is in this line; this is pre-eminently the major interest of life—given in fiction. What is the love-story, as rendered by this art?

It is the story of the pre-marital struggle. It is the Adventures of Him in Pursuit of Her—and it stops when he gets her! Story after story, age after age, over and over and over, this ceaseless repetition of the Preliminaries.

Here is Human Life. In its large sense, its real sense, it is a matter of inter-relation between individuals and groups, covering all emotions, all processes, all experiences. Out of this vast field of human life fiction arbitrarily selects one emotion, one process, one experience, as its necessary base.

"Ah! but we are persons most of all!" protests the reader. "This is personal experience—it has the universal appeal!"

Take human life personally, then. Here is a Human Being, a life, covering some seventy years, involving the changing growth of many faculties; the ever new marvels of youth, the long working time of middle life, the slow ripening of age. Here is the human soul, in the human body, Living. Out of this field of personal life, with all of its emotions, processes, and experiences, fiction arbitrarily selects one emotion, one process, one experience, mainly of one sex.

The "love" of our stories is man's love of woman. If any dare dispute this, and say it treats equally of woman's love for man, I answer, "Then why do the stories stop at marriage?"

There is a current jest, revealing much, to this effect:

The young wife complains that the husband does not wait upon and woo her as he did before marriage; to which he replies, "Why should I run after the street-car when I've caught it?"

Woman's love for man, as currently treated in fiction is largely a reflex; it is the way he wants her to feel, expects her to feel. Not a fair representation of how she does feel. If "love" is to be selected as the most important thing in life to write about, then the mother's love should be the principal subject. This is the main stream, this is the general underlying, world-lifting force. The "life-force," now so glibly chattered about, finds its fullest expression in motherhood; not in the emotions of an assistant in the preliminary stages.

What has literature, what has fiction to offer concerning mother-love, or even concerning father-love, as compared to this vast volume of excitement about lover-love? Why is the search-light continually focused upon a two or three years space of life "mid the blank miles round about?" Why indeed, except for the clear reason, that on a starkly masculine basis this is his one period of overwhelming interest and excitement.

If the beehive produced literature, the bee's fiction would be rich and broad, full of the complex tasks of comb-building and filling, the care and feeding of the young, the guardian-service of the queen; and far beyond that it would spread to the blue glory of the summer sky, the fresh winds, the endless beauty and sweetness of a thousand thousand flowers. It would treat of the vast fecundity of motherhood, the educative and selective processes of the group-mothers, and the passion of loyalty, of social service, which holds the hive together.

But if the drones wrote fiction, it would have no subject matter save the feasting, of many; and the nuptial flight, of one.

To the male, as such, this mating instinct is frankly the major interest of life; even the belligerent instincts are second to it. To the male, as such, it is for all its intensity, but a passing interest. In nature's economy, his is but a temporary devotion, hers the slow processes of life's fulfilment.

In humanity we have long since, not outgrown, but overgrown, this stage of feeling. In Human Parentage even the mother's share begins to pale beside that ever-growing Social love and care, which guards and guides the children of today.

The art of literature in this main form of fiction is far too great a thing to be wholly governed by one dominant note. As life widened and intensified, the artist, if great enough, has transcended sex; and in the mightier works of the real masters, we find fiction treating of life, life in general, in all its complex relationships, and refusing to be held longer to the rigid canons of an androcentric past.

That was the power of Balzac—he took in more than this one field. That was the universal appeal of Dickens; he wrote of people, all kinds of people, doing all kinds of things. As you recall with pleasure some preferred novel of this general favorite, you find yourself looking narrowly for the ''love story'' in it. It is there—for it is part of life; but it does not dominate the whole scene—any more than it does in life.

The thought of the world is made and handed out to us in the main. The makers of books are the makers of thoughts and feelings for the people in general. Fiction is the most popular form in which this world-food is taken. If it were true, it would teach us life easily, swiftly, truly; teach not by preaching but by truly re-presenting; and we should grow up becoming acquainted with a far wider range of life in books than could even be ours in person. Then meeting life in reality we should be wise—and not be disappointed.

As it is, our great sea of fiction is steeped and dyed and flavored all one way. A young man faces life—the seventy year stretch, remember, and is given book upon book wherein one set of feelings is continually vocalized and overestimated. He reads forever of love, good love and bad love, natural and unnatural, legitimate and illegitimate; with the unavoidable inference that there is nothing else going on.

If he is a healthy young man he breaks loose from the whole thing, despises ''love stories'' and takes up life as he finds it. But what impression he does receive from fiction is a false one, and he suffers without knowing it from lack of the truer, broader views of life it failed to give him.

A young woman faces life—the seventy year stretch remember; and is given the same books—with restrictions. Remember the remark of Rochefoucauld, ''There are thirty good stories in the world and twenty-nine cannot be told to women.'' There is a certain broad field of literature so grossly androcentric that for very shame men have tried to keep it to themselves. But in a milder form, the spades all named teaspoons, or at the worst appearing as trowels—the young woman is given the same fiction. Love and love and love—from ''first sight'' to marriage. There it stops—just the fluttering ribbon of announcement— ''and lived happily ever after.''

Is that kind of fiction any sort of picture of a woman's life? Fiction, under our androcentric culture, has not given any true picture of woman's life, very little of human life, and a disproportioned section of man's life.

# Law and Government

It is easy to assume that men are naturally the lawmakers and law enforcers, under the plain historic fact that they have been such since the beginning of the patriarchate.

Back of law lies custom and tradition. Back of government lies the correlative activity of any organized group. What group-insects and group-animals evolve unconsciously and fulfil by their social instincts, we evolve consciously and fulfil by arbitrary systems called laws and governments. In this, as in all other fields of our action, we must discriminate between the humanness of the function in process of development, and the influence of the male or female upon it. Quite apart from what they may like or dislike as sexes, from their differing tastes and faculties, lies the much larger field of human progress, in which they equally participate.

On this plane the evolution of law and government proceeds somewhat as follows: The early woman-centered group organized on maternal lines of common love and service. The early combinations of men were first a grouped predacity—organized hunting; then a grouped belligerency—organized warfare.

By special development some minds are able to perceive the need of certain lines of conduct over others, and to make this clear to their fellows; whereby, gradually, our higher social nature establishes rules and precedents to which we personally agree to submit. The process of social development is one of progressive co-ordination.

From independent individual action for individual ends, up to interdependent social action for social ends we slowly move; the "devil" in the play being the old Ego, which has to be harmonized with the new social spirit. This social process, like all others, having been in masculine hands, we may find in it the same marks of one-sided specialization so visible in our previous studies.

The coersive attitude is essentially male. In the ceaseless age-old struggle of sex combat he developed the desire to overcome, which is always stimulated by resistance; and in this later historic period of his supremacy, he further developed the habit of dominance and mastery. We may instance the contrast between the conduct of a man when "in love," as while courting; in which period he falls into the natural position of his sex towards the other—namely, that of a wooer; and his behavior when, with marriage, they enter the artificial relation of the master male and servile female. His "instinct of dominance" does not assert itself during the earlier period, which was a million times longer than the latter; it only appears in the more modern and arbitrary relation.

Among other animals monogamous union is not accompanied by any such discordant and unnatural feature. However recent as this habit is when considered biologically, it is as old as civilization when we consider it historically: quite old enough to be a serious force. Under its pressure we see the legal systems and forms of government slowly evolving, the general human growth always heavily perverted by the special masculine influence. First we find the mere force of custom governing us, the *mores* of the ancient people. Then comes the gradual appearance of authority, from the purely natural leadership of the best hunter or fighter up through the unnatural mastery of the patriarch, owning and governing his wives, children, slaves and cattle, and making such rules and regulations as pleased him.

Our laws as we support them now are slow, wasteful, cumbrous systems, which require a special caste to interpret and another to enforce; wherein the average citizen knows nothing of the law, and cares only to evade it when he can, obey it when he must. In the household, that stunted, crippled rudiment of the matriarchate, where alone we can find what is left of the natural influence of woman, the laws and government, so far as she is responsible for them, are fairly simple, and bear visible relation to the common good, which relation is clearly and persistently taught.

In the larger household of city and state the educational part of the law is grievously neglected. It makes no allowance for ignorance. If a man breaks a law of which he never heard he is not excused therefore; the penalty rolls on just the same. Fancy a mother making solemn rules and regulations for her family, telling the children nothing about them, and then punishing them when they disobey the unknown laws!

The use of force is natural to the male; while as a human being he must needs legislate somewhat in the interests of the community, as a male being he sees no necessity for other enforcement than by penalty. To violently oppose, to fight, to trample to the earth, to triumph in loud bellowings of savage joy—these are the primitive male instincts; and the perfectly natural social instincts which leads to peaceful persuasion, to education, to an easy harmony of action, are contemptuously ranked as "feminine," or as "philanthropic"—which is almost as bad. "Men need stronger measures" they say proudly. Yes, but four-fifths of the world are women and children!

As a matter of fact the woman, the mother, is the first co-ordinator, legislator, administrator and executive. From the guarding and guidance of her cubs and kittens up to the longer, larger management of human youth, she is the first to consider group interests and co-relate them.

As a father the male grows to share in these original feminine functions, and with us, fatherhood having become socialized while motherhood has not, he does the best he can, alone, to do the world's mother-work in his father way.

In study of any long established human custom it is very difficult to see it clearly and dispassionately. Our minds are heavily loaded with precedent, with race-custom, with the iron weight called authority. These heavy forces reach their most perfect expression in the absolutely masculine field of warfare, the absolute authority; the brainless, voiceless obedience; the relentless penalty. Here we have male coercion at its height; law and government wholly arbitrary. The result is as might be expected, a fine machine of destruction. But destruction is not a human process—merely a male process of eliminating the unfit.

The female process is to select the fit; her elimination is negative and painless.

Greater than either is the human process, to *develop fitness*.

Men are at present far more human than women. Alone upon their self-seized thrones they have carried as best they might the burdens of the state; and the history of law and government shows them as changing slowly but irresistibly in the direction of social improvement.

The ancient kings were the joyous apotheosis of masculinity. Power and Pride were theirs; Limitless Display; Boundless Self-indulgence; Irresistible Authority. Slaves and courtiers bowed before them, subjects obeyed them, captive women filled their harems. But the day of the masculine monarchy is passing, and the day of the human democracy is coming. In a democracy law and government both change. Laws are no longer imposed on the people by one above them, but are evolved from the people themselves. How absurd that the people should not be educated in the laws they make; that the trailing remnants of blind submission should still becloud their minds and make them bow down patiently under the absurd pressure of outgrown tradition!

Democratic government is no longer an exercise of arbitrary authority from those above, but is an organization for public service of the people themselves—or will be when it is really attained.

In this change government ceases to be compulsion, and becomes agreement; law ceases to be authority and becomes co-ordination. When we learn the rules of whist or chess we do not obey them because we fear to be punished if we don't, but because we want to play the game. The rules of human conduct are for our own happiness and service—any child can see that. Every child will see it when laws are simplified, based on sociology, and taught in schools. A child of ten should be considered grossly uneducated who could not recite the main features of the laws of his country, state, and city; and those laws should be so simple in their principles that a child of ten could understand them. . . .

In masculine administration of the laws we may follow the instinctive love of battle down through the custom of "trial by combat"—only recently outgrown, to our present method, where each contending party hires a champion to represent him, and these fight it out in a wordy war, with tricks and devices of complex ingenuity, enjoying this kind of struggle as they enjoy all other kinds.

It is the old masculine spirit of government as authority which is so slow in adopting itself to the democratic idea of government as service. That it should be a representative government they grasp, but representative of what?

of the common will, they say; the will of the majority—
never thinking that it is the common good, the common
welfare, that government should represent.

It is the inextricable masculinity in our idea of government which so revolts at the idea of women as voters.
"To govern:" that means to boss, to control, to have
authority, and that only, to most minds. They cannot bear
to think of the women as having control over even their
own affairs; to control is masculine, they assume. Seeing
only self-interest as a natural impulse, and the ruling powers of the state as a sort of umpire, an authority to preserve
the rules of the game while men fight it out forever; they
see in a democracy merely a wider range of self interest,
and a wider, freer field to fight in.

The law dictates the rules, the government enforces
them, but the main business of life, hitherto, has been
esteemed as one long fierce struggle; each man seeking for
himself. To deliberately legislate for the service of all the
people, to use the government as the main engine of that
service, is a new process, wholly human, and difficult of
development under an androcentric culture.

Furthermore they put forth those naively androcentric
protests—women cannot fight, and in case their laws were
resisted by men they could not enforce them—*therefore*
they should not vote!

What they do not so plainly say, but very strongly
think, is that women should not share the loot which to
their minds is so large a part of politics.

Here we may trace clearly the social heredity of male
government.

Fix clearly in your mind the first headship of man—
the leader of the pack as it were—the Chief Hunter. Then
the second headship, the Chief Fighter. Then the third
headship, the Chief of the Family. Then the long line of
Chiefs and Captains, Warlords and Landlords, Rulers and
Kings.

The Hunter hunted for prey, and got it. The Fighter

enriched himself with the spoils of the vanquished. The Patriarch lived on the labor of women and slaves. All down the ages, from frank piracy and robbery to the measured toll of tribute, ransom and indemnity, we see the same natural instinct of the hunter and fighter. In his hands the government is a thing to sap and wreck, to live on. It is his essential impulse to want something very much; to struggle and fight for it; to take all he can get.

Set against this the giving love that comes with motherhood; the endless service that comes of motherhood; the peaceful administration in the interest of the family that comes of motherhood. We prate much of the family as the unit of the state. If it is—why not run the state on that basis? Government by women, so far as it is influenced by their sex, would be influenced by motherhood; and that would mean care, nurture, provision, education. We have to go far down the scale for any instance of organized motherhood, but we do find it in the hymenoptera; in the overflowing industry, prosperity, peace and loving service of the ant-hill and bee-hive. These are the most highly socialized types of life, next to ours, and they are feminine types.

We as human beings have a far higher form of association, with further issues than mere wealth and propagation of the species. In this human process we should never forget that men are far more advanced than women, at present. Because of their human-ness has come all the noble growth of civilization, in spite of their maleness.

As human beings both male and female stand alike useful and honorable, and should in our governments be alike used and honored; but as creatures of sex, the female is fitter than the male for administration of constructive social interests. The change in governmental processes which marks our times is a change in principle. Two great movements convulse the world today, the woman's movement and the labor movement. Each regards the other as of less moment than itself. Both are parts of the same world-process.

229

CHARLOTTE PERKINS GILMAN

We are entering upon a period of social consciousness. Whereas so far almost all of us have seen life only as individuals, and have regarded the growing strength and riches of the social body as merely so much the more to fatten on; now we are beginning to take intelligent interest in our social nature, to understand it a little, and to begin to feel the vast increase of happiness and power that comes of real Human life.

In this change of systems a government which consisted only of prohibition and commands; of tax collecting and making war; is rapidly giving way to a system which intelligently manages our common interests, which is a growing and improving method of universal service. Here the socialist is perfectly right in his vision of the economic welfare to be assured by the socialization of industry, though that is but part of the new development; and the individualist who opposes socialism, crying loudly for the advantage of "free competition" is but voicing the spirit of the predaceous male.

So with the opposers of the suffrage of women. They represent, whether men or women, the male view-point. They see the woman only as a female, utterly absorbed in feminine functions, belittled and ignored as her long tutelage has made her; and they see the man as he sees himself, the sole master of human affairs for as long as we have historic record.

This, fortunately, is not long. We can now see back of the period of his supremacy, and are beginning to see beyond it. We are well under way already in a higher stage of social development, conscious, well-organized, wisely managed, in which the laws shall be simple and founded on constructive principles instead of being a set of ring-regulations within which people may fight as they will; and in which the government shall be recognized in its full use; not only the sternly dominant father, and the wisely serviceable mother, but the real union of all people to sanely and economically manage their affairs.

## Politics and Warfare

Ethics is the science of conduct, and politics is merely one field of conduct; a very common one. Its connection with warfare in this chapter is perfectly legitimate in view of the history of politics on the one hand, and the imperative modern issues which are today opposed to this established combination.

There are many today who hold that politics need not be at all connected with warfare; and others who hold that politics is warfare from start to finish.

In order to dissociate the two ideas completely, let us give a paraphrase of the above definition, applying it to domestic management—that part of ethics which has to do with the regulation and government of a family; the preservation of its safety, peace and prosperity; the defense of its existence and rights against any stranger's interference or control; the augmentation of its strength and resources, and the protection of its members in their rights; with the preservation and improvement of their morals.

All this is simple enough, and in no way masculine; neither is it feminine, save in this; that the tendency to care for, defend and manage a group, is in its origin maternal.

In every human sense, however, politics has left its maternal base far in the background; and as a field of study and of action is as well adapted to men as to women. There is no reason whatever why men should not develop great ability in this department of ethics, and gradually learn how to preserve the safety, peace and prosperity of their nation; together with those other services as to resources, protection of citizens, and improvement of morals.

Men, as human beings, are capable of the noblest devotion and efficiency in these matters, and have often shown them; but their devotion and efficiency have been marred in this, as in so many other fields, by the constant obtrusion of an ultra-masculine tendency.

In warfare, *per se,* we find maleness in its absurdest extremes. Here is to be studied the whole gamut of basic masculinity, from the initial instinct of combat, through every form of glorious ostentation, with the loudest possible accompaniment of noise.

Primitive warfare had for its climax the possession of the primitive prize, the female. Without dogmatising on so remote a period, it may be suggested as a fair hypothesis that this was the very origin of our organized raids. We certainly find war before there was property in land, or any other property to tempt aggressors. Women, however, there were always, and when a specially androcentric tribe had reduced its supply of women by cruel treatment, or they were not born in sufficient numbers, owing to hard conditions, men must needs go farther afield after other women. Then, since the men of the other tribes naturally objected to losing their main labor supply and comfort, there was war.

Thus based on the sex impulse, it gave full range to the combative instinct, and further to that thirst for vocal exultation so exquisitely male. The proud bellowings of the conquering stag, as he trampled on his prostrate rival, found higher expression in the "triumphs" of old days, when the conquering warrior returned to his home, with victims chained to his chariot wheels, and trumpets braying.

When property became an appreciable factor in life, warfare took on a new significance. What was at first mere destruction, in the effort to defend or obtain some hunting ground or pasture; and, always, to secure the female; now coalesced with the acquisitive instinct, and the long black ages of predatory warfare closed in upon the world.

Where the earliest form exterminated, the later enslaved, and took tribute; and for century upon century the "gentleman adventurer," i.e., the primitive male, greatly preferred to acquire wealth by the simple old process of taking it, to any form of productive industry.

We have been much misled as to warfare by our androcentric literature. With a history which recorded nothing else; a literature which praised and an art which exalted it; a religion which called its central power "the God of Battles"—never the God of Workshops, mind you! —with a whole complex social structure man-prejudiced from center to circumference, and giving highest praise and honor to the Soldier; it is still hard for us to see what warfare really is in human life.

Some day we shall have new histories written, histories of world progress, showing the slow uprising, the development, the interservice of the nations; showing the faint beautiful dawn of the larger spirit of world-consciousness, and all its benefiting growth.

We shall see people softening, learning, rising; see life lengthen with the possession of herds, and widen in rich prosperity with agriculture. Then industry, blossoming, fruiting, spreading wide; art, giving light and joy; the intellect developing with companionship and human intercourse; the whole spreading tree of social progress, the trunk of which is specialized industry, and the branches of which comprise every least and greatest line of human activity and enjoyment. This growing tree, springing up wherever conditions of peace and prosperity gave it a chance, we shall see continually hewed down to the very root by war.

To the later historian will appear throughout the ages, like some Hideous Fate, some Curse, some predetermined check, to drag down all our hope and joy and set life forever at its first steps over again, this Red Plague of War.

The instinct of combat, between males, worked advantageously so long as it did not injure the female or the young. It is a perfectly natural instinct, and therefore perfectly right, in its place; but its place is in a pre-patriarchal era. So long as the animal mother was free and competent to care for herself and her young; then it was an advantage to have "the best man win"; that is the best stag or lion; and to have the vanquished die, or live in sulky celibacy, was no disadvantage to any one but himself.

Humanity is on a stage above this plan. The best man in the social structure is not always the huskiest. When a fresh horde of ultra-male savages swarmed down upon a prosperous young civilization, killed off the more civilized males and appropriated the more civilized females; they did, no doubt, bring in a fresh physical impetus to the race; but they destroyed the civilization.

The reproduction of perfectly good savages is not the main business of humanity. Its business is to grow, socially; to develop, to improve; and warfare, at its best, retards human progress; at its worst, obliterates it.

Combat is not a social process at all; it is a physical process, a subsidiary sex process, purely masculine, intended to improve the species by the elimination of the unfit. Amusingly enough, or absurdly enough; when applied to society, it eliminates the fit, and leaves the unfit to perpetuate the race!

The inextricable confusion of politics and warfare is part of the stumbling block in the minds of men. As they see it, a nation is primarily a fighting organization; and its principal business is offensive and defensive warfare; therefore the ultimatum with which they oppose the demand for political equality—"women cannot fight, therefore they cannot vote."

Fighting, when all is said, is to them the real business of life; not to be able to fight is to be quite out of the running; and ability to solve our growing mass of public problems; questions of health, of education, of morals, of economics; weighs naught against the ability to kill.

This naive assumption of supreme value in a process never of the first importance; and increasingly injurious as society progresses, would be laughable if it were not for its evil effects. It acts and reacts upon us to our hurt. Positively, we see the ill effects already touched on; the evils not only of active war; but of the spirit and methods of war; idealized, inculcated and practiced in other social processes. It tends to make each man-managed nation an actual or potential fighting organization, and to give us, instead of civilized peace, that "balance of power" which is like the counted time in the prize ring—only a rest between combats.

It leaves the weaker nations to be "conquered" and "annexed" just as they used to be; with "preferential tariffs" instead of tribute. It forces upon each the burden of armament; upon many the dreaded conscription; and continually lowers the world's resources in money and in life.

Similarly in politics, it adds to the legitimate expenses of governing the illegitimate expenses of fighting; and must needs have a "spoils system" by which to pay its mercenaries.

In carrying out the public policies the wheels of state are continually clogged by the "opposition"; always an opposition on one side or the other; and this slow wiggling uneven progress, through shorn victories and haggling concessions, is held to be the proper and only political method.

"Women do not understand politics," we are told; "Women do not care for politics"; "Women are unfitted for politics."

It is frankly inconceivable, from the androcentric viewpoint, that nations can live in peace together, and be friendly and serviceable as persons are. It is inconceivable also, that, in the management of a nation, honesty, efficiency, wisdom, experience and love could work out good results without any element of combat.

The "ultimate resort" is still to arms. "The will of the majority" is only respected on account of the guns of the majority. We have but a partial civilization, heavily modified to sex—the male sex.

# Industry and Economics

Always the antagonist; to the male mind an antagonist is essential to progress, to all achievement. He has planted that root-thought in all the human world; from that old hideous idea of Satan, "The Adversary," down to the competitor in business, or the boy at the head of the class, to be superseded by another.

Therefore, even in science, "the struggle for existence" is the dominant law—to the male mind, with the "survival of the fittest" and "the elimination of the unfit."

Therefore in industry and economics we find always and everywhere the antagonist; the necessity for somebody or something to be overcome—else why make an effort? If you have not the incentive of reward, or the incentive of combat, why work? "Competition is the life of trade."

Thus the Economic Man.

But how about the Economic Woman?

To the androcentric mind she does not exist—women are females, and that's all; their working abilities are limited to personal service.

That it would be possible to develop industry to far greater heights, and to find in social economics a simple and beneficial process for the promotion of human life and prosperity, under any other impulse than these two, Desire and Combat, is hard indeed to recognize—for the "male mind."

So absolutely interwoven are our existing concepts of maleness and human-ness, so sure are we that men are people and women only females, that the claim of equal weight and dignity in human affairs of the feminine instincts and methods is scouted as absurd. We find existing industry almost wholly in male hands; find it done as men do it; assume that that is the way it must be done.

When women suggest that it could be done differently, their proposal is waved aside—they are "only women"—their ideas are "womanish."

Agreed. So are men "only men," their ideas are "mannish"; and of the two the women are more vitally human than the men, by nature.

The female is the race-type—the man the variant.

The female, as a race-type, having the female processes besides, best performs the race processes. The male, however, has with great difficulty developed them, always heavily handicapped by his maleness; being in origin essentially a creature of sex, and so dominated almost exclusively by sex impulses.

The human instinct of mutual service is checked by the masculine instinct of combat; the human tendency to specialize in labor, to rejoicingly pour force in lines of specialized expression, is checked by the predacious instinct, which will exert itself for reward; and disfigured by the masculine instinct of self-expression, which is an entirely different thing from the great human outpouring of world force.

Great men, the world's teachers and leaders, are great in human-ness; mere maleness does not make for greatness unless it be in warfare—a disadvantageous glory! Great women also must be great in human-ness; but their female instincts are not so subversive of human progress as are the instincts of the male. To be a teacher and leader, to love and serve, to guard and guide and help, are well in line with motherhood.

"Are they not also in line with fatherhood?" will be asked; and, "Are not the father's paternal instincts masculine?"

No, they are not; they differ in no way from the maternal, in so far as they are beneficial. Parental functions of the higher sort, of the human sort, are identical. The father can give his children many advantages which the mother can not; but that is due to his superiority as a human being. He possesses far more knowledge and power in the world, the human world; he himself is more developed in human powers and processes; and is therefore able to do much for his children which the mother can not; but this is in no way due to his masculinity. It is in this development of human powers in man, through fatherhood, that we may read the explanation of our short period of androcentric culture.

So thorough and complete a reversal of previous relation, such continuance of what appears in every way an unnatural position, must have had some justification in racial advantages, or it could not have endured. This is its justification; the establishment of human-ness in the male; he being led into it, along natural lines, by the exercise of previously existing desires.

In a male culture the attracting forces must inevitably have been, we have seen, Desire and Combat. These masculine forces, acting upon human processes, while necessary to the uplifting of the man, have been anything but uplifting to civilization. A sex which thinks, feels and acts in terms of combat is difficult to harmonize in the smooth bonds of human relationship; that they have succeeded so well is a beautiful testimony to the superior power of race tendency over sex tendency. Uniting and organizing, crudely and temporarily, for the common hunt; and then, with progressive elaboration, for the common fight; they are now using the same tactics—and the same desires, unfortunately—in common work.

Union, organization, complex interservice, are the essential processes of a growing society; in them, in the ever-increasing discharge of power along widening lines of action, is the joy and health of social life. But so far men combine in order to better combat; the mutual service held incidental to the common end of conquest and plunder.

In spite of this the overmastering power of human-ness is now developing among modern men immense organizations of a wholly beneficial character, with no purpose but mutual advantage. This is true human growth, and as such will inevitably take the place of the sex-prejudiced earlier processes.

The human character of the Christian religion is now being more and more insisted on; the practical love and service of each and all; in place of the old insistence on Desire—for a Crown and Harp in Heaven, and Combat—with that everlasting Adversary.

In economics this great change is rapidly going on before our eyes. It is a change in idea, in basic concept, in our theory of what the whole thing is about. We are beginning to see the world, not as "a fair field and no favor"—not a place for one man to get ahead of others, for a price; but as an establishment belonging to us, the proceeds of which are to be applied, as a matter of course, to human advantage.

In the old idea, the wholly masculine idea, based on the processes of sex-combat, the advantage of the world lay in having "the best man win." Some, in the first steps of enthusiasm for Eugenics, think so still; imagining that the primal process of promoting evolution through the paternity of the conquering male is the best process.

To have one superior lion kill six or sixty inferior lions, and leave a progeny of more superior lions behind him, is all right—for lions; the superiority in fighting being all the superiority they need.

But the man able to outwit his fellows, to destroy them in physical, or ruin in financial, combat, is not, therefore, a superior human creature. Even physical superiority, as a fighter, does not prove the kind of vigor best calculated to resist disease, or to adapt itself to changing conditions.

That our masculine culture in its effect on Economics and Industry is injurious, is clearly shown by the whole open page of history. From the simple beneficent activities of a matriarchal period we follow the same lamentable steps; nation after nation. Women are enslaved and captives are enslaved; a military despotism is developed; labor is despised and discouraged. Then when the irresistible social forces do bring us onward, in science, art, commerce, and all that we call civilization, we find the same check acting always upon that progress; and the really vital social processes of production and distribution, heavily injured by the financial combat and carnage which rages ever over and among them.

The real development of the people, the forming of finer physiques, finer minds, a higher level of efficiency, a broader range of enjoyment and accomplishment—is hindered and not helped by this artificially maintained "struggle for existence," this constant endeavor to eliminate what, from a masculine standard, is "unfit."

That we have progressed thus far, that we are now moving forward so rapidly, is in spite of and not because of our androcentric culture.

Bantam Classics bring you the world's greatest literature—
books that have stood the test of time. These beautifully
designed books will be proud additions to your bookshelf.
You'll want all these time-tested classics for your own
reading pleasure.

## Titles by the Brontës:

| | | | |
|---|---|---|---|
| ☐ | 21140 | JANE ERYE Charlotte Brontë | $2.25 |
| ☐ | 21258 | WUTHERING HEIGHTS Emily Brontë | $2.50 |

## Titles by Charles Dickens:

| | | | |
|---|---|---|---|
| ☐ | 21123 | THE PICKWICK PAPERS | $4.95 |
| ☐ | 21223 | BLEAK HOUSE | $4.95 |
| ☐ | 21265 | NICHOLAS NICKLEBY | $4.95 |
| ☐ | 21342 | GREAT EXPECTATIONS | $2.95 |
| ☐ | 21176 | A TALE OF TWO CITIES | $2.50 |
| ☐ | 21016 | HARD TIMES | $2.95 |
| ☐ | 21102 | OLIVER TWIST | $2.50 |
| ☐ | 21244 | A CHRISTMAS CAROL & OTHER VICTORIAN TALES | $2.50 |

## Titles by Henry James:

| | | | |
|---|---|---|---|
| ☐ | 21127 | PORTRAIT OF A LADY | $3.95 |
| ☐ | 21059 | THE TURN OF THE SCREW | $2.25 |

Look for them at your bookstore or use this page to order:

- - - - - - - - - - - - - - - - - - - - - - - - -

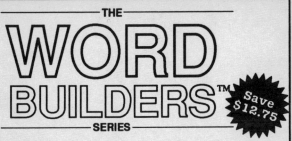